Elemental

Shadows of Otherside: Book 1

Whitney Hill

ELEMENTAL

Benu Media
6409 Fayetteville Rd
Ste 120 #155
Durham, NC 27713
(984) 244-0250
benumedia.com

Thank you for buying this Benu Media book. To receive special offers, release updates, and bonus content, sign up for our newsletter: go.benumedia.com/newsletter

ISBN (ebook): 978-1-7344227-1-9
ISBN (pbook): 978-1-7344227-2-6

Library of Congress Control Number: 2020903544

Cover Designer: Pintado (99Designs)
Developmental Editor: Jeni Chappelle (Jeni Chappelle Editorial)
Copyeditor: Dani Moran (Tessera Editorial)

For everyone who told me I should be a writer, all the fanfic readers who wanted to read more of my work, and everyone who's dreamed of seeing a character who looks like them on the cover of a book.

Chapter 1

Sometimes investigating a case went off without a hitch. Other times, whatever ruse I'd adopted didn't quite work, or something outside my control screwed my setup.

"Are you sure I'm not on the list?" I adjusted the wobbling box of sandwiches on my hip, hitched the insulated beverage bag on my shoulder, and cursed both my luck and the overheated air turning the office foyer into an oven. A gust tickled my cheek and the curls sticking out of the back of my cap in a short poof of a ponytail, tempting me to call on my powers to cool it. "They must have forgotten," I added.

The security guard who'd interrupted my attempt to follow an employee into the elevator reddened. He was big and hairy enough that he might have some jötunn or giant blood way back in his lineage. I eased away a half pace despite the lack of telltale earthy scent, just to be safe. Between my upbringing and my five years as a private investigator, I'd learned caution. Either way, I needed to get into this building. This job was for Callista. She didn't take failure lightly.

Scowling despite my accommodating step back, the guard bit off each word as he said, "Nobody here ordered lunch, missy. I already checked."

"Look, man, they're paid for. If—" I looked at the receipt, pretending I didn't know the name on the order, "Joseph doesn't take delivery, they go in the trash. Isn't there a break room or somewhere I can leave them?"

He eased the clench of his fists, not quite opening them, but relaxing away from the temptation to remove me. "Oh. Well, that explains it. Mr. Cumberland is on vacation."

A fact I had already inferred, having pretended to be an interested client to get an appointment on the calendar app this start-up used. The entire week leading up to the new year had been unavailable despite the office being open. I'd wanted a backup plan in case the easiest route—following an employee when there was no security guard on duty—fell through.

The research I'd done told me the VP of business development, Joseph Cumberland, had a reputation for surprising his team with catered lunches. It was easy enough to buy a load of meal boxes and borrow a cap with the sandwich shop's name on it, so delivery driver was my disguise.

I tried my best bored face and prayed that Joseph's title would outweigh the security protocol as the guard scrutinized me. My average height and weight meant I didn't look like much of a threat. At twenty-five, I could pass for one of the younger undergrad students at the nearby university and often did. Cute enough when I smiled, but no model, although the bright red sandwich shop polo I wore complimented my sienna-brown skin nicely. In short, not much of anything to take particular notice of…unless I was trying to follow a badged employee into a secure building.

The guard pressed his lips together as he made his decision. "Normally, you should be escorted in, but I'm short-staffed on account of Christmas. You go up to the third floor, you drop them sandwiches off, and you come straight back down, you hear?"

Bingo. Always have a backup plan.

"No worries," I said, restraining my smile to a tightening of my lips and lowering my eyes. The guard's diction had slipped away from Southern hospitality and toward down-home mob as he decided he didn't like me or the situation, but didn't have much choice. "I don't get paid what these kids do. Faster I get outta here, faster I can get more tips."

He grunted and waved me toward the elevator, the grand sweep of his arm carrying more than a hint of sarcasm.

I suppressed the impulse to return the gesture with a mocking curtsy. No use pissing him off when I was getting what I wanted.

As the doors to the elevator slid shut, I blew out a breath and shook my head. Even the most suspicious people tended to fall back on assumptions based on my appearance, providing opportunities to misdirect them. I wasn't an elf or a vampire and therefore couldn't cloud minds, but I still doubted any of my marks ever considered that I might not be human. Convincing humans that you're one of them without using magic is the greatest practical joke ever, and I get paid for it.

A harried-looking, younger twenty-something met me at the next door and pointed me to the break room before rushing off. Probably an intern, busting her ass to prove herself in a culture that would chew her up and spit her out if she didn't develop a stronger sense of self. I knew the look.

Start-ups had popped up like mushrooms after a rain in the Triangle—Raleigh, Durham, and Chapel Hill—with North Carolina's latest tax restructure. The influx of people from San Francisco and New York had brought money and big-city problems to a relatively smaller trio of towns. Business was booming, even if I turned down the illegal stuff. I could have made bank on cheating spouses alone.

This particular start-up had drawn the attention of the one person I couldn't say no to, and who didn't have to tell me why she wanted me to risk my PI license to bug a bunch of self-important healthtech blowhards. Video surveillance is legal in this state. Audio surveillance needs the consent of at least one of the recorded parties, and *that* I didn't have. Not that mundane law mattered to Callista, Otherside's hard-assed premier in the Triangle, my former legal guardian, and my current boss.

I spread the sandwiches on a long table as quickly as I could and lined up two one-gallon jugs, one sweet tea and one unsweet, alongside them. I was feeling decidedly unsweet as I thunked the jugs down a little harder than necessary, having taken this job gratis on Callista's orders. She'd been asking more of me lately, a lot more, and both the unpaid asks and the lack of explanation were grating. I wasn't a child or some low-level nobody. I was a Watcher. I'd earned some respect, but I wasn't getting it.

One of these jobs would eventually turn up something I could use. If she wouldn't give me the respect I deserved, I'd find a way to take it. I could bide my time until then.

With the beverage bag empty, I took a quick look around, then flipped up the cooler's false bottom and grabbed one of the small surveillance cams I'd hidden there. I stuck one to the underside of the cabinet closest to the wall. Everyone chatted at the proverbial water cooler, which, in this case, would probably be the adjacent beer fridge.

Tugging the bill of my cap lower, I wandered out, looking for a quiet hall and another opportunity on my way back through the office. My sharper-than-human hearing picked up chatter all on one side of the office, so I went the other way. The oppressive heating system kicked on again, and I relaxed my shields enough that the eddies of a disturbance in the air would warn me of someone coming. It was a risk, given the elven bounty on elementals like me, but I couldn't go back to Callista without being certain the bugs would pick up something good.

Jackpot. A tall bookshelf stood just inside an empty office with the CEO's name on it. I paused to listen for phone calls or clacking keyboards. Nothing. Heart thundering at the risk, I stood on tiptoes and pried off one of the little plugs that hid a screw hole at the top of the shelf, replacing it with an audio-only bug. If I got caught, Callista would do nothing to save me or my career, but after watching her draw stolen blood from every pore of an errant vampire with a single word, I feared her more than the human legal system. The empty office of the head of research and development mirrored this one across the hall, so I stuck my last audio bug on a shelf in there.

On my way back to the door, I glanced down the hall before running my fingers over the top of a framed, ugly-yet-typical abstract picture hanging next to the main entry. The amount of dust reassured me that this was not a place the cleaners thought about. I blew away the bunnies I'd dislodged and stuck another micro-camera there, where it could record people coming and going.

Job done.

The security guard ignored my little wave of thanks on the way out. Fine by me. I didn't like his attitude. On the plus side, it quashed any lingering sympathy I might have had for the trouble he'd be in when the board of this start-up read my report. Not that I'd had very much sympathy to begin with.

Humans. Easiest prey there was. It was almost unfair they didn't know about the rest of us: the beings of myth and legend, collectively known as Otherside.

While all of us lived by secrets and lies, my life was more obscured than most. Not just because of my job, but also because of what I was. Where most of the magic-using species were restricted to Aether, glamour, or life force, my talents laid with one of the four pure elements. That made me an elemental; my control over the element of Air made me a sylph.

Elementals are rare enough that Callista took me under her personal protection when Duke found me in foster care as a child. That protection came with some obligations once I was old enough to fulfill them.

Nobody in Otherside knows what Callista is, and nobody smart asks. Her petite frame and plain-yet-sweet features fool the stupid into missing a frightening intellect and overwhelming magical strength. The start-up's board had invited me to test their security, but it was only supposed to be an entry attempt—not unauthorized and illegal surveillance. But if Callista wanted a favor, she got a favor, no questions. For now.

I took care of some paperwork when I got back to the tiny office I rented in the big coworking space in downtown Durham, putting off the evening's scheduled meeting. Dawdling wasn't wise when Callista wanted an update, but I figured I'd earned some leeway. I had a business to run, after all, and it wasn't all as fun as tricking my way into swanky offices. There were bills to pay, emails to answer, and reports to draft.

At least, that's what I told myself. That I had a business to run. If I was honest, I was still mad about being strong-armed into the job. It was the sort of petty rebellion I'd been indulging in more frequently, and while it provided a minor satisfaction, the curdled ball of resentment in my belly grew a little larger and a little uglier with every uncompensated demand.

Lately, the demands had been for me to start using my magic in her service rather than for my best interests. After a lifetime of schooling—threats, really—in the dangers awaiting an elemental if I was discovered, I refused to draw attention to myself by using Air in an offensive against another Othersider. That meant I had to be useful in other ways. Gathering information was easier and safer as a private investigator than as a shadow in the dark, so business it was. My life and secrets depended on it.

Callista used it against me, reminding me that I both owed her and would need her intercession if an elf ever did stumble onto my secret. Hell, if anyone did. The high-blood elven houses had enough power in local and regional human government that someone might sell me to them for a favor. My logic said it would be better to leave well enough alone, and so far, I'd won the argument.

Evening tinted the sky orange by the time I left my office. A shift of the jet stream had brought a snap of cold Canadian air down south and the temperature had dropped alarmingly, especially for this part of North Carolina.

Everyone looked like a startled turtle as they tried to huddle under knit caps and behind wool scarves, hunched under their heaviest coats with arms crossed. Given that this was the South, only the recent transplants from northern states had anything adequate. I didn't feel the cold as badly as most, but it still bit through my jacket and made me hustle on the walk over.

Callista's pub sat on its own lot, conveniently close to the cluster of breweries north of downtown Durham, yet set apart. Part of that was the use of a magic that wasn't one of the four elements or Aether; I didn't know what it was, but it discouraged casual visits from mundanes. The pub was safe, neutral ground for Othersiders, where business could be conducted without worrying about what a human might see or overhear. Despite the mix of species present, some of whom had bad blood between them, nobody looked for trouble.

Part of it was Callista's reputation. She sold love potions and told fortunes with Lenormand or Tarot cards, but she wasn't a psychic or a witch as far as I could tell. That might be what the local religious folks called her when they dared speak about her behind her back, but she was more than that. Other in a way even the rest of us weren't. I'd once seen her kill a would-be burglar with a touch and I had no interest in instigating something that might draw that side of her forward.

The bar itself was completely unassuming, a chunky brick building with a metal liftgate at the back for deliveries. Inside, it was warm woods and low lights, almost like an English-style pub, but with enlarged Tarot cards framed on the walls. If anyone else tended bar there, I'd never seen them. She was always on duty when I visited.

I slipped in past some departing patrons, elves by the faint whiff of burnt marshmallow I caught as they passed. The elves didn't even glance at me, too low-blood or too drunk to catch the telltale tingle of magic as the woman's hand brushed mine in the narrow doorway. I shoved my hand into my pocket and slammed my shields up higher, counting myself lucky. It would have raised some uncomfortable questions had they noticed, the neutrality of Callista's bar be damned. Nerves had me slipping up.

"Arden Finch. I wondered when you'd get around to keeping our appointment," Callista said when I reached the bar. Her smile didn't reach her cool green eyes.

"Ma'am," I said in a cautious greeting as I slipped onto a bar stool. She knew what I was and had had a hand in raising me, but that didn't mean we particularly liked each other. I dug in my coat pocket for the rooted smartphone I'd bought specifically for this job and slid it over the bar. The only app on it was tied to the cameras I'd set up this afternoon. "It's done."

I told myself that the blast of December air following new patrons made me shiver, not her widening smile.

"Excellent, my dear." She filled a highball glass with Coke and dropped a wedge of lime in it, knowing I didn't booze in public. My insistence on appearing to do so amused her, so she played along.

I pressed my lips together, annoyed by her mocking smile. It was a bar. People tended to get nervous when it looked like you weren't drinking. Nervous people didn't play nicely and that always made my work harder.

"Still not willing to use your powers on a job? I have one that could benefit from your…particular talents."

The change in topic was both abrupt and unwelcome. I shifted on the stool and fiddled with the pendant that was the only thing I had left of my unknown father. It was one of the few nervous tics I hadn't managed to root out and I stopped as soon as I realized what I was doing.

Callista smiled, catlike. That she'd noticed my nerves made me grouchy all over again.

"You were the one who discouraged me from using them in the first place," I said, irritated enough to snap at her, though I kept my voice down. "And we had a deal. If I use my business to serve as a Watcher, I don't have to use my *other* skills. I don't need that kind of attention." It was an old argument, one I'd thought was settled.

Callista pouted and harrumphed as she cleared a few glasses from the bar. "Times are changing and you've gotten better at hiding yourself. Your shields are so tight I'd think you were human if I didn't already know. Besides, the djinn know about you and nothing has happened."

"Fine, but the djinn aren't—" I lowered my voice further and glanced around, "the elves." Preternaturally gifted humans and supernatural beings tended to have great hearing. My presence was bad enough without our conversation being overheard. It's not that I had anything against elves, except the fact that they'd kill an elemental like me upon discovery because of some stupid elven law going back to the days of Atlantis; they were sticklers for laws. Pretty shitty, but I tried not to take it personally. They weren't like the more individualistic djinn, prone to bending the rules for personal gain or pure whim. "Why push this now?"

She pierced me with a sharp gaze, but she'd pricked the one subject I wouldn't back down on. My life wasn't worth whatever had intrigued her enough to bring it up again—I was sure of it.

Never mind that I wanted, more than anything, to be able to exercise my powers freely. Allowing Callista to use me was not the way to gain that freedom. It would be a faster way to die, or another lever she could use against me. She was a master of manipulation.

"I've heard rumors," she said when I didn't look away. "The djinn are nosier than usual. The elves are boiling like a kicked anthill. The vampires have gone underground. Even the wereanimal clans are restless. Nobody seems to know why, and yet, everyone is on edge."

"Solstice fever." I shrugged and took another sip of citrus-spiked Coke. It happened at some point every winter. Something about the longer nights got everyone jumpy. Not surprising, given that most supernatural species are moon-bound and prefer the darkness, but then again…the jump of magic from that elf had been odd. That hadn't just been me; even a low-blood elf should have better self-control. Not that I would admit the thought, or the slipup, to Callista.

She read something in my face anyway. Another not-smile dimpled her round cheeks. "Perhaps. And perhaps you'll find yourself wishing you'd listened to me."

"Is that a foretelling?"

"Would you embrace your power and do this job for me if I told you it was?"

I snorted and pushed my half-finished drink away. "A dream and a bad feeling aren't worth my life."

"That might change before spring."

The cryptic words made me frown at her. Callista looked back at me with a bland expression that didn't match the charged history of our conversation.

"I'd say it's been a pleasure, but…well. You know where to find me." I gave a short wave and turned to leave.

"I certainly do."

I didn't look back, not wanting to see what might be in those cat-green eyes.

My walk back downtown was brisker than my walk over had been. A rabbit hopped away as I passed a vacant lot overgrown with grass and weeds, looking a little too big with ears a little too long, making my skin tingle in a way that was a little too close to magic. As a Watcher, I probably should have investigated whether it was a trickster hare rather than just a plain old rabbit, but I didn't care. Unlike everyone else, it wasn't bothering me, or asking me to do shit that would get me killed. I left Brer Rabbit to his evening and kept going for my car, parked in the garage across the street from the coworking space.

A freezing rain had started falling by the time I made it back to my place. Not very conducive to New Year's Eve fireworks, which was fine by me. The pops and sparkles were pretty, but only after I'd gotten over the wave of fear that someone had figured out what I was and fired a spell at me.

My lot was down a narrow gravel road and backed onto Eno River State Park, outside town, with lots of land on all sides. It wasn't convenient to anything except the woods, and that was how I wanted it. Good fences made good neighbors, but some things couldn't be hidden behind a fence. I liked being able to slip out the back gate and walk in the woods at night, or sit by the firepit I'd dug out of the backyard and listen to the music of the windchimes I had hanging around the property. As an elemental, I needed fresh air, the peace of the forest, and the nearby river. I could tolerate cities, but too long out of nature drained me.

I ran from the car and hopped up both the wooden steps of the wraparound porch, then stepped over the low, tied-off chord of magic creating a block of Air. I always left one in front of the door to trip up unexpected visitors. The nice thing about elemental magic was that only other elementals could see it at work. Anyone else would stumble and make enough noise to alert me. Paranoid, but effective, given that I was the only elemental around.

Callista's words needled me as I sipped a glass of prosecco on the couch, enjoying the peaceful glow of the fairy lights I'd strung up for the solstice and left up for the new year. The manipulative old hag never lied, but the truths she told never seemed to be the ones you heard. Her statement could be about my magic, or the start-up, or—given how carefully she'd phrased her words—nothing at all. That was the trouble with Callista. Untold power and layers of secrets wrapped around dangerous fragments of truth.

The start-up, though, that bore further looking into. Callista rarely took such an interest in mundane matters, which meant Verve Health Solutions was either a threat, or not as mundane as it appeared. Maybe both.

I reached for my laptop, then stopped with my hand hovering over it. "Take a day off," I muttered to myself. Tomorrow was a holiday, and after a busy December, I deserved to sip my bubbly without creating new problems for myself. There were plenty enough of those in the world as it was.

Chapter 2

WRAL's breaking news page reported a woman found drowned in Jordan Lake, which would have been tragic enough on its own without it having happened several times already since winter started. Not the same lake, but always someone found drowned or frozen to death. Nobody could remember so many water accidents happening in the winter, and local authorities were warning heavily about water safety and the risks of hypothermia.

Something about the drownings seemed off, but I couldn't figure out what. The police weren't considering the cases connected, so it was probably my overactive detective skills looking for links where there weren't any.

A rap on the door of my office pulled me out of the rest of the morning's news.

"It's open," I sang out. When the door opened, I had my professional smile on, ready to welcome the only client I was expecting for the day.

The man who stepped in was not that client. Tall and blond, well-built, a fighter's body. Not the thin, brunette head of the board from the start-up. A weighty, black gym bag hung from one shoulder, and I eyed it warily. He could fit any number of weapons in there. The air currents shifted as the open door let warmer air in, bringing the choking, burnt-marshmallow taste of Aether into the room.

He was a high-blood elf capable of some serious damage. Fuck.

My gut clenched and a wave of dizzy fear made me glad I was still sitting. Either I had been discovered, or I would be soon. Luck runs out and skill can't save you every time, which was why all my clients were human. It reduced the risk.

That, plus most Othersiders didn't seek outside help with problems. Justice tended toward the swift and very often fatal, carried out in parallel to the human system.

Knowing that and finding it worth my life to fly under the radar, I played human. Lived human hours, kept my powers under wraps, hid my true physical strength, and didn't go to any of the events in the Otherside community that you wouldn't find a human at. Spending time with some djinn and Callista was the most damning thing I did, and they were all known to have human contacts, particularly useful ones like PIs or blood bank volunteers. As far as I was aware, there was no reason to look twice at me.

So, what the hell was an elf doing in my office, reeking of Aether and a bad attitude?

I'd been sitting too long. Forcing myself to take a breath and hoping he wouldn't see me shaking, I stood, my eyes still on that bag. As I did, I checked my shields and pulled in my own magic as tightly as I could. At the same time, I forced my body to relax and thanked the Goddess that elven hearing wasn't quite as good as that of a vampire or were. Elves had the sharpest vision, but the tripping thump of my racing heart might go unnoticed.

The thoughts skittering through my head like marching ants froze when the burnt-marshmallow scent intensified as a blanket of silence fell. It was quieter than usual outside, the cold and the post-holiday slump keeping people indoors, but what little street noise there was vanished. The sound of the door shutting seemed thunderous in the artificial calm.

He'd done something to block sound. I shifted my feet, preparing to move but not embracing Air yet. If it came to a fight, the spell he'd cast would block out the noise of whatever I had to do to defend myself. Adrenaline spiked higher and cold sweat made my shirt stick to my back.

With a serious effort of will, I pulled my mind away from the terrible ways elves could kill me and back to the immediate issue. Maybe I could get out of this the easy way—by pretending I was only human and hadn't noticed his magic trick. "Welcome to Hawkeye Investigations. I'm actually expecting a client, but would be happy to help afterward."

He studied me, a small frown flitting over his brow before the scent of Aether lessened without losing the sound dampening. He'd tied off the spell. That suggested he didn't intend to stay long and would let it unravel after he was gone. Was that good or bad?

"I need you to help me find someone," he said, ignoring me. "I hear you're the best."

I'd have to play along. "Someone must have given me a good review." I pushed through the fear and smiled, keeping it small to demonstrate humility and respect for his problem even as my mind raced, seeking what little my djinn guardians had told me about elves.

Of all the supernatural community, elves were the ones who never sought outside help. They had their own courts, their own police force, their own government. Was this related to what Callista had said, about the elves being riled up for unknown reasons? "I can see why you'd be concerned. Why don't you take a seat and tell me about your missing person, Mr.…?"

"Sequoyah. Leith Sequoyah." He sat and my heart rate eased down a notch. Not here for a bounty. Yet. Maybe? Unless he was trying to do things the easy way as well.

He shifted his chair so that it had a better view of the door, the window, and me. It struck me as habitual rather than planned, an act of preparation rather than malice. Given what I'd heard of elven politics, I supposed he'd have reason for caution. "It's my grandmother," he said when he was settled. "We're deeply concerned. She's our family matriarch."

I'll bet she is. If she was the matriarch of a high-blood family, that meant she was probably a queen. This could be bad.

"Is there any history of Alzheimer's or dementia?" I asked, playing the ignorant human. Elves didn't have trouble with any of the age-related mental deterioration humans were prone to, and only someone not supernatural would ask.

Leith frowned and shook his head. "No. She's still quite sharp despite her age. What concerns us is that she disappeared rather suddenly and blood was found in her home."

My stomach plummeted. This was definitely bad. Not something I wanted to be involved in. "I'm sorry, but violent crime is something better handled by the police. I usually get called in for wives that have run off with their lovers, or fathers who have skipped child support."

"Please, Ms. Finch. If the police are involved it will become some sort of spectacle. My grandmother is very well respected in the community. Her reputation might not recover if there's a scandal. My family would like to handle this quietly."

I leaned back and crossed my arms, studying him. Something more was going on than he was saying. No police likely meant no elven law either. That they were outsourcing to someone they thought was outside the supernatural community meant they suspected someone inside it.

Red flags went up and started waving. What was going on for a high-blood elf not to trust the elven police? I could see them wanting to avoid other supernaturals—the vamps and the djinn in particular would love to get the upper hand on the elves—but the Darkwatch was supposed to be both excellent and beyond reproach.

I was curious in spite of myself. I'd been a Watcher and a PI for too long not to be intrigued by a tale as bizarre as this one, terrified or not.

"This could go badly for me if a crime was committed," I said, hoping he'd give me a clue. "I could lose my license if the police accuse me of evidence tampering, or obstruction of justice."

"If you find evidence of a crime, I promise I'll go to the police."

"You've already found possible evidence, if there's blood and a disappearance."

Annoyance tightened his features and a flicker of Aether nudged at my aura, just shy of my tightly held shields.

You bastard. What was it? Something persuasive?

"I'll beg if needed," Leith said, smoothing his face into something more earnest even as his shoulders tensed. "I really do need your help."

Social engineering was a bland way to describe manipulating people to achieve a goal that wasn't in their interest. It was one of my favorite parts of being a private investigator, and experience with it told me he was lying. Social engineering rule number seven: make sure your nonverbals matched your words. His didn't, and if I didn't react the right way, I was fucked.

My stomach tightened as I tipped my head to the side and made my eyelids droop slightly, the way I assumed they would if his spell was actually affecting me rather than sliding off my mental shields. He hadn't cottoned on to my being an elemental, or I'd be dead. Playing human was the only way I'd see the rest of the day.

Callista's words about my passing for human came back to me and his continued ignorance gave me the tiniest flicker of hope. What if I could use this as blackmail to buy my safety?

His shoulders eased as I said, "Well…it certainly would be a shame if she was unnecessarily drawn into a scandal."

"Yes," he purred, eyes narrowed to slits of ice blue. "It would. Won't you help me?"

When I hesitated, Sequoyah's flicker of Aether pressed harder. "Of course," I said, quick and breathy. I had to do this, whether I wanted to or not. If he realized his nudges of Aether were only skating off my shields, that would tell him I was an Othersider. If he broke through my shields and got a whiff of my magic I was equally as damned as if I didn't play along. Then no amount of blackmail in the world would matter. "Damned if you do and damned if you don't" had never been so literal.

He smiled to show perfect teeth. "I knew you were the right person to come to. How quickly can you start?"

Clicking randomly on my computer mouse to give the impression of checking my calendar, I tried to convince myself that I could still get out of this and avoid the risk of elven discovery. All I had to do was tell him I was booked out, even if I didn't have anything else on the schedule.

You need the money and you definitely want to know what the hell is going on, the slowly reappearing rational side of me said. *Plus, it's not worth the risk of him finding out you've slipped the Aether net. Grow a pair. Take the job.* Winters were usually slow, which was the other part of why I was annoyed that Callista hadn't paid for the surveillance equipment I'd needed for her job. Gear was pricey, and I couldn't expense it to Verve the way I had the sandwiches I'd used to make my entry.

I needed to give Leith an answer. It was Saturday, and I usually gave myself Sunday off in the slow season. With only one debrief meeting planned for today, I could start researching the case immediately…wait, was I really going to do this?

My heart started tripping all over again, but this time excitement blended with the fear. I was tired of hiding, and had had enough of Callista. This could be my out, if I dared. I'd need to learn more about what I was getting into first. That meant stalling him just enough to do research, yet not so much that he'd go elsewhere. "I need to wrap up another case. Monday afternoon, or after receipt of the initial retainer, whichever is latest."

"No sooner?"

Entitled prick. But desperate to avoid other options. This could be good, good enough to give me something to use. "I'm sorry. While I'm highly sympathetic and sensitive to the urgency of a missing person, I do have other clients. As I said, I was expecting one when you arrived. If you're deeply concerned that there's been foul play, then I have to insist on the police."

"No…no. Monday will have to do."

Too desperate to avoid Otherside. Enough that whatever this was might really give me a way out of Callista's service, if I played my cards right. And didn't get myself killed. With a tight smile, I stood and slid my card across the desk before opening my calendar for real and noting him in. "In that case, thank you for your visit. Please send me an email and I'll invoice you—" A stack of banknotes hitting my desk made me blink.

"That's five thousand dollars," he said.

"Okay, then." I put Sequoyah in a whole new tier of dangerous. Who walks around with that much cash? "That covers the initial retainer, plus some expenses. Monday it is. If you send over a photo and—"

He withdrew a manila folder from the gym bag he'd come in with, and dropped it to the desk before he stood, zipped the bag up, and walked out, pushing past a disgruntled Amy Ulster in the corridor. I hurried to swipe the money off the desk and into a drawer while she was distracted with scowling at the elf's back. It could go in the safe after I'd soothed ruffled feathers.

"Ms. Ulster!" I called, going to the door to welcome her in. "I'm so sorry for the delay."

Her glare swung to me and my smile hardened until it was fixed to my face. The feather-smoothing was going to take a while. Doubly so once I told her how many holes there were in her healthtech start-up's security. HIPAA compliance was a bitch.

* * *

The door finally shut behind a grudgingly satisfied board member. I slumped and rested my head on my arms. I needed to start researching background information on the Sequoyah case, but a headache throbbed in a band across my brow. People might ask for your help, but that didn't always mean they were happy to get it or that they were grateful for it. Some days they were decidedly *un*grateful.

"Well. It's not every day a high-blood elf asks for help. Especially from you."

I jumped at the masculine echo of my thoughts and glared at the djinni who had just materialized in my office. "Dammit, Duke! Ever heard of a doorbell charm?" Leith had me shook and the appearance of a djinni—even a friendly one—did not help. "Why bother giving me a callstone if you're not going to use it?"

Nebuchadnezzar, who everyone called Duke when they didn't want to summon him, grinned. He was wearing his favorite shape today, that of a gangly, youngish black man with laughing eyes the color of dravite, clothed in a sharp suit. "Guilty mind?"

"I have no reason to feel guilty," I snapped, still unsettled enough to play with my pendant before catching myself. It had been a while since a djinni had been able to drop in without me sensing them first. "He came to me. I know the rules, and the dangers."

"I am so very glad to hear that." He sat in the chair Leith had vacated and wrinkled his nose at the lingering scent of the elf's magic, but withheld comment. "Are you going to help him?"

"Yes."

Duke's arched eyebrow spoke volumes. "A dangerous choice."

"But mine to make." I sighed and slumped again. The djinn were nominally on my side, since they claimed my mother had been one, and Duke was more amenable to siding with me than most. A friend, even.

That didn't mean he'd look the other way if I got too involved with the elves. The two factions had been mortal enemies for millennia, since the drowning of Atlantis, maybe. Only the Détente and the need to remain hidden from the humans kept each side from attacking the other.

"It can't hurt to build goodwill just in case," I said, disgusted with myself as soon as the words came out of my mouth. An hour after my big rush of courage, and I was already falling back into old patterns, justifying my actions.

"Just in case." Duke's lips twisted in scorn. "If you think a little goodwill will save you from elven hunters—"

"I'm a fool. I know. Bounty. Death sentence. Elementals are too dangerous for elves to leave alive. We might do something to upset their precious balance. And so on."

Duke spread his hands and offered a slight smile. "On your head be it."

"It might very well be," a contralto voice intoned to my left.

I jumped again as Grimm materialized. As usual, she looked like Lana Del Rey's twin, only with hair the arterial red of fresh blood and sapphire-blue eyes. Her plum-colored skater dress swished as she moved to lean against my desk.

"Nosy djinn," I muttered. Louder, I said, "You two cannot just pop in here like this." An annoyed wave of my hand took in the windows, tinted for privacy but not so much that someone couldn't notice the abrupt appearance of two people. It had always been their habit to appear when they pleased, but it had been happening more frequently of late. Kind of like Callista's asks. It bugged the hell outta me.

Grimm scoffed and tossed long red hair while Duke just kept his teasing smile. This wasn't the first time I'd tried telling them off only to be dismissed, and it rankled.

"Also, we had an agreement," I reminded them, knowing it was pointless but ticked enough to say it anyway. "You're not supposed to be watching. Boundaries, remember?"

"Maybe, maybe not." Duke stretched long legs out in front of him. "Regardless, you can imagine my concern when I turned a thought your way and found a barrier of elven magic."

"What did he want?" Grimm asked.

I crossed my arms. "Nope, nuh-uh. We're not doing this."

"Not doing what?" She wrapped a crimson lock around her finger, looking coy until her eyes flashed to their natural ruby and back. The eyes were always a tell. She was nervous. Or pissed. Something, but not in complete control of her emotions. Fantastic. That made two of us.

I straightened from a reflexive hunch. Djinn temperamentality could be painful. "I'm not about to be in the middle of whatever plot you two have cooked up."

Grimm pulled a face. "Why would we—"

"Enough, Grimm." Duke uncoiled from the chair and resettled the suit jacket over his shoulders with a tug on the lapels. "If you're quite alright—"

"I am," I said firmly.

"Then if you're certain you wish to take this path, perhaps we could offer some help?" The way Duke eyed me as he said that made me wary. When Grimm didn't object, I grew even more suspicious.

"Info would be welcome," I said carefully, wondering what he wanted even as a shuddery thrill ran over me at the thought of finally learning more about the people who wanted me dead. I probably should have known more about elves than I did, but I'd been sheltered in Callista's care, raised almost completely apart from the rest of Otherside and given only the barest information needed to avoid outing myself the first time I encountered another Othersider on my own. After I'd turned eighteen and moved out of Callista's house, I hadn't dared to risk drawing elven attention by investigating them.

Neither Duke nor Grimm had ever been forthcoming before; that they were now said something more was afoot. Maybe Callista was right. And maybe this was another of her ploys. Either way, I needed information. But there was a catch. Djinn never simply offered anything; there were no gifts. None without barbs, anyway. "Perhaps I could share a tale in return," I said, certain that if they were here and offering, they wanted something more than simply to check on me.

Grimm looked up from her fingernails, her pout vanishing. "Something about your work?"

"And about Callista."

That got their attention.

Chapter 3

One of the only reliable things about djinn is that they love a good story, especially if it's true. It's partly the information gleaned and partly the entertainment. When you're immortal, things like money lose meaning. Knowledge and secrets, though, those always had value.

Duke had offered first, so my story would wait until he shared. We made the quick walk to a nearby coffee shop and ordered, gathering our drinks before finding a table. I scribbled notes on the receipt, planning to write off the meeting as a business expense. It was research for the Sequoyah case, if not exactly what I'd planned on doing today.

Grimm lounged on a section of the long bench along the shop's back wall, her careless sprawl almost indecent in the clingy dress she wore despite the wintry bite outside.

I sighed. She was hunting. I should have known she'd have multiple reasons for coming to see me. There were always layers with her. With all djinn, but especially her.

Duke noticed as well. "Grimm," he said. The warning note made her roll her eyes, but she sat up and dropped the sultry air. "Thank you." He sipped his coffee, some blend of hot chocolate, spices, and espresso, which was the reason we always met at this particular café on Main. I settled back against my chair and blew on my chai. Duke might have to go first, but he'd get to it in his own time.

"How much do you already know?" he asked after finishing half his cup.

"Only what you two have already told me over the years and what I've seen from a distance," I said in a quiet voice, trying to rein in my bitterness. They knew exactly how much I knew: next to nothing. It annoyed me more than it used to. I'd done what I'd been told, and minded my own business thinking it would keep me safer, contented to stay ignorant and stay alive. But what if I'd known more *before* an elf walked into my office to hire me? Duke and Grimm had been doing all this extra checking up lately, but it took that for them to volunteer something useful?

That hurt. It shouldn't have, but it did. Especially with Duke. He'd been all about tough love when I was younger, but he hadn't been the mean girl Grimm could be sometimes.

I glanced around the shop, double-checking the clientele before continuing. It was mostly empty at this time of day but caution never hurt. "They're matriarchal, and led by queens, who are usually the eldest and most powerful women in the family. The Darkwatch could take on the human SWAT and win easily but they prefer to keep a low profile. High-blood are purebred, low-blood have interbred with humans and have weaker magic and lower status. Magic is Aether-based and opposite to djinn— unlike you, they can only affect others with magic, and not themselves." I paused and considered.

"You forgot vicious, manipulative, oh, and they hate elementals so much that they'll—"

"Grimm, if you can't be constructive, go hunt elsewhere." Anger simmered under Duke's words.

"Defending *them*?" she hissed.

"No, I just don't need you to bugger my deal," Duke snapped. "I called you as a courtesy. If you can't act like you have three thousand years under your belt, then get out."

I held my peace and kept an eye on the café. The highly individualistic and self-interested djinn always squabbled among themselves. Drawing their attention only got you dragged into the argument, and usually not on the side you thought you agreed with. Besides, Grimm was just being nasty by rubbing my nose in a fact I was already well aware of. Living three thousand years didn't make you wise; it made you petty.

They stared at each other. Duke's eyes flickered this time and Grimm looked away first. "As I was saying," he said, turning back to me.

I bit my tongue to stop myself from pointing out he hadn't actually been saying anything.

"You're right about the families. Family is of the utmost importance, especially the female head. She passes her name and house to all of her offspring, who are tattooed with a house sigil when they come of age, although only a female heir can ascend to the head of the family. She'll have bodyguards, a mix of family and high-ranking members of allied houses."

"Look for a tattoo, watch out for muscle. Got it," I said.

He leaned forward. "The most dangerous thing about *them* isn't their powers, or their combat skills. It's that they always act collectively. I would argue that *we*—" he gestured at Grimm and himself, "—are more powerful one-on-one. But they do nothing alone. Whatever your client wants, there will be at least two more backing him. And there will be at least three on the other side. All things must be balanced, always."

"And all things come in threes." I forced myself to take another sip of chai. The milky warmth sat poorly today, curdling in my stomach. One high-blood was bad enough. Three or more on any given side? Recipe for disaster, or even more of one than there already was.

"Just so. And if this problem of your client's involves a female, especially if it's a queen…"

I tried to look interested and curious, rather than guilty.

He smiled as though my lack of response had told him anyway. "Well. If that's the case, it'll be more than three. Was he a fighter?"

"Who?"

"Your client."

"Nice try. That's not the work story I was going to tell you. And I need more about—them, first." Being circumspect in public was tiring sometimes, however necessary. "Weaknesses. If I have to do this playing mundane, how do I protect myself? I've relied on avoidance up until now."

"Lead. Bullets will do." Grimm leaned forward and rested her arms on the table with a toothy smile. "If you don't have a gun, get one. Then there's the arrogance; it keeps them from considering options. The groupthink Duke considers beneficial can be a crutch or a hobble if it keeps them busy finding consensus instead of acting. And they breed slow, needing their environment to be in balance before the cows will become fertile. The faster you kill them, the more you tip the balance in our favor."

"Other than lead, you're out of luck if you can't catch one alone," Duke said. "They can weave their magic together to make it stronger. Some have specialized individual talents."

I scowled, as much put off by Grimm's slurs as what they were telling me. "So, you're basically telling me I'm screwed even more than usual when it comes to elves. They're stronger, more powerful, cooperative, and I can't use my magic unless I'm going to die anyway."

Duke tilted his head to the side. "That's about right, yes. Why do you think we kept you away from them?"

"Shit. If they're that powerful, why are they in a balance with, you know…" I dropped my voice. "The coteries and the clans?

Why not run Otherside by themselves? Other than Callista, I mean."

Grimm scoffed. "I just told you. Population replacement. The coteries can grow as large as they like, subject to the pool of available blood to support their population in any given area. Weres could turn humans if they didn't consider it filthy, but they'd rather mind their own business and fuck like rabbits. Marshmallows?" She sneered as she used the slur for elves. "They *can't* create more of themselves unless their environment is stable. Why do you think they're such hippies? Half of Greenpeace is elven by now."

"The Détente just formalizes everything and keeps population numbers in check without anyone losing face," Duke said before sipping his coffee.

I nodded. I hadn't really thought about it before because I was unwilling to draw attention to myself by asking questions, and had accepted it by default. Only now, when I had no choice, was I beginning to see what that willful ignorance cost me. The milk was definitely souring in my belly now.

"Of course, getting involved in *their* business might disrupt the balance, not to mention upset some people," Grimm said softly. Anger burned in her gaze, though whether it was at me or at the situation I couldn't tell.

Either way, there were too many reasons why I had to take this job despite it being stupid and potentially deadly to do so. Money could be returned and I could find another way to get more independence, but if it got out that I'd somehow slipped an Aether net, the knowledge of another faction in the Triangle—even a faction of one—could do as much to unbalance power as a missing elven queen. Worst-case scenario had it toppling an elven house.

The resulting chaos would draw the vampires from Raleigh and Charlotte, maybe even the weres out in Asheville. More djinn would definitely be drawn from the ethereal plane; they appeared wherever there was an opportunity for mischief. Nature abhors a vacuum, and so does the supernatural community. While Grimm might think otherwise, *not* acting could be as dangerous as being seen as partial to the elves.

Then, of course, there was my status as a Watcher and the corresponding obligations owed to Callista. Oh, and her little bad feeling about everyone in town being stirred up.

I sighed and pushed the chai away, my gut churning too much to want any more. It had gone cold, anyway.

Grimm and Duke were looking at me expectantly when I had gathered my thoughts. I didn't want to think about this anymore, frustrated by the fact that I couldn't just stay in my bubble and mind my business, so it was time to reciprocate. But how much to tell them?

"Callista is pushing again. About…you know. Me. What I can do."

Duke's eyebrows lifted before he could find a blank expression. He'd been present for the original argument and I was almost certain that his siding with me was the only reason Callista had relented. "Has she given an order?"

"Not yet. But she'll want to know about one of them coming to me."

"That she will." Duke tried to catch Grimm's eye over their mugs. She ignored him a little too obviously, pretending an interest in a woman on the other side of the shop. With an exaggerated eye roll, he said, "*They* are seeking outside help. She's pushing a matter that has been settled for a decade. The weres…well. Never mind them. What was this work story?"

Grimm's attention snapped back to us as I made a mental note about the weres. I gripped my mug and recounted the story of infiltrating Verve—and Callista's unusual interest—to my tea. Resisting the urge to squirm at telling Callista's business to djinn, even if they were my friends, made the words come out stiffer than they should have.

"The thing that bugs me about this is that she's never taken such a direct interest in a mundane business before," I concluded. "I've passed her the tidbits I picked up in the course of whatever case I'm working, but she's been asking more and more lately. Just with Otherside at first, digging into records, or working my friends in the police department for more information, but now a direct action against a human business."

"Curious," Grimm said. She clacked long, lacquered nails on the table in an uneven cadence and exchanged a look with Duke. His lips thinned.

"What's going on, guys?" First Callista, now these two. Was anybody going to tell me what the hell was going on? Hadn't I earned that? Irritation crept into my voice as I said, "Why do I feel like there's something you aren't telling me?"

"There's always something we aren't telling you," Duke said with a sly wink and a smile to take the sting out of the words. "How could we possibly tell you of all the whispers we've gathered over the years?"

Grimm didn't reply. Sometimes I suspected she knew what Callista was. If she did, she was frightened or bribed enough to keep the secret. If it was the former, I wasn't sure I wanted to know what could frighten Grimm badly enough to prod her about her silence. Not yet, anyway. Curiosity almost always got the better of me, as it had with Leith. *One thing at a time.*

"Not reassuring," I said.

"It wasn't intended to be," Duke said, rolling his eyes. "It is simply the truth."

My brow pinched into a scowl. "It's *a* truth."

Duke tipped an imaginary hat at me. Grimm tapped faster.

"Fine," I said. "You're not going to tell me whatever secret or plan has you both so agitated."

Duke looked skyward, exasperated. "We're not—"

"You are. Keep your secrets, it's just what you do." I leaned back in my chair and crossed my arms. "Tell me this, though. Why be forthcoming about *them* now?"

Another look passed between the two djinn before Grimm said, "Up until now you had enough sense to stay the hell away from them."

"Just like you taught me," I murmured. A suspicion was forming in my mind, a tangled snarl of thoughts and happenstance, but I couldn't find the end of the thread yet. It bugged me, but I pushed it aside to consider later.

Beside me, Duke twitched. "I'm being summoned."

"I told you not to give that fool an amulet." Grimm didn't believe in being summoned. She tended to kill anyone who discovered her full name. Even I didn't know it, although I could reach both her and Duke via callstone—a pendant of polished hematite, enchanted to enhance its ability to connect and ground energy from the ethereal planes in this reality. Basically, an interplanar cell phone.

"Sometimes these academics come up with the most interesting theories, though. Negotiating with them is almost as entertaining as leaving false scents for wolves and watching them run themselves silly." He rose and headed for the door. Grimm and I followed him out.

A burst of sharp, cold air slapped us, and I grimaced. Were we not in public, I could have tamed it, thawed it, and wrapped it around us like a shawl before letting it go on its way to delight someone with a brief kiss of heat. As it was, I had to stand there and shiver as it tugged at my cobalt blue scarf and whisked away the coffee shop's warmth.

Duke ignored it, untouched by the cold as he turned a corner into an alley and disappeared before he'd gone three steps.

"He's going to get us caught one day," Grimm said. Her arms were stiff when she pulled me into a goodbye hug. Something was bothering her.

That was fine. Something was bothering me, too, several somethings.

As I made my way to my sporty little hatchback, I went over our conversation. Djinn could be hard to read. Most have had hundreds or thousands of years to decide who and what they wanted to be, so they were always putting on mannerisms and changing forms, an endless game of metaphysical make-believe.

My thoughts turned to the funny feeling in my gut. Duke, Grimm, and Callista were always so adamant about keeping me safe. It had taken finding an old elven book while snooping in Callista's library one day for me to believe the need for it. The illustrations still gave me nightmares. We might all have been more civilized these days, but it didn't mean I went looking for trouble.

Still, though…something was making my sixth sense tingle. I'd learned not to ignore it, especially in investigations. I'd never cared until now that my only knowledge of elves was that they were dangerous hunters who would shatter my magical shields, and subject me to tortures I could barely imagine before turning me into their plaything or killing me. That had been drilled into my head and formed the basis of endless training in how to shield my power.

Everything else I'd gleaned by listening at doors or overhearing quiet conversations and putting the pieces together. Fear had shepherded me away from the topic for decades. Now that I had no choice but to face it, little things were standing out. Details that didn't quite line up, looping into an uncomfortable snarl in my usually clear thoughts.

The drive home passed in a blur. I tripped over my own block of Air on the way in, cursing as my keys flew from my hand and clattered across the deck. I crouched as the tree next to the house rustled, not from wind, but from a body. My mouth went dry. Had Sequoyah figured out where I lived? Was this the trap springing closed?

"Who's up there?"

When no answer came, I risked pulling on Air to send a wind blasting through the branches. A disgruntled raccoon chattered as one broke and left him dangling by two paws, his rear half swinging in empty air, striped tail bristling.

"A fucking raccoon. Goddess." I waited until the raccoon found his way back up before bending to scoop up my keys. The fat, furry creature's scramble might have been funny if my heart wasn't racing. Maintaining a constant vigilance was impossible but I had to be better than this with elves walking into my office.

With most of the afternoon left, I settled in to do some initial research on the Sequoyah case. Leith had compiled a light dossier, including a photo, basic statistics, and a few comments about things that had seemed off lately: a fight with one of her friends, spending more time away from home, overheard phone calls with tense tones.

Deciding it would be ageist to assume Sybil wouldn't have a social media profile, I did a quick internet search. Her name was unusual enough that she was the only one with an exact match result. Facebook and LinkedIn, both with the same profile picture Leith had provided. Her importance in the community was confirmed both by her social media accounts being completely public and her outreach posts about local politics and environmental issues. Each post was fiery, yet gave the sense of being carefully crafted, providing me a better idea of her personality than the dry summary Leith had included.

I reviewed everything, taking notes about how frequently she posted, what about, who she interacted with, who interacted with her more than the other way around, and when her last update was. She'd been quiet for a day before Leith had come to me, in contrast to her habit of posting at least twice every day.

Nothing on social media gave any hints as to why she would have disappeared, though, unless she'd simply grown tired of being so publicly available. It could happen.

I set work aside for the evening when my stomach started to rumble and reheated some leftover lamb stew. It wasn't until I was halfway done that I pulled the first threads free of the tangle that had been bothering me all day: whatever Grimm and Duke were up to touched on me somehow, and it involved elves.

That scared me enough that I lost my appetite. I already knew they wouldn't tell me the what or how unless I had enough knowledge to confront them, so I'd just added a new mystery to a plate that was filling too quickly for comfort.

Chapter 4

The next morning, I reluctantly took Grimm's advice and called in an order for a lead dagger to the tomtar blacksmith Callista kept on retainer. Commissioning a weapon specifically to fight elves felt like asking for trouble, but trouble had already walked in my door and hired me. Callista's protection, such as it was, wouldn't help if I was dead. If I wanted to stand on my own, I'd need to be ready to defend myself.

I wasn't the only one paying for protection with service. Tomtar were one of the few fae species that had magic rather than glamour and their smithing skills made them valuable. They were rare in this part of the country, with most of them being concentrated in the areas of Swedish migration in the Upper Midwest. Without the threat of Callista's retribution, Nils and his family probably would have been kidnapped long ago.

The promise of a carton of cigarettes guaranteed me a rush order, but it still wouldn't be ready for another week. Lead just wasn't as available as it had been before humans understood that they were almost as susceptible to lead poisoning as elves. Nils had grumbled over the inconvenience, but he'd get it done.

I spent the rest of the day doing winter maintenance chores and tending the air plants hung in glass bulbs throughout my house. That done, I lit some sandalwood incense and settled into my armchair to read by the fire. My new case wasn't the only thing I needed to research. I also needed to figure out what

Callista and the djinn might be hiding from me. I reviewed the few old books I had and jotted notes of what I remembered from childhood conversations. There might be a clue to my past buried in them somewhere. Nothing jumped out at me, but I could be patient.

When Monday rolled around, I met Leith at his family's home. He hadn't been keen on my seeing the scene for myself, pushing back when I called first thing in the morning. Explaining that reviewing the setting first-hand might give me a clue had gotten me a grudging appointment to meet here during his lunch hour. *What do elven toughs do as a day job?*

Jordan Lake seemed too peaceful a place for there to have been a violent kidnapping. The Sequoyah family home backed onto a secluded beach in the woods, down a winding dirt road and behind a chain-link fence hung with aggressive "no trespassing" signs to discourage lost hikers from entering the family land. I couldn't decide if the eight-bedroom house was quaint or spooky.

Leith waited on the wrap-around porch, hands on his slim hips, a lock of blond hair twisting in the wind. For all that I'd resolved to take the case, mental commitment couldn't override the reflexive spike of fearful adrenaline. Last night's thinking had reminded me that the only way to overcome a fear was to face it. Until I overcame my fear of dying at elven hands, I wouldn't find the clues to what Grimm and Duke were hiding from me, or what so bothered the elves that they would seek outside help. I pushed aside the instinct to get back in my car, and waved an acknowledgment before going around to the rear of the hatchback.

My kit rode there, containing the various tools of the trade for a PI. The Nikon D750 and its three lenses came inside with me at night, but the binoculars, tripod, and a small case with a voice recorder and spare memory cards stayed in the car. A notepad and tablet lived in the camera bag with my wallet; I'd shelled out extra for a nice leather bag that could serve as a purse or a backpack. Never knew when I'd be on a case or find a clue, so it paid to be both prepared and able to blend in.

The house's security cameras were well-hidden, but I spotted them. "Was there any footage of that night?"

"Nothing useful," Leith said, annoyance pinching his tone.

I let it go, though I found his reaction odd. Once inside, I snooped around with Leith looming over my shoulder, and hoped he took my shivers for being cold, not the carefully leashed terror twisting my stomach. It got easier once I got to work, focusing on what was in front of me rather than waiting for a trap to spring.

"Visit your grandmother often?" I asked, reminding myself that I had to do my job. With any other client, that included interviews.

"Of course. I saw her daily." His tone was biting, and I didn't push. Whatever had him in a mood wouldn't be helped by my putting him even further on the defensive than I had by insisting on coming here.

He'd left the scene as he'd found it. A few drops of blood stood out on the ash wood of the floor, like you'd see from a broken nose or a split head. Nothing I'd be too terribly concerned about if someone hadn't been missing. Some furniture had been shifted out of place, judging by the divots in the rich Oriental rug. A fire poker had fallen from its rack, faint dustings of soot showing where it had dropped and rolled.

"I can see why you were worried," I said, trying to make small talk to break the uncomfortable silence.

My client made no reply, simply watching with crossed arms and a face like a thunderhead as I crouched to check under the couch and armchairs for other clues.

After strolling around the room to get a sense of everything, I went back and took pictures, dictating notes to the recorder after each one so I'd remember the context and why it stood out later.

Leith grunted when I started recording and leaned carelessly against what had to be an antique table.

When I was done, I stood in a doorway and tried to reassemble what might have happened. "You think the blood is hers?"

"Why wouldn't it be?"

The surly tone put my back up enough to push away some of my fear. "There was a struggle, so the perpetrator's, if you think she was taken. You're sure you don't want the police to investigate this? Or maybe I could take a swab in for you?"

"No. No police, no swabs. I told you, Ms. Finch, we can't afford a scandal. And she wouldn't want her DNA on file to be abused."

Sighing, I shook my head. While I couldn't blame him for not wanting elven DNA in the hands of human police, his attitude was making my work unnecessarily difficult. "Can I see the rest of the property?"

"Why?"

"So I can do my job. I investigate, Mr. Sequoyah, and there's more to this house than a living room with displaced furniture and a few drops of blood."

He studied me with hard eyes before sweeping a hand to the hallway behind me. Was there something he didn't want me to find? Or maybe elves were territorial, like weres and vamps?

Not knowing made me grumpy. I could be missing clues because I had to play human and had allowed fear—and Callista's guardianship—to keep me ignorant all these years. The rest of the Othersiders might not have wanted me, or feared what I was, but I was still a part of the supernatural community. It was past time to reexamine some of the things I'd been told.

By the time we'd made it through every room, cold sweat dampened my back and I was glad for the jacket hiding it. "Outside, please?" The words came out tighter than I'd intended. I hated being afraid, and I hated being ignorant. Being both while having a tall, stacked, magically powerful elf at my back put me in a terrible mood.

With poor grace, he led the way back to the main room and out to the back porch. I paused to look out over the lake, lapping smoothly against the frost-rimed shore. An empty dock extended over the water. Two Adirondack chairs faced toward the lake on the platform at the end of it. A boat was hauled up on the beach, its engine tilted up to keep the propellers out of the sand, the interior protected by a snap-on cover. I tried to decide if it should be dirtier for presumably having sat outside all winter, but I didn't know anything about boat maintenance, nor did it seem important to the immediate scope of the investigation.

"Is there anything else on the property I could take a look at?"

"Nothing that's any of your business."

Taken aback by the curt tone, I nodded and kept walking. He wasn't comfortable with me being here. I needed to leave before I pushed him from defensive to offensive.

"I think that's all I needed to see, Mr. Sequoyah. I'll get out of your hair now."

He thanked me, stiff and formal, and I nodded again, picking my way over fallen branches toward the driveway. After replacing everything in the car's hatch, I climbed in and sighed as I settled in the seat, relieved not to have him standing over me anymore. I waited until I was down the private drive and back on the main road before loosening up on shielding my power. My shoulders twinged as they eased, having been locked around my ears. Had Leith noticed?

Something about the meeting bothered me. How was Leith so sure the blood belonged to his grandmother? Smell, maybe? The elves had been hunters, once. I hadn't heard of them having a particularly good sense of smell, but maybe that's just because everyone knew weres had the best and vamps weren't far behind. My senses were better than human, so it stood to reason his were too. He'd know what she smelled like; to me, the whole place just smelled of the burnt-marshmallow-and-herb scent of elves.

Then there was his general reluctance to let me see anything else in the house. It might have been territorial protectiveness, but what if he was hiding something? In most violent cases, the perpetrator was someone close to the victim. *The perp's not usually bold enough to come to a private investigator for help if it's him, though. You're reaching.*

I huffed and put my foot down on the gas. Highway 751 was a fun, winding drive through the trees until it passed by the big Southpoint mall and traffic got more congested. I turned onto 54 and headed toward Chapel Hill.

Leith might not have been willing to go to the police, but I was.

Not that it was the wisest course of action by any means, bringing mundane police into a supernatural investigation against the wishes of my client, but I had to start somewhere. In any case involving missing persons, I headed to the local police department after doing the initial open source research—Google and social media profiles. If there was already a case in progress, sharing information could get it solved faster. If there wasn't, having a few more people keeping their ears open usually didn't hurt.

The police weren't always happy to see me, some being of the opinion that I got involved a little too often in matters better handled by "professionals." Not that they weren't, but I resented the suggestion that I wasn't. And hey, I helped at least as much as I obstructed. Most of the time.

Even so, I had a few friends on the force, and bringing them lunch worked better than calling and bugging them. Detective Tom Chan in Chapel Hill had used me as a resource on more than one occasion when they needed a social engineer or an extra interviewer. Some people wouldn't talk to a cop, but they loosened up around me.

I mulled over Leith's request and his curt behavior at the house. It was rare that someone would ask me not to go to the police; usually I was just a faster option than the overworked PD. In any case, Chapel Hill didn't have jurisdiction over Jordan Lake. I was just consulting a colleague. A fine line, but I was already putting myself at risk just being on this case. It was a little late to worry about following the rules.

After a quick stop for pizza, I continued to the police station. The whole town of Chapel Hill was green and well-to-do—part of why the elves preferred it to the rest of the Triangle—and the police department sat in a pleasantly wooded lot about a mile north of the University of North Carolina's main campus. Students burdened with overfull backpacks whizzed past on bikes as I approached, and I twisted in my seat, checking that there weren't any more before turning in.

My favorite officer was on desk duty. "Rachel, how's things?"

"Arden! Long time, no see, although I guess that's a good thing." She smiled and tossed a fall of short, auburn hair out of her eyes. "Who ya looking for?"

I smiled back. Rachel was one of those people who radiated sunshine and made it difficult not to like them. I hoped police work didn't tarnish that. "Is Detective Chan in today? Sorry, I should have called ahead, but I'm coming from a scene." I hefted the pizza boxes I'd stopped for. "I brought y'all some lunch."

"Oh, bless you. I'm starving." She snagged a piece and spoke around a bite. "Let me check the duty roster…yep! He's here. I'll page him."

"Thanks, Rachel." I let her take the boxes back to the breakroom, and sat down to wait. Chatting with Rachel would have been more interesting than using my camera's Wi-Fi connection to back up the day's photos and scanning the faded fliers on the message board, but she was working and I didn't want to get her in trouble.

"Arden! I wondered if we'd see you this month. And with bribes, as always."

"Detective," I said, rising to shake the hand of the plainclothes cop coming toward me with a slice of pizza in hand.

He grinned, dark eyes twinkling. "I keep telling you to call me Tom."

"I know, I know. Habit, though." I tried to be professional when we were in front of the public. Or in front of other cops, for that matter; being too casual could easily be misinterpreted, to my detriment. "I've got a case," I said as he led the way back to his desk. It was on the open floor but had low cubicle walls to give a semblance of privacy.

"I thought you might. You never stop by just to say hello." His mock pout reminded me that I'd promised him a coffee date, one that never quite stuck. "What kind of case?"

"Missing person." He sobered, switching to professional mode, and I gave him the details Leith had shared, along with my observations at the house.

"Unusual of you to go against client wishes," Tom noted. He'd doodled a dog with his free hand while I talked and he pretended to focus on that, retracing a few lines, before looking up at me. A tactic I'd seen him use to seem disinterested when he really wasn't. I shrugged and he narrowed his eyes. "So, what is it about this one that's making you do it?"

"For someone who wants his grandmother found, my client isn't exactly being…forthcoming." I frowned and chewed my lip. "I dunno, Tom, call it a hunch. I don't think he did it, but I think he knows more than he's telling me and is worrying so much about the optics that his priorities are a little screwed. You haven't heard anything?"

"Nothing about a grandmother going missing, no. And nobody in lockup or psych matches the description, though I could check in with Apex and Pittsboro PD."

"I'd appreciate that. You'll let me know if anything does come up?"

"Of course. Won't even insist on that coffee date."

"Thanks, Tom."

"Keep me posted. Might not be a criminal case, but…"

"Yeah. There might be a 'yet' on the end of that."

* * *

My next stop was the Raleigh morgue, in the opposite direction of both my office and my home, and another example of where showing up in person usually yielded more direct results than a phone call.

"Hey, Doc." I offered the grande Americano I'd picked up in case it was one of those Mondays.

"Ah! My little bird comes bearing gifts," he said with a smile. I used to think that was what made him a psychic—sylphs identified strongly enough with birds that we didn't eat poultry—but no, he was referring to one of the tattoos across my upper back, a hovering kestrel fighting the East Wind. Doc was a tattoo snob, so when he complimented me on it when I came in wearing a tank top last summer, I took it as high praise.

For reasons I had yet to figure out, Dr. Michael Miller had never had a problem with me stopping by his morgue. Most people he chased out with admonishments about disturbing the dead, and a stern warning not to come back in his refined Southern drawl, but me, he liked. It was nothing sexual; Doc Mike had no interest in women. My best guess was that he was a sensitive of some kind and sensed some kind of kindred spirit in me as a magic user. He might be a psychic, a witch, maybe even a latent necromancer. It had made our initial meeting awkward, but he'd warmed up to me, and became one of my best sources.

Whatever his motivation, it made my job a hell of a lot easier on the rare occasion a case involved a missing person. Showing respect helped too, just like with the cops.

He accepted the coffee and leaned back in his chair to take a sip. I waited in patient silence. Never bother Doc Mike before he'd had a chance to enjoy his coffee.

He sighed in pleasure before returning his attention to me. "What can I do for you, Arden?"

"I've got a missing person. Just doing my due diligence."

"Of course, of course." He tapped at his keyboard, pecking the letters to his password in individually. If I ever needed to come here after-hours, I knew how to access his computer. "Name?"

"Sybil Sequoyah." I spelled it for him. "Female, DOB given as July 23, 1942." She was probably older than that. Elves might look human, but they had much longer lifespan.

Doc Mike repeated the name and birthday as he entered it. "Mmm. Nope. Nobody locally." A pause while he clicked around. "Nothing in the statewide database, either. Photo?"

I dug in my backpack and withdrew the manila folder Leith had given me along with his money. The professional headshot from her social media profiles was held to the top of the inside with a paperclip. I pulled it free and showed it to him.

"No. Not a one like her, now or ever." He reached for the photo. "Exquisite bone structure. And so much willpower in her eyes. I'd remember her alive or dead. If she's dead, she's not here."

I sighed. Doc Mike had an excellent memory for not only his charges, but those in the database across the region. If the queen was dead, she was probably buried somewhere the human police wouldn't find her. "Thanks, Doc."

"Do I want to know why you don't look happier?"

"No. You really don't."

He studied me, sharp, brown eyes boring holes into mine. "You be careful, little bird. You're the only one of my visitors who brings me proper tribute."

I laughed as the heavy feeling of the last few days lifted a little. Doc Mike might have preferred the departed but in a world of people who wanted me dead, it was nice to know he might be sad to see me on his table.

Chapter 5

Striking out at the police station and the morgue was both good and bad. It meant no new clues, but it also meant Sybil Sequoyah might have just tripped over a chair, bumped her head, and checked herself into a hospital. I doubted that was the case, though. My gut said something had happened.

I went back to my office in Durham, and made calls to all the local hospitals. None had checked in an elderly woman matching Sybil's description, or by that name. Wherever she was, it wasn't on the record, which meant it was time to dig.

I started with the list Leith had provided of her favorite places and regular weekly stops. She hadn't gotten out much, but everyone I spoke to mentioned that she always had a man with her. Not the same man every time, but usually tall and well-built. Attractive in a way nobody could put their finger on, whether dark or fair. Sybil would joke that they were her boyfriends but when I showed a picture of Leith a few people recognized him as one of the men.

So she would have had a bodyguard with her, and occasionally that person was her grandson. Who had been with her the night of the disappearance? I called Leith to ask.

"Mr. Sequoyah, would your grandmother have had someone with her the night she disappeared?"

After a long pause, he said, "She should have."

"Any reason you didn't mention that before?" I tried to keep my voice light. He was getting on my friggin' nerves with all of this evasion and teeth-pulling.

"Because it should have been me."

That rocked me back. Embarrassed anger colored his words as he said, "I'd stepped out to run an errand and left her alone. She said she'd be fine. When I got back, she was gone. The footage from the security system was scrambled."

The silence following his statement dared me to criticize him. I let it sit as a few puzzle pieces fell into place. Was this why the Darkwatch wasn't being called in? Because he was embarrassed?

I sighed. Men and their egos.

"Is there anything else you may have…forgotten to mention?"

"Not that I can recall."

Liar. There had to be something. Even if it was just that he was playing a dangerous game of cover-your-ass. "Could I see the footage?"

"I told you, it's scrambled."

"I might have someone who can unscramble it."

"You can do that?"

"Yes."

Another pregnant pause. Again, I counseled myself to patience.

"If it will help you solve the case, I'll send it over. We have to find my grandmother."

"Thank you, Mr. Sequoyah." Finally, some headway. "You can send it to me via Dropbox or leave a USB at the reception desk at my office."

"Of course." The earlier anger had melted away and his tone grew smooth and lilting. "You're a resourceful woman, Ms. Finch. I'm so glad that I came to you."

"It's my pleasure to help."

"Hm. Yes. A rare woman, indeed."

What the hell does that mean? I avoided addressing it, feeling the creepy-crawly discomfort of a man fishing for a date with a woman just trying to do her job. Not happening with him for so many reasons, and the switch in behavior from his grandmother's house was both weird and off-putting. "Shall I wait for the USB or...?"

"No, no. I'll Dropbox it. Please let me know as soon as you learn anything."

"Will do."

"I can't wait."

I shivered as a click signaled the end of the call. *What a weirdo.* Still, a paying client was a paying client, even if he was an elf. And speaking of clients...it was past time I checked in with Callista. Her number was saved to my favorites, not because she was one, but because I knew what hand was most likely to shelter me if something happened. As long as I didn't displease her.

"Arden. I've been waiting to hear from you."

"I figured." With a wince, I tucked the phone between my shoulder and my ear, and started tidying the office to leave for the day. "Sorry. Long day, strange client. One you may be interested to hear about, actually."

"I see. Go on."

My eyebrows shot up at not being lectured on civility. Must be a slow day at the bar. "An elf came to see me."

"And you're still alive? I always knew you were a clever girl."

"Yeah. Well. I couldn't hide forever, right?" When she didn't answer, I kept going. "So. His grandmother is missing. Won't go to the cops because he doesn't want a scandal. Getting information out of him is like pulling teeth, though, and I'm starting to feel like something else is going on, even if it's just that he wasn't where he was supposed to be when she disappeared. Have you heard anything more than whispers about itchy weres and bitchy elves?"

"Yes, actually."

My breath caught. Was she finally going to bring me in on something?

"There's a rumor going around the bar that an elven girl has gone missing. High-blood, so they're keeping it quiet. This new disappearance interests me, my dear. It interests me greatly." Her voice wrapped around my brain in a way that would have been seductive if it hadn't raised all the small hairs on my body in dread.

What the hell is she?

"Thanks." I slumped in my chair, and rubbed at a spot on my desk, disappointed that she hadn't shared something bigger even as I wondered about two high-blood elves going missing.

Something clicked. "Callista…I'm wondering if this grandmother might be a queen. Massive house at Jordan Lake, supposed 'boyfriends' accompanying her everywhere. My client could pack a wallop with Aether, but I suspect he's avoiding the Darkwatch as well as the human police."

"She might be. And he might be."

The walls were back up. Great. She'd shared that tidbit in the hopes of using me some more. "Any hints? Fun facts? Things I should know in order not to get my head cut off?" *Anything more than rumors? Something that might be important enough to you that I can use this case as leverage to get you to back off?*

"You've spoken to your djinn."

It wasn't a question. Interesting. Had they spoken to her? "Yeah."

"So. Keep your shields up and you'll keep your head."

I ground my teeth at hitting another wall as far as information about elves was concerned. Why was everyone so close-lipped?

I couldn't keep the sullen note out of my voice as I said, "Fine. I'll keep you posted."

"You do that, dear one."

I hated when she called me that. I'd never felt dear to her. I started to hang up, then remembered the other reason I was checking in. "Oh—do you need anything more on Verve? My contract with that client is complete for now, so..."

"No. We just needed eyes and ears. You're starting the new year off well. I'm pleased."

"Sure." The call clicked off with the clatter of Callista's landline receiver and my stomach knotted at the thought of someone at Verve finding the bugs. I was good at my job, but accidents happened. The cleaners might have started being more diligent. Hopefully Verve's board would think it was done before I'd done the penetration test. The job had been to get in and report weaknesses, not find surveillance devices.

Still seesawing between resentment and anxiety, I dropped the phone in my bag, locked up, and headed out. Power games with Callista couldn't happen until I had something worth using. If there was scrambled video footage to review, I had to pay a visit to a werewolf.

Roman Volkov was who I went to when I had tech problems outside my expertise, or needed some new toys. He was also occasionally my fuckbuddy.

I hadn't realized he was a wolf until the first time we'd slept together. An eerie energy had slipped over me when he'd climaxed, like Aether but not, and a whiff of woodsy musk had tinged his sweat. I'd frozen, wondering if I'd given myself away as well, but he'd made no sign that he'd noticed anything out of the ordinary.

Grimm, in one of her more gossipy moods, had told me that the Volkovs were a powerful werewolf family in Asheville. There were whispers of a banished runt and I thought I'd found him.

He wasn't a physical runt. Just shy of six feet—tall, for a werewolf—and bulky with muscle, Roman probably could have rolled my little Honda hatchback as easily as playing flip cup. No, he was a magical runt, which was likely the reason he was here in north Durham and not out west in the mountains with his kin. Weres are a tough bunch, whether wolf, leopard, jaguar, coyote, fox, tiger, or otherwise. Weakness was barely tolerated in lesser pack members; in ruling families, it was dealt with by banishment or murder.

From the tales he'd told, Roman had been on his own since puberty. He'd picked up an odd mixture of skills, all focused around machinery or technology, several barely legal if not outright illegal, and all useful to me as a private investigator.

So. A visit to see the wolf in the woods.

He didn't answer when I called ahead and I debated the wisdom of just turning up. Werewolves, I knew for a certainty, were territorial. The last time I'd surprised him he'd gone all grumpy and growly. A glance at the moon showed a waxing crescent, though, so I'd risk it. He had said he wanted to see more of me.

Roman's place was on the other side of Eno River State Park from mine, in the cluster of trailer homes across from the Cabe Lands trailhead. A few old-school muscle cars roared down the narrow road as I drew close, and I hugged the dirt at the edge. I was just pulling up in front when my phone rang. Roman's name appeared on the car's center console display in the moment between parking and turning off the engine.

Rather than answering, I walked up and knocked. I had a moment to ask myself again if it was a good idea to visit a werewolf unannounced before the door swung open.

"Well," Roman drawled, a lock of brown hair falling into his eyes as he looked me up and down. "I wondered if a call meant you were coming by."

"Bad time?"

"Not at all. Especially if…" He trailed off and gave me the eye again, a heated smile tugging at his lips.

Relieved, I grinned back and cocked a hip, glad I'd worn my nice black jeans today. "A little work, a little play."

"Ass *and* cash. You're my favorite client, Arden." He stepped back and swung the door open, trailing a finger down my arm as I passed him. I didn't know if the casual touches were something general to all weres, specific to wolves, or a quirk of his in particular. I enjoyed it since there weren't many others I could risk being so intimate with. Keeping my shields locked down over my aura took away from the experience, but it was better than nothing.

He kissed the nape of my neck as he slid my jacket off and I mentally rearranged the order of business for the evening. Time was of the essence in a missing persons case, but I'd pulled a thirteen-hour day already. Detective Chan or Doc Mike would call if anyone matching Sybil's description turned up. Spinning my wheels and burning out wouldn't get her found any faster. Time to take a breather.

A puff of cold air teased along my back as he shut the door and hung up my coat. Then his arms slipped around me from behind. "Haven't seen you in a while," he murmured, lips moving against my ear. "I missed you."

Warmth surged as a tingle ran over me. I'd missed him too, missed being able to relax and delight in being desired. I tilted my head to the side so he could kiss my neck. "You mean you don't sleep with all your customers?"

"Only the hot ones who bring me something more interesting than a blown spark plug or a flat tire." His hands rose to cup my breasts. "So…just you."

I didn't know what to say to that, so I turned around and kissed him. We weren't dating, but that sounded like a declaration of exclusivity. Not that I was sleeping around, but to me, being a girlfriend meant you should tell your partner a few things. Like, that you're an elemental.

Part of the reason I messed around with Roman was because he was weak enough magically not to notice me, but strong enough that he'd probably survive being collateral damage. That being said, I didn't want to find out if he was willing to risk being collateral damage.

He also knew better than to push, accepting my kiss and cupping my ass. I tugged his t-shirt up and ran my nails along his flanks. His hips bumped mine, encouraging me backward toward the couch. Roman was happy to see me, and another flush of heat raced over me. It *had* been a while.

For once, he'd forgone a belt and was barefoot. Getting his jeans off took coordination with the kissing and his lips moved against mine in a repressed laugh when he had my pants open and down first. His hand moved lightly at the apex of my thighs, rubbing rhythmically until I was gasping and ready. We broke to strip out of our shirts and roll on the condom he'd pulled from his wallet before he lowered me to the worn sofa, then kicked off his jeans and boxer briefs.

The faint hint of musk grew when he pressed down on top of me to reclaim my mouth. I slipped a hand down to stroke him, drawing a groan.

"Don't tease me, Arden, please."

"But it's what I do best."

With a growl, he caught both my wrists and pinned them over my head in one of his bigger hands before nipping my neck. "Naughty bitch," he breathed between kisses. I laughed and offered a token struggle purely because it excited both of us. He ended it by guiding himself into me.

Work and worries drifted away as he moved. This simple, easy joining was what I'd needed after the stress of the last few days. No strings, no complications, just a man who always made sure I came first.

When he freed my hands to grasp my hips I dragged my nails down his belly, spurring him on just that little bit more I needed to tip over the edge.

Between being stressed and not getting laid in weeks, my control slipped. Fortunately, my eyes were closed and the flicker from their usual rich, deep amber to glowing gold didn't give me away. A light breeze did, though, making Roman shiver. I clamped down on it in a panic and lost the thread of the orgasm, but he was too busy losing himself to his own to notice. *Too damn close.*

He rested his head against mine before pulling out and the woodsy, musky scent of werewolf grew. "That was…something was…" Shaking his head, he tugged the condom off, and shifted to squeeze behind me on the couch. I rolled to my side to make space and tried not to tense. "I guess I just really missed you."

Much too close. I stroked his arm and tucked closer, hoping my body would distract him. He made a pleased noise and buried his nose in my hair. "You smell like a thunderstorm today," he murmured. "Crackly. Like tinfoil."

Like my magic. Fuck. Roman might be weak for a werewolf, but he was strong enough to catch the scent of *other*. "Huh. That's weird," I said. "You just smell like sexy man."

He hummed contentedly at my back, and his breathing slowed as he slipped into a postcoital nap. I dozed as well, taking comfort in feeling safe for the first time since Leith had entered my office. I could get used to this…if I didn't have so many secrets.

"Want a drink?" he mumbled just as I was on the edge of really falling asleep.

"Nah, thanks."

He pushed himself upright and grabbed the bottle of bourbon on the side table, pouring a splash into the glass next to it. "I bet you're a firecracker when you've had a few," he said after a sip, eyeing me over the rim.

"You have no idea," I murmured as I stretched out to put my feet in his lap. There were reasons I didn't drink in company. Reasons that had nothing to do with holding my liquor and everything to do with the energies that could be released when I wasn't in my right mind. A weird little quirk in my magic that I wouldn't willingly demonstrate to him or anyone else, not since the accidental first time.

Roman got that look again but let the comment go. "You had business as well?"

"Yeah. You know anything about video?"

"A bit." He smirked, which could have been for anything from knowing how to do a deepfake to wanting to make his own dirty movie. Knowing Roman, it was probably both. "What about it?"

"If I had one that was damaged, could you recover it?"

His grey eyes lit up, shifting from stormcloud to bright steel in excitement, and he started rubbing my feet. "You bring me the best work, babe. Sure, I can probably reconstruct it."

"Perfect." I stretched my arms overhead and settled against the cushion.

"You gonna get me the file tonight?"

"Yeah. Later. When you're done." Chuckling softly, he dug a thumb into my arch hard enough to make me moan with pleasure. "Maybe after a little something else as well, if you keep that up."

Chapter 6

I left Roman's later than I'd intended but with enough of the weighty fear eased to feel refreshed. He leaned on the doorjamb to watch until I was in my car, heedless of the freezing winter air he was letting in, and waved. I beeped twice in farewell before making a U-turn and pulling away.

The drownings had him worried. The evening news had said another body had been found, an older woman. Not old enough to be Sybil, yet a pattern was emerging that she might fit into. Female, upper-middle class or affluent, ties to Chapel Hill.

Were they all elves? That was where they had their territory in the Triangle. Would the missing girl from Callista's rumor be next? Would Sybil?

All this trouble with elves and now they were coming to me for answers. Maybe being Roman's girlfriend wouldn't be so bad. It would be nice to have someone at my back. I squeezed the steering wheel hard enough for the leather to creak. No. Too risky. We had a good balance now and if either of us wanted more, too bad. It would suck to lose a safe source of companionship if he wanted more, but it was better than revealing myself or mucking up a valuable business arrangement.

When I pulled into my driveway the headlights fell on Duke, leaning against the big oak in the front yard, heedless of what the bark must be doing to his suit. Something was bothering him; Duke was always more casual than he should be about his powers but this was too much even for him.

He ignored my grumbling and followed me up to the house, using Aether to go ghosty and walk through the block of Air when I stepped over it. He couldn't see it, but he'd tripped over it enough times not to bother trying to guess where I'd moved it at each visit.

"What brings you here?" I asked as I closed the door behind us and leaned over to tug off my boots.

"A vision," he said.

"A vision. About…"

"You."

"Me," I said, clutching my pendant, and not liking this at all. A vision had brought him to me as a child. He'd brought others. Having been raised among humans for my early years, I hadn't known what they were. Their whispers from the ethereal plane had caused me physical pain that had me hiding under the blankets every night for months. "Traumatic" was an understatement when describing living in a mundane foster home with the attention of the djinn. It wasn't until they'd told Callista about me that I was adopted into her care and named a sylph.

"You," he repeated, hands in his pockets as he studied the floor. "Arden…something is coming. In the vision, everything around you is cold and dark. Colder than ice. Darker than death."

I stared at him, heart in my throat. It took a few attempts before I could ask, "Is it the case?"

"I can't say."

"Elves? Do they know what I am?"

"I don't know."

I fisted my hands, not sure if fear or anger was topmost but fed up either way. "Dammit, Duke, what *do* you know? I can't go around afraid like this. I won't! I feel like I'm gonna hurl every time something new happens and I am seriously not here for this. Not now, and not from you."

He looked up and studied me, the shining black gold of his eyes pained. "Maybe we were wrong to keep you so ignorant of them. We thought it would be enough to hide you. All hidden things are found, though, aren't they?"

"Then tell me something!"

"No."

That rocked me back. "What? Why?"

"Anything I say now could tip the balance. I probably shouldn't have told you about the vision, but…well. It could just be a metaphor and not a true seeing."

"Your metaphors are seriously creeping me the fuck out right now."

"How's your werewolf?"

I blinked, thrown by the change in subject. "What does Roman have to do with this? Is he part of the vision?"

"No. You smell of wolf."

"And you're changing the subject."

"Am I?"

"I'm really not in the mood for—"

He vanished.

"Damn the djinn!" I hated when they did that. Their talents with Aether laid in manipulating themselves and light, the converse of elves. Invisibility, flight, illusion, shapeshifting, and, annoyingly, teleportation were all on the table. Unless formally summoned, they only finished the discussions they had an interest in.

Once again, I was left with more questions than answers and the feeling that my life was even less in my control than I'd thought an hour ago. The frustration that had been simmering since the Verve job flared. My little air plant bulbs swayed as I indulged myself in letting off steam in the form of a draft, sending it whistling through my small house just strongly enough to make the curtains flutter.

I have to be better than this. I didn't know who might be close enough to sense what I was doing, or if anyone could. Childish shit like that could get me killed if I forgot myself and did it where others could see.

* * *

My phone rang at an ungodly hour the next morning. I shook myself awake, and glared at the caller ID in the darkness afforded by quality blackout curtains. It was neither a number in my phone's contacts list nor the Google Voice number I'd set up for the business. Who called at seven in the morning?

"Finch," I mumbled.

"Arden? It's Mike Miller."

I sat up, suddenly much more awake. "Doc? You found Sybil Sequoyah?"

"No. But I found something else strange. Given your experience with some of the odder cases, I thought you might find it useful to take a look."

"You're the best, Doc. I can be there in fifty minutes. Maybe less."

"See you then."

In an effort to be quick rather than stylish, I zipped up a thick, cobalt-blue hoodie over a black t-shirt and jeans, slipped into my heavy, black leather boots, and made it to the morgue far faster than was safe given the sheen of ice on the roads.

Doc Mike was waiting for me when I strode into the morgue, practically bouncing on his toes. He handed me a neatly folded heap containing what looked like a mask, bonnet, apron, booties, and gloves.

I raised my eyebrows at him. "I totally thought you were going to show me on a video screen or something."

"Normally, I would. But this is…hmm. It's just weird." He smirked. "Hope you haven't had breakfast."

My stomach flipped. "I never do but I really don't like what you're suggesting." Not saying anything else, the good doctor waved me ahead of him, down a hall, and through a set of wide metal doors. In the scrub room, I got suited and booted, wrinkling my nose at the overpowering scent of wintergreen coming from the mask.

"You'll be glad for it later," Doc Mike said as he handed me safety glasses, and led the way through.

Two bodies were laid out on slabs, both female. One of the women had been dark-skinned in life, the other fair and older, but death had leached the color from both of them. I grimaced behind the mask. Nobody liked being reminded of mortality.

"These are the latest drowning victims. The brunette came in early this morning. No ID."

"I hadn't heard there'd been another."

"She's been kept out of the press."

"Why?"

"That's what I wanted to talk to you about." He moved to the side of the nearest corpse. "Up until now, we've been treating these as separate incidents. It's unusual for so many people to drown in a winter, but there was that stupid YouTube challenge going around. Polar bear dare, or something. Two of the cases were younger, so we figured stunts. Dumb kids whose luck ran out and whose friends were too afraid to help."

"With you so far."

"Then some older ones came in, old enough we didn't reckon they'd be doing silly stunts. Still, accidents happen."

"I hear a 'but' coming."

"But here's where it gets weird. Three of them had marks like this." He gestured me closer, and I tried to breathe more shallowly as he pulled the woman's arm away from her body with gentle hands and rotated it. Two shallow puncture wounds, green with old bruising, dotted the inside of her elbow.

Holding my breath, I leaned closer, glad now that he'd invited me in rather than simply sending me pictures. A snake large enough to make a bite impression that wide would have had much longer teeth and left a deeper wound, and they weren't active at this time of year, so it wasn't that. The last time I saw anything with fangs that could make marks like that was back when Grimm was in a vampire phase and using Aether to look like one of them.

The punctures had to be vampire bites.

Someone in the community has been naughty. This was exactly why we had Watchers and I blessed my lucky star that he'd called me. Callista needed to know that the vampires were getting sloppy and while I really did not want to be the one to tell her, it was better me than someone else. Doc Mike was a good guy, and sometimes her cleanup methods could be extreme, not to mention the likelihood that tattling would piss off the vamps.

"Copperhead?" I said, trying to throw him off.

He scoffed. "Come on, Arden. Don't you live near Eno? You know the snakes are hibernating now. Besides, I ran blood tests just in case they had somehow all managed to disturb a sleeping snake. There's something not right about the level of coagulation I'm seeing in the results, and there's no venom in any of the bodies."

This is bad. I cleared my throat as a sour taste coated the back of my tongue. "Not a snake, then," I said reluctantly. "What's your hypothesis?"

"For now? Some kind of drug with a new delivery system. Fast-acting, since I didn't see a trace of anything other than the anticoagulant in their system."

I nodded, relaxing until he added, "But there's something else."

"Oh?" How much more of a clusterfuck was this going to be?

"Tattoos." With the same respectful care as before, he replaced her arm, tilted her head, and thumbed her ear aside. A graceful tattoo danced on the skin of her neck, sort of like kanji but not, in a script I recognized from that book of Callista's— the one that had scared the bejeezus out of me as a teenager. It was an elven House sigil.

Someone was definitely targeting elves. Which meant my next question was whether Sybil would be the next to turn up.

"The same tattoo on all of them?" I asked, dreading the answer.

"No. The same on three of them. Two others had the same one to each other, but different to this one, and the last had a third. All the same style though. Again, could be one of those trends—I remember when those damn birds-turning-into-dandelion-fluff tattoos were all the rage—but they're the exact same tattoos, all behind the ear or under the clavicle."

"Let me see if I understand what you're saying. Three vics with weird drug tracks. All six with similar tattoos in similar locations. All found drowned around the Triangle."

"That's the sum of it, yes."

"Have you spoken to anyone else about this?"

He gave me a sharp glance. "It's noted in the report I'm about to send to the local police departments. Why?"

Good to know. Hopefully he won't suspect me when the cleanup crew does their job. I fidgeted as guilt crawled over me. Secrecy sucked.

I didn't want to tell on him, but Otherside's secrets had to be preserved. I had a duty.

Do you? A little voice whispered in the back of my mind. *Do you owe any of them anything? They're hiding things from you. Are you really part of the community? Enough to risk Doc Mike?*

I shook my head to clear it away. Now was not the time for doubts. None of us knew who Callista's other Watchers were; we each operated as a self-sufficient cell. If I failed to report this and someone else did, there would be some explaining to do. Besides, whether I was accepted by the majority of the Othersiders or not, I wasn't human. The last attempt to come out had ended with the Salem Witch Trials, and I was so not here to be burnt at the stake.

Doc Mike was still waiting for my response. I shrugged and said, "I was just wondering if there was a second opinion on the marks and tatts. This is definitely out of the ordinary. Can't say I've seen the like."

"Hm. No, my colleagues hadn't seen anything like it. I figured it was peculiar enough to call you, given your history with the weird cases."

I nodded, hoping he never connected *weird* with *Otherside*. "I'll keep my ears open and my eyes peeled. You know how nosy I am." My grin was lost behind my mask.

He laughed and gestured toward the door. I hotfooted it out of there, nerves prickling with anticipation as I stripped out of the protective gear and disposed of it in the biohazard bin. A scrub in the sink, and I was ready to go.

It was early to be at work, but I was up and dressed. A small business took hustle to run, even at the rates I was able to charge. That, plus every hour that passed decreased the likelihood of a good outcome in the Sequoyah case. Might as well go in.

Having run through the crime scene, police department, morgue, and hospitals on Monday plus frequented locations yesterday with no luck, today was for searching records and if that failed, interviewing friends and family. Roman hadn't been sure how long it would take him to get something useable out of the video, if anything was recoverable at all, so until he came back with an update it was old-fashioned detective work for me.

I went back through the folder, reconsidering my theory that Sybil might have grown tired of being in the public eye all the time. If she had, maybe the blood at the family home was Leith's. After reviewing my notes on the last three months of her social media posts, she seemed like the type who might have bopped her bodyguard on the nose and walked out the door without him. Was that why he was embarrassed and avoiding the Darkwatch?

Stop speculating. Find the facts, I reminded myself.

If she had slipped Leith, she might have started a fresh profile. Duke had said elves always acted collectively. Social media provided an outlet and a connection to billions; maybe it served as a comfort to Sybil Sequoyah as well. An image search with her profile picture didn't turn up anything interesting, though.

Leaning back in my chair, I scrubbed my hands over my face, and stared at the ceiling. Dead end after dead end. A lot of PI work went like this, slow and slogging, until patience and diligence was rewarded with success.

Or not. Some cases just didn't have happy endings. This was starting to feel like it would be one of them. While each missing person case was different, they also had their similarities. Something was off about this one, and I couldn't put my finger on what it was.

Chapter 7

I spent the rest of the afternoon scouring the various databases investigators used and calling a few of my colleagues around the Triangle. No joy. When six o'clock rolled around, I realized I'd missed lunch. *Not good. You need to eat.*

Evening was prime time to interview people who worked the standard nine-to-five, and I wavered guiltily, tapping at the screen of my phone. The device flickered obligingly while I dithered, waiting for me to press my index finger to the back to unlock it. It wasn't just Sybil's friends and family I needed to call; it was Callista as well. I'd been so caught up in the Sequoyah case that I'd neglected my responsibilities as a Watcher.

I grimaced and rolled tension-tightened shoulders. *They can wait a little longer.* I'd known that one day Doc Mike would stumble on something that would make him a liability. The more dangerous Othersiders usually covered up their mistakes—vamp victims drained in the heat of passion, djinn deals gone wrong, the occasional maladjusted werewolf or witch who'd lost the Way—but medicine and genetic tests were getting too good not to notice the ones that slipped through our fingers.

Wait a minute. Genetic testing…if that's what Verve is working on, it would explain Callista's interest. I massaged a tight muscle in my shoulder as I debated doing a search, then rejected the idea. My plate was more than full and sticking my nose in now might buy me some bargaining power for Doc Mike, but it might also get that nose snapped off.

Food first, then questions of loyalty. I knew better than to speak the thought aloud, especially given Duke and Grimm popping in the other day. Anyone could be listening, and unless the spell was directed at me, I'd miss it. The downside of shielding so strongly was the hampering of my ability to detect passive magic unless it was being woven right on top of me.

A new barbeque restaurant had opened between my office and Callista's bar. Reasoning that soul food would be good for the soul, I bundled up, and walked over.

The restaurant had that good, heavy scent of woodsmoke, roasting meat, and sharp, vinegar-based sauce wafting from five hundred feet away. The inside was almost too warm after the brisk evening nipping at my cheeks, and condensation from steaming food and the diners' breaths fogged the windows. Family-style seating at high-top tables ran down the center of the room, with lower tables for smaller or shyer parties around the edges. It was the kind of place Roman might like, and I wrestled with the question of whether bringing him here would be too much like a date for what we were doing.

On the cashier's recommendation, I ordered a plate of Lexington-style barbeque, collard greens, and mac and cheese so thick it stuck to the roof of my mouth. Good stuff. Made me glad I wasn't one of the oread, earth elementals. They avoided eating anything hoofed, or so I was told. Chicken I could live without; everything is supposed to taste like it. But a good pork shoulder? Nope. Definitely glad poultry was off my list and not this.

I hesitated at the door on my way out and fiddled with the edges of my black knit beanie, knowing I should go see Callista and not in the mood for it. I didn't want to argue for my friend's life, the preservation of his place of business, or his sanity, on top of my ongoing issues with my boss. If I'd had time to come up with a plan then I'd have gone, but I had nothing. Just excuses and a jumble of puzzle pieces that should fit together and didn't. "Fuck it," I muttered. When I had something to bargain with, I'd speak to Callista.

Halfway across the overgrown lot that served as a shortcut back to the main part of downtown, a shift in the breeze brought me a scent that put my hair on end. Burnt marshmallow. Alerted to a threat, I eased my shields the barest hair needed to sense active magic. There was something faint, almost not there, at the edge of my awareness. I wouldn't have sensed it without looking for it, even with my shields down. Whoever it was didn't want me to know they were there.

I was being followed. *Shit.* I shouldn't have risked the shortcut. I swallowed against a suddenly dry mouth. The night's cold bit deeper, driven by fear. Hefting my backpack, I lengthened my stride, and started drifting back toward the populated part of town. In my hurry, I nearly tripped crossing the railroad tracks in the dark, and used catching myself as an excuse to speed up into a jog.

When I made it to the nearest building and the halo of a security light, I turned back, reaching into my bag for the knife I carried just in case. There was nobody there. Peering into the darkness behind me revealed nothing. No footsteps sounded under the distant vehicle traffic. I couldn't catch the scent of elf anymore. "Great," I muttered to myself as I kept walking. "Now you're imagining things."

"Don't be so sure."

I spun back at the voice, knife up, only to have it knocked away as I was pushed out of the light. A hand gripped my arm and pulled me around into an alley, before shoving me back and moving out of my reach. My feet were the only ones that made a sound as they scuffed along the broken concrete of the sidewalk, and all the food in my stomach made me nauseous as I realized I was dealing with an Othersider. Humans never walked that quietly or moved so quickly.

"You're the private investigator," the man's voice said. His face was hidden by a ski mask, and darkness clung to him more heavily than was natural. His lean form was head and shoulders taller than me with the scent of roasted marshmallows overpowering his herbal, masculine scent. An elf.

"I don't know what you're talking about," I panted, trembling and shielding for all I was worth. I had a shotgun loaded with buckshot at home for protection against human thieves and trespassers, but didn't have the insurance rider to carry a handgun while I was working. The steel knife, now somewhere on the ground, was the best thing I had; knives couldn't be traced as easily as bullets, and if I was dealing with Otherside, that was important. Most of us avoided guns; they were too noisy and left too much evidence for human crime scene investigators looking for clues, or Watchers trying to do cover-ups.

Not that any of this helped me now, when I needed something more than a bad attitude and magic I didn't dare use. Adrenaline surged. "Back the fuck off!"

"You're sticking your nose where it shouldn't be. That's a mistake. Give me your bag."

My bag? He has an elemental trapped and wants my bag? That was almost as weird as the complete lack of inflection in his tone. My stomach churned harder and my mind raced. Fight was not going to work. Getting away was better, anyway. *Flight it is.*

I tried to run, only to be blocked as he slid in front of me. He was faster than a human would be, and I couldn't show my own speed without giving away that I was something more than human myself. If he hadn't caught on yet, I didn't want him to.

"Fine, take the fucking bag!" I held it out. Better that than my life.

He snatched it and dug my camera out with gloved hands. The faint *snick* of the memory slot being opened told me the card was being pulled out. The camera was replaced with a rough jerk, which confused the hell outta me. Why only take the memory card? Why not take the camera as well? If he was trying to deprive me of photos, the joke was on him. They were in my Google Drive, delivered when I did my wireless backup.

Duke's voice echoed in my head as the elf backed up, keeping an eye on me as he pocketed the memory card: *Whatever your client wants, there will be at least two more backing him. And there will be at least three on the other side.* Was this my guilty party?

"Stop. Digging," he said, his voice hard but still empty of passion, anger, or excitement. "This is the only nice warning you'll get."

"You call this nice? You son of a bitch, who the fuck—"

"There are things that go bump in the night, Finch. Quit investigating and don't rouse them." He dropped back a few paces before turning and walking away, melting into the shadows far faster than should have been possible, and leaving me with shivers running down my spine that had nothing to do with the cold. Leith had come to hire me, and that was bad enough. This elf had some kind of bone to pick with me.

Quit investigating what, though? The Sequoyah case? Doc Mike's bodies? And who the hell was he that he knew my name?

Standing in a dark alley wasn't going to get me any answers. Pushing away from the wall, I found and sheathed my knife before heading directly for my car, each step falling harder until I was running. Breath came ragged and sharp, the cold, dry air slicing my lungs until the metallic taste of overexertion coated the back of my throat. I was heaving when I reached the car, and my hand shook so much that I was glad it had remote entry. All

I had to do was slip my fingers over the handle and pull when the hatchback chirped a welcome. Managing a key would have been beyond me.

The events replayed like a movie as I raced home, not caring that I was speeding again. This evening wasn't the first time I'd been threatened, hence the shotgun at home and some self-defense classes that obviously weren't up to an elf in the dark. Some people didn't like being found; others reacted violently to being the dupe of social engineering. All of that, I understood. I'd singled them out personally, so they retaliated. Working with humans meant I'd always been strong and fast enough to dodge out of trouble.

But this? I had no idea who this was or what was in it for him despite him knowing my name.

The lack of emotion from this guy scared me more than anything else, like frightening me and stealing my memory cards was simply a job, just a thing he had to tick off a to-do list for the night. Pick up some groceries, fill up the gas tank, rough up the private investigator, take the memory cards but leave the far more valuable camera. That spoke of professionalism. Professionals meant money. Money meant someone powerful among the Othersiders had taken an interest in something I was doing.

Not good.

I paced my living room when I got home, trying to think it through and put everything in its logical place. I clutched my callstone, the polished hematite warming in my hand but remaining dormant. Calling Duke or Grimm tempted me despite the fact that I'd be giving information away for free if I talked to one of them about what had happened, but I didn't activate it and make the connection. I wanted info, not to see them, so all I did was pace, rubbing the stone with my thumb as I tried to organize my thoughts.

"For Ishtar's sake, Arden, what is your bloody problem?"

I jumped and whirled at Grimm's voice behind me, wavering as the djinni arched an eyebrow at me.

"I didn't call you," I said. "Go away."

"Call me or not, you obviously wanted to. Either way, you're fondling that damn callstone hard enough to give Duke and me the shits with all the anxiety you're putting off. What is it?"

Shaking my head—whether to convince her or convince myself, I wasn't sure—I backed up toward the couch.

Grimm folded her arms and rolled her eyes. "I'm serious. Either put the stone away or talk to me." Her expression softened. "You know, like we used to?"

Crossing my own arms, I looked down at my feet, annoyance flaring at the hole in the toe of one sock. Grimm and I *had* been close once, almost sisters, if you could be sisters with someone three thousand years your senior. Duke had discovered me, Callista had raised me, but Grimm had been the one I'd confided in until I'd figured out that she didn't really want much to do with me unless I could give her information. We'd grown apart after that, and I was sure she was hiding something from me, but maybe I had to give something to get something.

I let my shoulders slump, not looking up as the soft scuff of her footsteps came closer. Said nothing when her hand landed gently on my shoulder and tightened in the suggestion of giving me a hug.

Stop being a child and be an investigator. What would I do if I treated this situation as a case? Something was going on, and the elves weren't the only suspicious party.

Grimm hummed softly as I relaxed into her embrace. "Tell me what happened."

"There was an elf," I said, pausing when she tensed. "He told me to back off the case. Scared the blessed bejeezus outta me."

She leaned back, flicking ruby eyes over me. "But no more than that?"

Disgusted, I pulled free, and threw myself into my armchair. This was part of why I'd stopped telling her everything. Aside from the feeling that she was going behind my back, nothing was ever bad enough to merit true concern. "Not unless you count stealing the memory card out of my camera and being freaky as hell disappearing into the night like some sci-fi villain."

"Don't get pissy," she said, coming around the couch, and sitting on it with crossed legs. "I know you must have had quite a fright, but at least you're still alive. Did he use any magic?"

At least you're still alive, I smart-mouthed in my head. If I hadn't been trying to figure out her angle I'd have said it out loud. Sass always ticked her off enough to leave. "No," I admitted, "Nothing active, anyway. He reeked of it though. Grimm..." Feigning hesitation, I looked down and picked at a fingernail.

"What is it, honeysweet?"

"I'm scared." I pitched my voice high and quiet, the same lost-girl tone I used when I needed men to find me harmless. It wasn't that hard; I really was scared. Underneath it was anger at how I'd been treated, but I didn't want her to see that. Yet, anyway. "All of a sudden, elves are everywhere. And I just feel like..."

The soft swish of fabric signaled Grimm moving from the couch to kneel beside the chair and rest her head against the arm. "Talk to me," she purred. The same voice she used whenever she thought I might say something useful.

With a shrug, I said, "I feel like I'm in over my head. Not like when an investigation goes bad, but like, for real. This is bigger than me, isn't it?"

She traced the pattern of one of the knots in the hardwood floor, the slow movement of her fingers betraying that she was considering lying to me. "It is," she said.

My breath caught in surprise before I could remember to keep it steady; I'd expected her to brush me off again.

The red depths of her eyes swirled when she looked up at me. "Change is coming, such as I haven't sensed in a thousand years or more. We need to be careful now, all of us, or the world will be remade to someone else's vision. Do you understand?"

"No," I whispered, transfixed by the shifting molten lava of her gaze. This was more than I'd expected from her, a glimpse of the secrets she held so close. After months—years—of being kept in the dark, was I finally about to be brought into the loop?

A grimace flashed so quickly I might have imagined it. "Arden, I know Callista mentioned that all of the communities in Otherside have been on edge," she said in a flat voice. "Stop being stupid and don't get involved. Nothing good will come of it."

I jerked back in surprise at the bitter exasperation that had replaced honeyed words, and she blinked, then smiled. The sense I'd gotten at the coffee shop, that all was not right, redoubled at the obvious ploy.

"I'm sorry, love," she said, picking at her dress before tracing one of the geometric shapes patterned on the skirt. "Look, please just be careful. Can you do that for me? I wish you'd drop the Sequoyah case. It's dangerous."

"That's obvious," I said. First the anonymous elf, now Grimm. The elf I sort of got. He might well be implicated by something in the investigation. But Grimm? Normally, she'd be egging me on, if only to try pumping me for information later. She hated elves.

Sudden insight kicked me in the ass. Grimm knew exactly why Otherside was on edge and thought something in this case would tip it into boiling over. Her bad temper—or worse-than-usual temper—probably stemmed from having the same objective as an elf: getting me to drop the case and go back to minding human business.

Forcing a fake smile of my own, I set the callstone on the low table on the other side of the armchair to placate her. "I'll be careful. If I can hand the case over to the police without risking secrets, I'll do it, okay?"

Grimm rose, bending to kiss my forehead. She hadn't done that since I was a child, before my powers kicked in, and our relationship changed. "Good girl. Be safe and be smart." Her lips faded with the rest of her as she shifted realities and disappeared.

For such a smart, experienced being, she had never been good at telling when I was lying. I suppose that would have taken too much introspection.

Chapter 8

There comes a day when you just get tired of being tired, and scared, and lonely. With the previous night's odd mugging and Grimm's complete lack of sympathy, I'd hit my limit. Ambushed by two high-blood elves in the space of a few days, driven to find solace in the arms of a werewolf who didn't know that I knew he wasn't human, trying to find a woman who would probably lead the charge in cutting off my head so I could escape Callista, feeling duty-bound to turn in a friend for the sake of laws that didn't protect me, having one of my oldest and only friends lie to me…it was too much for a single week. I'd had enough of the bone-deep fear that had dictated my moves and limited my power.

As I trudged into the office the next day, I felt like a cicada nymph crawling up a tree, preparing to shed its skin. Duke and Grimm had both said that something was coming. Fine. Let it come. I needed to take ownership of my own life instead of stumbling about, spooking at shadows. Just last week, I'd reveled at the sense of power that came with being a social engineer, talking my way past the security guard, playing my role so well nobody knew what I was really there for, and delivering results that had gotten me a hefty payday.

Who was this person giving herself ulcers when her own personal boogeymen were so convinced by her mask that they'd hired her none the wiser?

Grimm's visit had gotten me thinking. I didn't even know how much of what I'd been told was true. I didn't know the true limits of my own magic, only the carefully managed and tightly controlled practice activities Callista had allowed when I was growing up. I'd never done more than get surly at the restrictions placed on me, always playing the dutiful, grateful foster child trusting that those who provided her sanctuary were looking out for her best interests. My little rebellions had increased over time but in the end, I always did what I was told.

It was time to change that. I needed to move beyond the shelter of ignorance, and get more first-hand knowledge of the other species in the Triangle. I needed to embrace the skills I used when working human cases to build my own power base, my own fortress. I had never been so in need of advice and information, yet Duke, Grimm, and Callista were still hiding something from me. Riddles and visions, secrets and misdirection.

For a few minutes, I got so steamed that I debated dropping the case entirely, a full-scale resistance against Watching the situation and reporting back to Callista. Then I remembered Grimm's push to do just that and Leith's cloying magic as he nudged at me to agree with him. A magical compulsion probably wouldn't be broken without severe trauma. I wasn't sure being jumped in an alley qualified. Besides, it wasn't the first time I'd been threatened on the job. Probably wouldn't be the last.

Callista herself wouldn't tolerate it, either. The situation with Doc Mike I could explain away by saying I was working on it as part of the current case, and needed to know if anything else came in. Throwing everything else to the wind in a fit of pique would be a disaster.

So. A plan. With an effort, I focused on breathing, imagining a wind blowing away the hot shreds of anger and frustration, leaving me coolheaded.

The basis of every good plan was information. I needed to exhaust all available avenues with the elves, then consider expanding the scope of the investigation. Unfortunately, interviewing those who knew Sybil turned out to be worse than dealing with Leith.

Humans fell over themselves to provide information in these situations, each thinking that their small piece of information would be the one to crack the case. Call me cynical, but I didn't think it was an effort to be helpful; most just wanted the notoriety that would come from being the one who *knew* something. The chance for their fifteen seconds of fame on the evening news.

Elves, on the other hand, proved to be reluctant witnesses. None of them wanted to talk, either on the phone or in person. Evasive answers left me with no more information than I'd started with. The whole elven populace couldn't be complicit in Sybil's disappearance, so this had to be circling the wagons, the hush-hushing that Callista had mentioned. Leith probably hadn't told his people anything more than that Sybil had gone missing, if he'd said anything at all.

Heaving a sigh, I dialed the second-to-last name on my list, prepared for yet another complete waste of time. "Hi, this is Arden Finch with Hawkeye Investigations. I'm looking into a missing person. Do you have a few minutes to chat?" A small gasp on the other end was more than I'd gotten from anyone else, and I perked up. "I'm sorry if this is a bad time, Ms.—"

A whispered voice interrupted, "Is this about Katherine?"

Frowning, I wrote *Katherine, friend of Elaine Harper—missing?* on the notepad in front of me. What were the odds that someone in the same circle as Sybil was also missing?

"What can you tell me about Katherine?"

"Oh, thank goodness. I didn't think—but anyway. I haven't seen Katherine since Monday. We met for lunch. She seemed normal, I guess, for how much stress she's under with her family pushing her to marry."

"I see," I said, scribbling those details. "I'm so sorry to hear that. Could you confirm what Katherine looks like, what she was wearing?"

"Umm…she's my height, so like…five foot eight? Slim, she works out. She missed spin class with me yesterday. She's a brunette. Brown eyes. Pretty."

"Any tattoos or identifying marks?"

Elaine hesitated, and my attention sharpened. "She has a little tattoo behind her ear. Something…abstract."

Holding back a sigh, I rubbed my forehead. She'd just described the woman I'd seen yesterday morning at the morgue. I got as many more details as I could about Katherine before asking, "Has anything else strange been going on?"

Silence.

"Ms. Harper? Please, I know this must be difficult, but in any missing persons case it's important to see if there are patterns, especially new ones. It could help us find her." I winced, hoping she didn't hear in my voice the knowledge that her friend was already dead.

A deep breath. "She's been going to a bar in Raleigh. Claret. Her family wouldn't approve. Please don't tell them. Please find Katherine."

The dial tone buzzed. Not what I'd been hoping to get out of the conversation. Still, something to repay the favor of Doc Mike's calling me. I called and told him what Elaine had said, then started looking into a bar called Claret. Maybe the drownings and disappearances really were related and not just an extreme case of solstice fever driving the Otherside communities mad.

Maybe looking at a fresh angle would lead me back to Sybil.

An idea formed as I tapped my pen against my desk: what about the vampires? If both a rogue elf and Grimm were hot for me to drop the case while another elf wanted me to dig into her missing friend and all of Otherside was anxious, what might the vamps know?

While the only connection I had between the Sequoyah case and the drownings was that they involved elves, I hadn't been told to drop the case until *after* I'd been called in to look at the drowning victims again, the ones with vampire bites. It was a stretch and yet…something about it felt right to me.

Claret first. Then I'd figure out the vampires.

I pulled up the bar's website. It was one of those establishments that got around North Carolina's booze-to-food ratio law by making itself a members-only club. Usually that meant paying a dollar or two for a membership card and adding your name to a list. It was one of dozens in downtown Raleigh, a few blocks away from the capitol building.

Raleigh was the biggest sister of the three cities making up the Triangle. Where Chapel Hill was a blend of staid academia and yuppies in minivans, and Durham was the gritty, hipster comeback kid, Raleigh was where the money and power gathered in glittering towers of glass and steel.

Even if Claret wasn't a vamp bar, it seemed pretty damn likely that I'd run into vampires tonight.

Their main base was out in Charlotte, the banking capital, a two-and-a-half-hour drive southwest. Raleigh was the state capital, though, and the vampires wouldn't leave all the power plays to the politically adept elves. There had to be a balance, always. The elves got Chapel Hill. The vamps got Raleigh. The rest of us—a couple of small were clans, a handful of fae, Callista, and me—got the neutral ground of Durham.

For cities close enough to be given a designation tying them together, getting anywhere in the Triangle was ridiculous. Most people chose their preferred area and either refused to leave it or bitched at length if social obligation required them to go to one of the other points. My house at Eno, on the northwestern side of Durham, was about as far away from Raleigh as you could get while still being in the Triangle, and I was not looking forward to a long drive home after a night out.

"Tough shit," I told myself as I pulled my backup dress out of the self-assembled closet I'd installed in my office for just this reason. "Part of the job."

A quick change in the bathroom had me in a midi-length black dress with sequins on the cap sleeves. I wound my curls into a tight, high bun, applied a smoky eye, and slipped a pair of go-with-anything black pumps in my bag. The knife that usually went in my backpack went in a thigh sheath. *Et voila*, the private investigator transformed into a young professional going out for thirsty Thursday drinks and a bit of a prowl.

Downtown was packed, as usual, but I got lucky with parking and slipped into a spot alongside the curb a block away when another car left. A quick change into my heels, a little black clutch, and I was ready. The DSLR camera would have to stay in its lockbox in the back for now. My smartphone would do in a pinch.

Claret gave me the shivers even before I'd gotten to the door. The windows were blacked out, covered over with a UV-reducing film. A neon-red scrawl told you where you were, the letters a thinner, more slanted version of that Lobster font that was all over the internet for a while. The lights and door details were old brass, with real fire dancing behind glass in the lamps. The closer I got, the more a psychic weight of some kind pressed on me. A human might not have noticed it.

I shuddered. Something—or someone—powerful was nearby. I hadn't expected that, and it made me nervous. Were they inside Claret?

A small queue of professionally dressed men and women stood outside the bar. Some were smoking, others were waiting to get a membership card and enter. I joined the latter, teeth clenched, digging in my clutch for a few crumpled dollar bills, and hoping I wouldn't need more than three.

After paying my membership and exchanging a friendly—if forced—smile with the doorman, I strode in as though I'd been there before. My eyes adjusted quickly to the dim light, and I groaned inwardly. Wine bottles rested in floor-to-ceiling racks. A menu handwritten in chalk and punny signs quipping things like, "Wine a bit, you'll feel better!" decorated every square inch of free wall space.

Just my luck. Wine was what I tried to avoid most of all. Not that I disliked it. No, very much the contrary. But it was one of the oldest alcoholic beverages invented and the fastest to unlock the magical side effects I sought to ward off. If I wanted to fit in enough to get information, though, I'd have to have a glass.

Just the one. If it takes more than that, I'll leave.

I ordered a South African Shiraz and savored the first sip, rolling it over my tongue before letting it slip down my throat. This was a vice I didn't allow myself often.

"Now there's a gal who knows how to appreciate the finer things," a melodic, faintly accented voice said. I opened my eyes and found a petite, dark-eyed woman with long waves of emerald green hair grinning at me. She held out a hand. "Maria."

I shook it, slightly in awe of her delicate features and elegant bearing. "Arden."

"Good to meet you, Arden." She grinned and a dimple formed in one cheek. "Is this seat taken?"

"No, be my guest."

Her smile widened as she took the seat with a delicate hop. "I don't think I've seen you here before."

"My first time. It was…recommended to me." Why was she so mesmerizing? The smallest frown marred her brow for half a second, and I realized that I'd been gazing into her eyes. I glanced away, embarrassed and hoping she didn't think I was some kind of weirdo.

"I love when we get recommendations," she said, her voice huskier than it had been.

"We?"

"Oh! I'm the proprietor. We cater to some…particular tastes, here at Claret. Word of mouth is our surest source of new blood." She grinned as though she'd said something clever.

The penny dropped. "Ah."

She meant literal new blood. Maria had to be a vampire, and the bar a front to find new willing donors. I swallowed hard, wine forgotten. When Elaine had said her family wouldn't approve of Katherine visiting this bar, I hadn't made the connection between the bites on some of the drowning victims and a bar in Raleigh.

Maria leaned closer. "What's your type?" she asked. For a minute I thought she was asking my blood type. Maybe she was, but her fingernail dinging against my glass gave me an out.

"Bold, with a hint of spice," I said, deciding to play the game. Who better to get information from than the bar's owner?

"Mmm. Me, too." Maria was close enough to kiss, if I turned my head. I wanted to. Not knowing how much a vampire could affect me stopped me.

She inhaled and froze. "What are you?" she whispered, her breath warm on my neck.

It was my turn to go still. "Pardon?"

"Don't play games with me. I can smell the blood in your veins. You aren't human, and never were. So, what. Are you?" Her lips brushed the side of my neck.

My heart thudded. Was it that easy to be discovered? But no, she didn't know, she'd never encountered an elemental, or she wouldn't have asked. I tilted my head enough to meet her eyes again with a sideways glance. "Ask Callista," I murmured, mouth barely moving.

Her eyes widened. "Watcher," she hissed, easing away as though I were a snake she didn't want to startle. I said nothing, and made myself take another sip of wine, trying to pretend this was all in a day's work when I'd never been so unsure in my life. She blinked and took a breath she probably didn't need before sliding off the stool. "Come with me, please."

It was my turn to recoil. "Where?"

"My master would like to meet one such as you."

Stomach knotting, I said, "And I suppose there's an easy way and a hard way?"

"There always is. Call it a courtesy. Or don't. I'd love to do it the hard way."

Chapter 9

Given that I had no interest in discovering what the hard way would be, I stood, leaving the mostly full glass of wine on the bar. Maria clasped her hands at her waist, and led me to a small, narrow hallway hidden behind a curtain in the back wall.

"This isn't ominous at all," I muttered under my breath. I hated being underground.

"As I said, think of it as a courtesy." Now that she wasn't trying to seduce me, Maria's tones were more clipped. She tapped a code into the numbered panel at the end of the hall, and waved me through. A spiral stair went straight down into a shadowed basement. The pressure of power I'd felt outside grew, and I gritted my teeth as I started descending, hoping I wasn't going to find myself regretting this entire trip.

The stairs ended in a small room with a few chairs. Maria took the lead again, pushing through another set of curtains hanging behind the foot of the stairs, and unlocking another coded door. When it swung open, the dancing glow of firelight beckoned. The swish of air from the door brought with it the scent of vampires, heavy with iron and ash, and I wondered how I'd missed it on Maria upstairs. Glamour? Perfume?

"If I don't walk out of here unharmed, Callista won't be pleased," I said, regretting the high-heeled shoes. I wouldn't be able to run in them. Invoking her name once had gotten enough of a reaction that I used it as a shield now, never mind that

Callista herself was probably not all that pleased with me just now.

Maria only stared at me. I stayed where I was.

"Your blood won't be touched, girl," a resonant male voice called from deeper in the room.

"There. You have my master's assurances," Maria said with a slight sneer.

Ignoring it, I stalked past her only to stumble to a stop at the sight of the space beyond.

Black leather sofas faced each other across a wide ebony coffee table. A burgundy rug with abstract geometric details picked out in black and white stretched beneath, defining a more intimate area in the larger room. The fireplace crackled with a dancing fire to my left, a chair that could only be a throne looked over the room from the back, and the right wall was incongruously empty. I wasn't sure what to make of it all. Throne room? Entertainment? No idea. I clutched my purse to stop myself from rubbing my arms at the thick layers of power coating the room.

The vampire on the couch backing the fire waited for me to take in everything before beckoning me forward. "Come. We hold to the Détente, even if Maria would rather break it to taste you just now." He was small and spare, almost gaunt, with dark brown hair pulled back in a long braid and a gold torque glinting around his neck. He was also the source of the terrible weight of power. A master, surely—but maybe also *the* Master?

"What brings a Watcher to my place of business?" he said as I took slow steps forward, gesturing me to the opposite couch when I paused again.

I took a minute to settle myself, crossing my legs and smoothing my skirt, wondering how he'd learned I was a Watcher in the time it took for us to come down the stairs. Could vampires talk mind-to-mind?

He waited. Nothing in him betrayed the slightest hint of impatience, and an indulgent half-smile played over his full lips.

"I'm looking for someone," I said when I was as collected as I was going to be. Maria's glance at her master was quick, but I caught it. They knew something.

"Before we discuss business…my name is Arden Finch, and I mean no harm to you or yours." Best to make that clear right off the bat. I was in unfamiliar territory with no clue as to the protocols, and no idea who he was in the pecking order. *That might be a good thing to sort out, given the strength of the magic in here. If he's not the boss, I need to find out who is.* "May I presume you're the Master of Raleigh?"

"Indeed, you may." He smiled approvingly, appearing almost human except for the beating power coming off of him in waves. "So well-mannered. Much better than the last Watcher. That didn't end so well. For him."

I had no idea what had happened with the last Watcher and no desire to repeat it, given Maria's flash of fangs. My gut tightened, and my heart sped up as I tried to keep my face blank.

My host said, "I am Torsten and you are welcome here."

"Thank you," I said. He nodded as though accepting obeisance. It irritated me, and I bit my tongue to keep from saying something stupid. No need to make him revise his opinion of my manners before I'd even learned anything. "I'd like to ask about some people who might have visited your bar."

"You may."

I pulled the photo of Sybil from my purse, along with printed screenshots from Katherine's and Leith's Facebook profiles, and lined them up on the table. "Have you seen any of them?"

Torsten gestured Maria to look with a lazy flick of his fingers. His eyes stayed on me, unblinking.

"This one has been here," she said.

I twitched, startled out of a trance, and the master vampire grinned to show a slip of fangs. I pulled my eyes away from his, refocusing on Maria.

She was pointing to Katherine. "She was a long hunt," she added, glancing at her master, who nodded. "But worth it."

"Elves let you feed on them?" I frowned, trying to put that together. I'd always assumed vampires restricted their predation to humans. If they weren't…I went cold despite the heat of the room. Something like this could upset the power balance if it got out of control.

Torsten smiled, showing his fangs again, clearly trying to get another rise out of me. "Times are changing."

I thought of the other two victims Doc Mike had mentioned. With six dead, three with vampire bites, I wasn't sure it hadn't already gotten out of control. "She wasn't the only one, was she?"

Maria shifted, almost a squirm.

"Answer her," Torsten said, his playful mien vanishing.

"No."

The whispered admission drew his eyes from me at last. Crackling anger replaced bored indulgence so quickly I gasped. "You've been naughty, Maria," Torsten snarled.

"Master—"

"Silence." He turned to me, dismissing a quivering Maria, and I went rigid with the force of his regard. He was the source of the psychic weight that had been pressing on me outside, so strong that I'd sensed him one floor up and a block away. "Assure Callista that I will handle this, and thank her for sending someone so…tactful…to bring it to my attention."

"Of course," I said, hardly daring to breathe, and leaving him with his assumption. I was down the rabbit hole now, with no idea how much farther it went, entangling myself in whatever arrangement the vampires had with Callista on top of whatever elven mess I'd been dragged into. The only way out was forward. "And the other two? You're sure you haven't seen them around?"

Torsten leaned forward with the sinuous grace of a snake. "The older woman, no. The man…" He picked up Leith's picture and stared at it, then flapped it gently as though to jog his memory. "I'd have to smell him to be sure. We had trouble during the summer. Maria?"

"The fight. Yes." She was still shaking. What happened to bad vampires to make her more afraid than I was? Clearing her throat, she said, "There was a man—an elf—stirring things up. He'd come in every few days and try convincing any other elves in the bar to leave all this cross-species hedonism behind. He had some group he wanted them to join instead, elves only. Their name had something to do with red, although for all I know it was the wine. Or a euphemism." She rolled her eyes. "When they wouldn't listen to him, he wanted us to bar elves from coming here, or to discourage them from coming back."

"Ridiculous, of course," Torsten said, rolling his eyes as he tossed the photo on the table and slouched against the couch. "It's a free country, after all. If they're of age…well." He ran his tongue over his teeth. How did he manage not to cut himself on his fangs? "We don't seduce elves—" a dirty glance at Maria "—often. But why should we turn down willing donors, whatever their race? America, land of opportunity and equality. The great melting pot."

Something about the way he said that made me think he wasn't from here originally, or recently.

"I wouldn't want to get between you and your…hunts. Like I said, I'm just here for information about these three. You've been most helpful. Thank you." I scooped up the pictures.

"Anything we can do to assist," he said. "We wouldn't want to send the wrong message, now would we?"

I wasn't sure what the right answer was to that, so I said nothing. After stuffing the photos back in my purse, I rose and straightened my dress. When I looked up to say goodbye and get the hell out, they were staring at me again. "Is there…something wrong?"

Torsten and Maria exchanged glances before he said, "You've looked us both in the eye."

Fuck. What did I do? I swallowed, hard, before getting an apology out. "I'm sorry, this is my first time visiting with vampires. If I've misstepped—"

Torsten's full-throated laugh interrupted me. Maria just looked hungry again, the keen expression replacing the fear Torsten had instilled in her. I fidgeted, clutching my purse and trying to edge toward the door, until he cut off suddenly. "That's precious. Tell me, what are you?"

"Why?" I said stupidly, mind racing. His gaze bore into mine, and he leaned forward again. That pressing weight intensified and I shook my head, trying to dislodge it, to shake him loose.

"What. Are. You."

"I'm…"

For a minute I didn't know. There was only the emerald flame of his eyes, the pressure to let him in, to tell him everything there was to know about me. It was too much to think or breathe around, let alone speak.

A whisper of air caressed my cheek. *Air.* Air was my refuge, the element that made me what I was. I knew that, owned it, found myself in it. With a shuddering gasp, I shook off the weight, stumbling as I tripped over my own feet in an effort to get away from him and out from between the couch and the table.

Irritation tightened his features before he leaned back and looked to my left. My head snapped around to see another person had joined us. The door opening had been the source of the draft that'd saved me. "I'm sorry if I've interrupted…" the new vampire said.

"You're not now, but you will be if this isn't important," Torsten snapped. The man glanced at me and then back at Torsten, who flipped a hand at me. "Go, girl. I've never encountered a creature that could hold my gaze and then break it. That entertainment has bought you your freedom—this time. Pray you don't become too interesting."

I didn't quite run out of the room. I just walked faster than I ever had in my life.

"You're already far too interesting," Maria's voice said behind me when I reached the stairs.

I jumped and spun, not having heard her follow me out. She reached for one of my curls with supernatural speed, pulling it straight and letting it spring back before I jerked away. I *hated* when people touched my hair.

Pouting, she said, "It might be worth hunting another elf to see if you come back."

"I don't think Torsten would agree," I said, fright and the feeling of having my space invaded driving me to snappishness.

Remembered pain flickered in her eyes, followed by anger when she realized I'd seen it. "No. I don't think he would. Run along, little whatever-you-are. And be careful. The night is full of us." She stalked back into Torsten's room with a sway of her hips, and shut the door firmly behind her.

For once, I didn't feel like snooping around. I had no interest in being the newest vintage served at Claret, and it was the second night in a row I'd been warned about the real dangers after nightfall.

"Stupid," I cursed myself as I hit the top of the stairs and pushed through the curtain. I'd forgotten the first rule of vampires: don't ever look them in the eye. Though lacking the elven control of Aether, their personal glamour could bespell, especially if they wanted something, and double if they were old. I'm not sure if I was more afraid that Torsten had wanted something, or that I'd been able to withstand giving it to him. That was *not* how one stayed under the radar and out of trouble.

And yet…I'd learned something. I had a partial immunity to glamour. Partial, because without the distraction of the door opening, I would have told Torsten what I was, and anything he asked afterward. The memory quickened my pace again. I pushed through the curtains, feeling like everyone in the bar was watching me, and got the hell out of Claret.

Biting winter air nipped me as soon as I was away from the heat lamps in front of the door. I took in a lungful, pausing to close my eyes and savor it before continuing to my car. With fresh air came clarity. Maria and Torsten hadn't told me everything, I was sure of it. Whether it was to do with my case or their mysterious deal with Callista, I didn't know. I wanted to—a natural curiosity came with being a PI—but it wasn't the kind of thing that would be good for my health to pursue. These weren't the humans I was used to dealing with, and that wasn't the case I was investigating.

A hand grabbing my elbow yanked me both out of my thoughts and into a shadowed alley three steps away from my car. "Let go!" I said as I tried to jerk away. Instead of being released, I was pulled closer against a body. I opened my mouth to scream, only for a hand to clap over my mouth.

"So sweet the struggles. Fight me, fight me. Your blood will sing the sweeter song. The more you—" the voice cut off in giggles as the insanity and encouragement to fight sent me from scared to terrified. I forgot every self-defense class I'd ever taken and flailed in a useless, ineffective panic.

"Put her down, Aron."

The order cut through enough for me to recall my training, although none of my self-defense efforts—the instep stomp, the solar plexus slam—made a dent.

"Ms. Finch. Arden! Stop. Moving."

The instructions had to be repeated before I was able to take hold of myself enough to obey. Whoever had grabbed me clutched harder, a strange whimper-growl emanating from the voice box pressed against my ear.

"It's mine, mine for me. Not you, not yours."

"Aron. Do you remember what happened last time I had to come out and get you?"

Quiet threat oozed from the voice, and oppressive power weighed on us. Torsten. Aron whined like a kicked dog, squeezed one last time, then let go so abruptly that I stumbled and fell.

Heedless of my dignity, I scrabbled away on all fours before finding my feet again. My headlong flight to my car was halted by Torsten's arm blocking the exit to the alley, his hand pressed to the wall.

"Wait," he said, his attention on Aron. In a louder voice, he called, "Maria, make sure Aron gets home."

I pressed as close to the brick as I could as Maria slipped past and coaxed Aron away. When they were gone, Torsten turned to me. "Were you bitten?"

"I don't—" The hand I reflexively clapped to my neck at the question came away bloody.

Torsten caught my chin and turned my head to the side. "Stop struggling," he said between gritted teeth. A harsh accent came out, something northern European, maybe. "Your scent is intriguing enough without spicing it with fear."

Ice formed in my belly, and I stood as still as I could, sharp, shallow breaths creating heavy puffs against the chill night.

"A scratch. He nicked you, nothing more. Fortunately for us all, he's not stronger. We don't need a full rakshasa on the loose. Still…" Torsten's voice trailed quieter with each word, until he released me. His lips thinned as he pressed them together. "We owe you a debt."

"I'll take a favor." My voice shook and my mouth was dry. "I just want to get the f—" I swallowed the swear with effort, remembering his appreciation of courtesy, "—to get out of here. Please and thanks."

"A favor. Fine. Go."

He wasn't happy about it, and I didn't care. I went, a corner of my mind trying to figure out where I'd heard the word *rakshasa* before.

It didn't matter. Whatever had just happened, it was time to get as far away from vampires as I could.

Chapter 10

The evening didn't catch up with me until I got home and was sitting in the relative safety of my armchair. Tea sloshed over my hand as it started shaking, and I set the mug aside with a hiss. I'd kept it together on the drive home, clenching the wheel at ten and two like a teenager on their driving exam, but now that I wasn't dodging the Triangle's notoriously terrible drivers, there was nothing to distract me. With the weather being as cold as it was, I lit a big fire in the fireplace. Even so, I trembled as though trapped outside in a blizzard.

In allowing limits to be placed on my powers and taking only human cases, I'd done myself a serious disservice. Anger sent tendrils through my chest, giving faint hints of warmth that the fire hadn't as I looked back over the years.

Only recently had Callista changed her mind about wanting me to use my powers; it couldn't be a coincidence that other matters were coming to a head as well. Duke and Grimm had always been wary of my seeing or hearing too much about elves. The feeling that they'd wanted to keep me dumb blended with the *how dare* feeling of being attacked twice in one week, stoking anger into rage. I pushed up from my comfy chair to light some incense, then paced with fists clenched when I couldn't settle again.

"What the hell is happening?" I whispered to myself. Elves drowning and disappearing. Vampires straying outside their agreements. Callista getting extra nosy. I turned everything over and over in my head, but couldn't find the connection unless it was to do with the bites. Even then, I couldn't find the connection between those events and Sybil going missing except for all of the victims being elves.

"Now you're assuming a series of random events are connected. Great," I snarled aloud, to break the circling thoughts. Making those kinds of assumptions led either to stunning breakthroughs or sloppy, wrong detective work. I needed to find Sybil, now, because every day that passed made it more likely that she'd turn up dead.

Deciding that Roman should have made some headway with the videos, I dialed him. He picked up on the first ring.

"Arden, how'd you know I was about to call you?"

"That's good timing." I bounced on my toes, hoping he had something. "How's the video coming?"

"I think I've almost got something. The quality won't be great, but you'll probably want to take a look."

"Will it be ready tomorrow?" Just thinking of doing anything more tonight made me want to scream. I'd had so much more than enough for one day. But I had to solve this case.

Roman must have heard the tension in my voice. "What's wrong?"

"I—nothing. It's fine. I'm just…busy. Tired." I bit my tongue to stop from telling him about Claret, reminding myself that I was playing human and shouldn't know about vampires, or Watchers, or any of it.

"Are you sure? You don't sound so good."

I chewed my lip, desperate to say something. When nothing coherent pushed its way forward I said, "Yeah, I'm sure. Just busy. Thanks, Roman."

"Okay, babe." He didn't believe me but, true to nature, wasn't going to push. "I'll work on this footage a little longer tonight, and send over whatever I end up with in the morning. Sleep will do you better than staying up all night waiting for it."

"You're the best. Invoice me as well, okay?"

"Course. Can't have ass and cash without the cash. See ya, Arie."

I hung up, wondering why the pet names had increased. Something in the video? The other night?

The other night...

I plopped back into my armchair as a thought occurred to me. Roman had said I'd smelled like thunderstorms but hadn't known why. Leith had been in my office and used a pretty heavy spell without noticing that I was shielding from it. The vampires hadn't recognized my scent, either, and Torsten had to be at least a few hundred years old if he was Master of a city. *Assuming he really is the Master, and you weren't just introduced to a front man.*

The important thing was, nobody had made the connection that I was a sylph. *Have they forgotten about elementals?* My breath caught. I didn't want to dare to believe it. *Holy shit. What if nobody knows what to look for anymore?*

Sipping my tea, I considered the idea that far from waiting for an obvious fuckup on my part, the simpler and far less ominous reason none of them had taken a crack at me—crazy vampires aside—was that they just didn't know what I was. Nobody knew what Callista was, either, and she wasn't under a death threat.

Nobody knows. The thought sounded ridiculous in my head, so I repeated it out loud. "Nobody. Knows. Can they?"

Which then begged a new question: why shouldn't I practice my powers in the privacy of my own fenced yard? Hadn't Callista hinted it might be a good idea if I did?

Our conversation at the bar echoed in my head. "A dream and a bad feeling wouldn't be worth my life," I'd said.

"It might be before the spring," she'd replied.

I jiggled my knee and chewed on a hangnail. Had she known what I was about to be pulled into? There were some in the community who thought her psychic. I'd just assumed she was putting the pieces together from all her Watchers. The effect was the same. She knew something, and I would be as stupid as Grimm thought I was if I ignored it.

The thought of practicing percolated in my brain, trickling through me in a mixture of anticipation and denial. Denial because it had been so deeply ingrained over the years that I shouldn't risk it. Anticipation because with all the extra shielding over the last week, my power was starting to feel like a wetsuit that was a size too small: tight to the point of compression, and uncomfortable in a way that made me want to squirm.

"Fuck it," I said, pushing up from the chair and going for my coat. Hiding forever was a statistical impossibility, and I didn't want to be helpless and hobbled in a world where so many others had a leg up.

The chill night called, a haunting woodland song of scritching branches, the slap of damp pine needles, and the occasional screech owl.

I stood in the center of my small yard, head down, controlling my breathing as I centered myself. It had been ages since I'd last done any serious exercises. I had passive Air powers that would manifest if I didn't work to control or shield them—vocal mimicry, seeing and sensing distortions in air flow, keeping the air around me at a comfortable temperature, and purifying the air in spaces I spent a lot of time in. Birds were more tolerant of or even drawn to me, like a real-life Disney princess. But those would happen like breathing. I'd been strongly encouraged to control them as much as I could, but not punished for them when I slipped.

Active powers, like whirlwinds and whips or arrows of Air, were forbidden.

Why should I keep playing by everyone else's rules? Compliance benefitted them, not me. It kept me impotent. And that impotence made me a tool.

Time to change that.

Dropping my shields after holding them so close was like peeling the second layer of skin from an onion. When I was finally free, I filled my lungs with an even deeper breath than before, taking in the smell of woodsmoke from my chimney. Held it. Released it to let the eddies made by my exhale swirl around me, taking on a life of their own as I extended a finger of elemental power and nudged them.

That felt damn good. I did it again.

In moments, I stood at the eye of a small hurricane centered around me. When I forced it faster, the trees edging the yard whipped and bowed. When I slowed it, only the windchimes hanging off the back porch shifted, not even enough to knock against each other.

Next, I made little tornadoes. Then I shifted to trying to use Air as a scoop to shift a pile of yard waste. I was too heavy-handed, so a splatter of mud decorated the side fence as leaves and sticks went flying. Strength, I had. Finesse would need practice.

For the moment, I enjoyed the rush of power.

An adrenaline rush raced through me, leaving me breathless and giddy. Tingles sparked along my skin, making my hair stand on end. A giggle bubbled out, the sound startling me. I didn't make noises like that.

What can I do that's useful, and not just blowing wind?

Focusing, I thickened the air, forcing it to be a heavy and unmoving wall. Then I tried making blocks like the one in front of my door, but more of them, just to see how many chords of magic I could handle. The exhausting evening started catching up with me, and the magic unraveled before I could get beyond three.

Come on. Push through.

I clenched my fists, trying to stop their shaking, and tried thinning the air closest to me. Thinking of high mountaintops with less pressure, I sent oxygen molecules fleeing, creating a mini vacuum. That turned out to be stupid, and I let go of the chord of magic as I was suddenly gasping for breath. "Finesse," I reminded myself once I'd caught it. Too much, too fast, without enough focus.

The temperature had dropped even further while I'd been practicing. Cold seeped through my coat. My ungloved fingers were numb, and when I let go of the last thread of Air, the exhaustion intensified, a dragging weight on my shoulders that nearly buckled my knees. *Time to go inside.*

I went to bed that night suffused with the excited guilt of a child who had peeked at her solstice gifts.

* * *

The nice thing about being self-employed was that there was no one to answer to if I decided to work from home.

Not having practiced in so long meant I had something akin to a hangover. A throbbing head and a hint of nausea made me curl up tighter under the sheets with a groan. The irony was that if I'd practiced drunk, I wouldn't be experiencing these aftereffects. Regular practice would reduce them over time, but a bottle of wine would have served as a shortcut even as it unlocked different, more unpredictable, abilities.

I rolled over and slapped at the nightstand for my phone. The glow of the screen didn't help my headache, but it distracted me from my stomach. When I opened my email, the first one was from Roman. It had no subject line.

"i should double my rates," he'd written, leaving out capital letters and ignoring punctuation. "couldn't salvage the audio though sorry." Intrigued, I opened the Google Drive link he'd included and clicked play.

It was surveillance video from the Sequoyah house at Jordan Lake, having the appearance of degraded footage cleaned up and originally taken by a high-def security camera. I loved those things; they made it so much easier to catch someone dead to rights. The timestamp was last Wednesday evening, three days before Leith had come to see me.

Sybil Sequoyah sat in half lotus, meditating or doing yoga, maybe. As I moved to scroll the video forward, a man entered the scene. Tall, with wavy dark hair in a medium-length cut—the kind that took money and scissors, not just a set of clippers in your bathroom at home. Rolling to my belly, I peered closer at his profile as Sybil ignored him. Had she known his step?

The man paused, apparently waiting for acknowledgement. When he didn't get it, he started speaking. Without the audio I had no idea what about, but it brought Sybil to her feet, a slow, graceful uncoiling. She might be elderly, but there was strength and power in her limbs. I could see the snap of anger in her eyes, even in a recording.

So. She'd argued with this man, someone she seemed to know. More often than not, it wasn't a stranger who would hurt you—my alley encounters this week aside. It was your friends, or family, or close acquaintances.

He reached for her arm. Shook her. I hissed with outrage to see a man easily six-two and built with lean muscle wrap his hand around this woman's whole bicep, and jerk her to face him. His face wasn't angry, though. It was intent.

"What were you trying to convince her of?" I murmured. The discussion got heated, and he tried to pull her with him. She resisted, slapping him across the face. He let go, his expression clouding as he fingered the gouge one of her rings must have left on his cheek with one hand, and reached into a pocket with the other. The video glitched, pixelating, then cleared once more before disappearing into more pixels, and then static.

"What the hell?" Had he had some kind of device in his pocket? Or had he been going for something else?

Either way, I needed to talk to this man. He might have been the one who had taken her. If not, he was one of the last people to see Sybil Sequoyah.

I threw back the covers in a sudden burst of energy and called Roman on my way to the bathroom.

"Seriously? Seriously, Roman, you sat on this all *night*?"

"Like I said, babe, you sounded like you needed a break."

"Someone is missing!"

"And if you run yourself into the ground trying to find them, who does that help?" A faint growl underscored his words and I paused, mouth open, again getting the feeling that he was starting to care more than a simple fuckbuddy should. *Shit.*

"I'm sorry," I said, trying to de-escalate before he went wolfy and territorial. "I'm just afraid we won't find her."

"You will."

"I mean…you know."

"Alive and unhurt."

"Yeah. Damn." I sighed. Intuition told me that it was probably already too late, but I had to keep looking.

"It'll be okay, Arie. Whatever happens, it's not your fault. It's the person who did this to her." His voice carried the weight of a long, knowing sadness, and I stopped myself from asking who'd hurt him. I didn't need more to worry about just now.

"Thanks. I'll sort out your invoice within a week."

"Arden—"

"I have to run. I need to meet with my client. Thanks, Roman. Bye." I hung up before he could say anything else, and ignored the phone's buzzing to step into the shower. Roman didn't deserve it, but my head hurt too much to be nice to more than one person today, and I had a feeling I'd need that energy to avoid strangling Leith Sequoyah.

Chapter 11

I cleaned up and dressed in record time, and called Leith on my way into town. He agreed to meet me at my office, and I spent the wait building up my shields. The scent of Air magic had been commented on before, and if I could smell when an elf was using Aether, I had to assume that practicing would intensify my own scent. My insides tightened, as much from anxiety as from squeezing my power back into its box. I was gambling my life on the revelation that nobody remembered what an elemental smelled or felt like.

When I pulled up the reconstructed video on his arrival, surprise flickered to apprehension, and then to neutrality. He scowled at the footage, and his neck flushed red when the man, my new suspect, approached his grandmother.

"That's Troy Monteague," he said with a snarl. I flipped to a new page in my notebook and wrote down the name. We watched as Troy reached for her arm, shook her. "What the— he's one of her…people."

"Her people." *Bodyguards*, I supplied mentally when he just stared at me. "Do you know why they would argue?"

"No. But Monteague is relatively new. Still finding his place and learning her ways."

"I see," I said, although I wasn't sure I did. Filler words are a glorious assistance to quick thinking. "I should have asked this earlier, but have you received any ransom demands?"

"No. I would have mentioned that up front."

Like you mentioned that there was a video? Nodding, I asked, "Do you know where I can find Mr. Monteague?"

"I think he lives in Carrboro. I don't know his address, but I know he goes to a martial arts class between there and Durham most days. He drives one of those Acura hybrid SUVs. A black one."

I noted the information. *Big enough to comfortably seat a VIP or cart a body, while still being eco-friendly. What else would an elf bodyguard drive?* When I looked up, he was staring at me with a mixture of masculine heat and anger. "Mr. Sequoyah?" I said in a low voice, not understanding the look.

"Are you going to find her or not?"

I stiffened at the accusation in his voice and the snap of frustration in his icy eyes. "I'm doing everything I can. There are alerts and requests for information out. I was down in Raleigh yesterday following a possible lead. And—"

"Raleigh?" He stiffened. "Why? She didn't go there often. Maybe once or twice a year."

"I understand," I said, reaching for patience. This had to be hard on him. The video must have made it harder, and there was the matter of what Maria had said about his trying to keep his people out of the bar. "But nobody at her regular places has seen her. I have to widen the search. Have you reconsidered going to the police?"

"No. No, I don't want them blowing this up into some kind of scandal." The word *scandal* seemed to remind him that I was his only chance at avoiding one. He became smooth, even oily, again. "I'm sure you're doing everything you can."

Aether built, leaving a faint taste of marshmallow. A tendril of it eased toward me, and I forced myself not to react to the terror that he'd discover me.

His smile sent chills down my spine. "And if you can do anything else, I'm sure you will. I feel confident." A strong nudge on *you will*—more compulsion.

"Of course I will." I didn't know how I pushed the words out of my dry mouth, but I added, "You have my word."

Nodding as though that was exactly the answer he'd expected, Leith saw himself out. Again, he'd left his spell to unravel, and I resisted the urge to bat it away. There was nothing I could touch, either physically or with Air.

Fear faded along with his footsteps, leaving space for excitement to spark. I finally had a lead. Something real and tangible to go after.

This had been one of the more frustrating of my investigations. I'd taken missing persons cases before—for runaway spouses. Those were easy as blowing leaves in the wind. If a break hadn't come from the video, I didn't know how much longer I could have continued working this case without insisting Leith go to the police. The window had been closing even before the video.

If I couldn't track down this Troy Monteague and get something solid by Monday, I would refund Leith's money, and tell him to turn over everything I'd learned to the authorities. The sense that something wasn't right with all of this lingered.

With a jiggle of the mouse, I woke up my computer and tapped in a search for martial arts studios between Durham and Carrboro. Time to find a mystery man.

Sometimes it was as easy as searching combinations of known names, hobbies, hangouts, and workplaces to get a hit on something like a tournament or some other event. Hoping this would be one of those times, I tapped "Troy Monteague" into Google, and added "martial arts."

No joy.

I tried again with different disciplines, forms, and spellings. Still nothing. That meant I'd be doing this the hard way, making a note of all the possibilities between Durham and Carrboro, and doing some sleuthing.

A good chunk of the morning was gone by the time I'd made a list and gotten through calling. I couldn't, of course, simply call and ask if so-and-so was a member somewhere, even when I was able to perfectly mimic the voice of someone else. Most places had a policy against giving out member information. What I did instead was try a small ruse built on a pretext. In other words, I presented myself as someone else—like I had when pretending to be a sandwich delivery driver at that start-up.

This time was tricky, though. If a martial arts studio was anything like a gym, they'd either be small enough to know him personally, have one of those fancy membership systems with a photo attached, or both. The next time he was in, they'd likely do what they're trained to do: make friendly, conversational banter and welcoming comments that showed they were personally interested in the well-being of their members. Comments that might have included someone calling to look for Monteague.

The pretext I used couldn't be something like returning a credit card, where I'd just be expected to call the bank. It also couldn't be something most people would automatically ask about, or they'd alert him that someone was looking for him.

I went with a friend trying to plan a surprise party. Something innocent enough that it wouldn't make anyone uncomfortable if it came out, but still better kept quiet. Even if it wasn't a big deal, nobody wanted to be the asshole who gave away the surprise.

Finally, I struck gold with a krav maga training center that said yes, Troy Monteague was a member and no, they couldn't host the surprise party there because of the disruption to other members. I let the guy who'd answered the phone go after getting several assurances that he wouldn't ruin the surprise.

The afternoon and early evening passed in surveillance, sitting in the coffee shop next door to the studio in the strip mall, and waiting for a black Acura MDX hybrid to drive through the lot. I'd grabbed a schedule earlier under the pretense of possibly joining, hoping the semi-permanent odor of human sweat would cover up my own scent, and scratched off a class for each hour that passed without my suspect.

I was getting ready to call the whole thing a wash when the purr of a nice engine brought me out of the article I was writing about social engineering, having pitched it to *PI Magazine* in an effort to drum up more business. The caliper logo on a sleek, dark SUV flashed in the headlights of a car passing the other way as it pulled into a spot right in front of the coffee shop window.

Act normal, I reminded myself as the man I'd seen in the video got out, tugging a duffel bag that could have been the twin to Leith's out with him. He looked around, eyes darting to take in stucco-covered pillars, the wider lot, anywhere that could hide someone.

He didn't look at the woman sitting in plain sight directly in front of him.

I kept my eyes on my screen, looking up when movement in my peripheral vision indicated he was moving to my right, toward the krav maga studio. After giving it a solid ten minutes, I got my stuff together and headed out, glancing in the window as I walked past.

There he was, doing warm-up exercises in a t-shirt and exercise bottoms, looking light on his feet and frighteningly athletic. This was the place.

Clutching my key between my fingers in case the masked assailant was still following me, I made my way through the parking lot to my car, got in, and drove around the block before coming back. With two exits out of the parking lot, I had a fifty-fifty chance of picking the one he'd leave from. Carrboro was southwest of here, so I chose the exit closer to that direction, parked again, and settled in to wait a little longer.

An hour was a long time to sit alone in the dark with your thoughts. Mine kept drifting toward the video and what this man might have wanted with Sybil, then bouncing back with an admonition that he might have been trying to help or warn her. With no audio, there was no context. Elf or not, I couldn't assume he was guilty just because I'd been threatened.

When Monteague left, he drove right past me, making it easy to ghost out behind him and trail him home.

I kept driving past the house he parked in front of, a small but tidy duplex in an older neighborhood that didn't match the value of his car, muttering the house number under my breath until I'd turned a corner. After a quick stop to write the address down, I headed home.

* * *

Detective Chan confirmed that there were no priors or warrants out for Troy Monteague of Carrboro, so either he wasn't that kind of dangerous, or he was, and just hadn't been caught yet. It also assumed Troy Monteague was really his name, and he didn't have a rap sheet under a different name. Whichever it was, cornering him wasn't wise.

Desperation was the mother of stupidity.

I waited for him outside Harris Teeter, having gotten up early enough to stake out his place and tail him on his morning errands. It was public, there were cameras, and people were used to being approached outside grocery stores, whether by charity fundraisers or the homeless.

"Hey there, sir," I started when he emerged, sidling up and matching his stride. His shoulders tightened but he didn't look at me. The scratch on his left cheek had already healed in just over a week, leaving a faint, old-looking scar. A human would still have a scab, or a fresh-looking, half-healed mark. *Note to self: elves heal fast.*

"Don't carry cash," he said gruffly.

"No worries, I'm not here for cash. I'm a private investigator."

His fingers loosened on the cart, preparing to move, and I let myself drift farther out of his reach. "Whatever it is, I have nothing to say," he growled.

"Look, I'm sorry to bother you like this. I'm just trying to find out something about an elderly woman who's gone missing." His jaw clenched, and I pushed on with, "She was last seen in this area. Maybe you've seen her around?" I held up the picture of Sybil, and he flushed deeper than the wind nipping our cheeks would account for.

"Nope." He didn't even glance at the photo.

"You sure?" My gut was saying both *run away* and *he knows something.* I gritted my teeth and forced myself to keep pace with him.

The cart slowed as he finally looked at me. Hazel eyes like moss on sandstone fixed on me with an intensity that stopped me in my tracks, my survival instincts finally kicking in. Troy Monteague leaned forward, and a prickle of Aether stung through my shields. I was already two steps away, and still trying to increase the distance between us, before my brain caught up with whatever impulse that zap had instilled.

"Right. Haven't seen her. Sorry to bother you," I said again, completely rattled. He might be even stronger than Leith, and now he knew someone was looking for him. *Shit.* And what had he done to my shields? Had he discovered me?

I hotfooted it back to the storefront before either of us could consider that too carefully, and showed the photo to a few more people until a black SUV roared out of the parking lot. That ended up being lucky, because I found a man who said he was her hairdresser, who gave me more info for my timeline and the name of Sybil's favorite spot at Jordan Lake: the New Hope Overlook. Apparently, Sybil loved to watch for bald eagles. Talked about them every time she was in for her twice-monthly trim.

The odds that she would be there were slim, but so many people went to favorite places to escape troubles in their daily lives. What if the blood on the floor was Troy's, from that cut, and Sybil had gone to the overlook, and had an accident?

It was far-fetched, especially given that a much more likely explanation was available. Troy was my suspect. He'd done *something,* even if it was just setting her off. His involvement didn't have to be malicious for it to cause guilt. He was her bodyguard, and she was missing. That looked bad enough.

I sped back to my office to assemble some notes, and make sure there was a record of everything I'd learned. If he had done something to Sybil, it wouldn't be hard for him to track me down. Whatever he'd done to my shields had me spooked, and I wanted records in case I went missing. He'd certainly behaved suspiciously enough that I was certain he knew something. Worse, if he'd gotten through and picked up something from me, I could be his next target. My skin prickled as I grimly put together a folder with duplicates of all my notes, and put it in my top drawer. I hoped I was just being paranoid. Either way, caution had kept me alive. It might help avenge me, too, assuming anyone cared enough to do so.

After that, I mapped out the locations to which I'd followed Troy, adding the Sequoyah property at Jordan Lake to try establishing a radius. However adventurous people were, most had their patterns for daily life. Preferred shops, regular classes, work sites, that sort of thing.

My focus didn't last long. The idea that Sybil had had an accident had taken root, gripping my mind with burning intensity. I couldn't shake it loose. After trying and failing to talk myself out of it, I fished my callstone out of my purse, and concentrated.

"Duke? Grimm? I could really use some help."

The stone flared from hematite grey to red. Grimm answered in a drawl. "Hello, lovely. What kind of trouble are you in?"

"I need you to follow someone for me." I rapped my fingers across the desk, rapid-fire, then stood to pace when that didn't do enough to dispel the nervous energy.

"A hunt. How delightfully wicked of you to call."

"Grimm…it's an elf."

She hissed but said, "I'm still listening."

"He knows something, but he also knows I'm on his tail. I just need someone to keep an eye on him, take some notes of his whereabouts, who he talks to, that kind of thing. You in?"

"What are you paying with?"

I sighed. "You couldn't just do me a favor?"

"A favor!" She laughed. The rich, mocking chuckles ran chills down my spine. "A favor. Djinn don't do favors even for our favorites, you know that."

"You owe me, Grimm."

"How do you figure that?"

"I know you're hiding something from me. About elves."

"I'm hiding lots of things," she said, completely undeterred. "There are so *many* horrible things to hide about them. You'll have to be more specific."

"Fine. You help me with this, and I won't tell Callista about the rakshasa," I snapped, finally remembering who had mentioned the creatures. Grimm's vampire phase had ended when she'd driven a vampire mad prematurely, creating a rakshasa. I'd overheard her talking to Duke and kept quiet, filing it away for future research.

The information I'd dug up in secret later came flooding back. Vampires could hypothetically live forever, but they didn't have the elves' evolved resistance to mental deterioration. Eventually the virus that turned them needed more iron and human-based proteins—more blood—than could reasonably be sustained, and the host needed to be put down before they could expose Otherside. Some lines were more prone to failure than others, and apparently the failure could be induced. Hence, rakshasas like Aron, Torsten's scion from the alley.

Dead silence met my stab in the dark.

"I mean it, Grimm."

"You'd tattle on me? How did you even find him, anyway?"

Does that mean Aron was her fault? "I'm a PI. It's literally my job to find other people's secrets." I had no evidence that Aron was the rakshasa she was responsible for, or if there was another one somewhere between Raleigh and Charlotte, but she didn't know that.

"Bitch."

I huffed, exasperated. Asking her for help was not a good idea, but my gut said I needed to find Sybil right now. "Fine, yes, I'm a bitch. Are you going to help me or not?"

"Callista never finds out about the rakshasa."

"As long as you tail this elf until I tell you otherwise. Without harming or interfering with him."

"I hate you."

"No, you don't." Grimm's dramatics got tiresome. If it wasn't for the fact that I needed eyes on Monteague, I'd have ended the call. Never end a call with a djinni until you've secured a clear verbal agreement. "Let's hear it, Grimm."

"Fine. I will follow your elf and take note of his whereabouts until you no longer require my *assistance*. He will remain unharmed and unbothered so far as I am able to manage. But if he comes after me, I'll rip out his fucking throat and use his skin as a costume for All Hallow's Eve."

"Thank you." I gave her all the information I had. "I need to go check on a lead. I'll keep the stone on me in case you come across anything."

The stone flashed again, back to plain hematite, and I ran for the door.

Chapter 12

The nagging sense that I needed to go and look for Sybil grew until it stabbed at my mind like a hot poker. New Hope Overlook was one of the more remote spots at Jordan Lake, even farther south than the Sequoyah property. Houses grew smaller and the land they sat on sprawled, except for the occasional rich-looking subdivision. Working farms and horse boarding stables alternated with tractor repair garages and garden nurseries. Vultures in the trees marked where the stripped bones of deer carcasses lay, the victims of icy roads, blind curves, and not enough stopping time.

The winding two-lane road didn't have a posted speed limit, so I floored it, going as fast as I dared on the slick surface. I was starting to wonder if I'd made a wrong turn when I spotted the brown tourism sign indicating the New Hope Boat Ramp, which was the trailhead for the overlook.

The parking lot hosted only two other cars—not surprising at this time of year, but not encouraging when I was looking for someone. The boat at the Sequoyah house had been pulled out for the winter, but there had been a small garage at Sybil's house. One of the cars might be hers.

My heart sank when neither of them matched the make and model from the file Leith had provided. Stubbornness drove me back to the car for a quick change of shoes to the hiking boots I'd thrown in the hatchback's cargo area. *She could have gotten a rideshare*. Something told me I needed to look, a sense I sometimes thought might be related to Duke's gift with visions. I'd never had a bad hunch in all my years as a private investigator. I wasn't going to set this one aside.

With footwear better able to withstand frozen mud, I was off. The overlook was about a third of the way around the loop, according to the unhelpful map posted at the start of the trail.

"At least I'll get my exercise, even if I don't find her," I said with a sigh. A glance at my phone made me wince. The area was so remote I wasn't even getting cell service. Maybe it was just a dead zone in this spot?

It was already early afternoon. The sun had crested and started to fall. If I was going to get out there and back before the park closed, I needed to hustle.

This trail was wilder than the ones near my place at Eno. Dead leaves lay thicker. The paths were narrower, less defined. Rotting redcap mushrooms popped out of the forest debris at random intervals, creating surprised splashes of color against the winter browns and greys. The thuds of a woodpecker hunting grubs kept pace with my footsteps. I couldn't run with all the roots and rocks underfoot, not without risking an ankle, but I hiked as fast as I could, thighs burning on the hills.

A thick, moist scent, heavy with wet and rotting vegetation, reached me after half a mile. The lake, it had to be. And then there it was, a dull gleam under the grey skies, visible in glimpses through the pine and yellow poplar.

Although I could see the lake, there was still a bit of a hike around its meandering edges to the overlook. If I hadn't been in such a damn hurry it would have been beautiful, despite the slippery mud and sliding gravel making footing treacherous, and the cold biting through my coat.

Finally, I came to a sign pointing away from the trail loop to the overlook. A break in the trees opened into a small clearing with an angled wooden bench, jointed like half a hexagon and set between a gap in the trees to look out over the water. It would have been pleasant to sit and watch the shifting waves had I not been stressed out and driven to find some hint of Sybil Sequoyah. I went to the edge of the small cliff making up the overlook, peered down, and saw…nothing.

"Damn." The word carried all my bitter disappointment. I searched the area, kicking over heaps of sodden leaves to find nothing more than damp sticks and discarded plastic bottles left by inconsiderate hikers.

Coming back to the edge, I hugged myself, and stared out over the lake. Ice frosted the rocks along the edges, and a lone motorboat cut across the water. Smaller waves grew larger, slapping against the rocky shore below with a hollow sloshing sound. *Why did I think she'd be here? Why would she be? Stupid. Grasping at straws.* My intuition had betrayed me for the first time.

The waves sloshed again as I turned to go. I frowned, pausing to pay more attention to the way sound moved in the air. *Why does it sound hollow?* I grabbed a thin, young tree and leaned out farther over the edge of the escarpment. The mud coating the stone showed footprints leading down to the icy sand of the shore. They looked relatively old, having had time to widen, settle, and stiffen, and they were deep. Someone heavy. Or someone carrying something heavy? Difficult to tell with the distorted mud. Either way, there was no reason for them to be down there. I had to look closer.

I stripped off my gloves, and scrambled down the slope in a crabwalk, scraping my bare hands in my hurry. The rock at the bottom was slippery with a treacherous mixture of lingering ice and splashing cold spray, and I had to grab a projecting tree root to stop from sliding onto my ass and straight into the water. Once I'd caught my balance, I looked around.

My eyes met the dull, glazed gaze of Sybil Sequoyah, dead at least a few days, wrapped in a heavy blanket, and dumped on the tiny suggestion of a beach created by a hollow under the cliff. The waves rocked her gently, threatening to tug the blanket free.

I gasped, going stiff with shock. The intuition that had nagged at me all day had been leading me here, and I'd nearly dismissed it, turned around, and gone home.

"Goddess," I whispered, my chest tight. In all the missing persons cases I'd handled, I'd never found anyone dead. I nearly dropped my phone fumbling it out of my jacket pocket. One bar of service.

I hesitated, mind numb, staring dumbly at the screen. Who did I call? Leith, as my client, who wanted to avoid police involvement? Callista, for a cover-up? Or the human authorities?

Calling the police for an Otherside death went against everything I was trained to do as an Othersider and a Watcher. We dealt with our own problems quietly, without fuss and without leaving hints that could reveal us. Callista could have a crew out here in less than an hour to recover the body.

And if they did, the trace evidence that a human CSI might uncover—anything I might use to improve my position—would be gone. If they found something it could still be disappeared later, but my connections with Doc Mike and Detective Chan might give me something I could use against Callista and the elves.

You really think you're more important than the community? Sybil's dead eyes mocked me. Maria's comments about Leith's behavior at the vampire bar echoed in my mind, alongside his creepy shifts in behavior and the heavy-handed magical attempt to make me do what he wanted. Then there was Grimm's insistence that I leave the case alone. Whatever the fuck was going on, nobody wanted it out in the open, which meant something big. Something I could use if I had the courage to reach for it.

My thumb quavered as I stabbed in 9-1-1.

I don't remember what I told them. I stayed on the line until first responders arrived, like the nice lady had asked, and then hung up to answer questions. A boat arrived first but couldn't get close enough to do anything given the shallow, rocky lake shore. I stood there shivering, listening with half an ear as the woman in the boat gave instructions to a land-based team on a long-distance radio.

Even telling myself that Sybil was likely dead hadn't prepared me for this. I'd taken the case with the same measure of confident optimism I had for locating deadbeat child support parents—I'd find her, tell Leith she was okay, and move on to the next case. I'd been avoiding thinking about what I'd do when I found her, trying to maintain a professional distance from the fact that she was an elf and I was an elemental.

None of that mattered now.

A troop of footsteps and a shift in the air movement overhead announced the arrival of more first responders. Hands extended down, and I scrambled to reach them, awkward and clumsy with cold and shock. A metallic blanket settled over my shoulders as an EMT gently tugged at my arm to guide me toward the bench, out of the way of the firefighters rigging ropes to prepare a way down. The EMT filled a Styrofoam cup from an insulated flask and pushed it into my hands. I drank automatically, and gagged at the bitterness of coffee. I hated coffee.

The man said, "Sorry, ma'am, it's all we've got and we need to get you warmed up."

I nodded and forced myself to take another sip, doing my best to focus on his questions. I'd arrived at the boat ramp around one-thirty. I didn't have any medical concerns other than being fucking freezing—unusual for me, not that I told the EMT that. Then came a police officer with her questions. Yes, I was the private investigator who'd called in the discovery. No, I don't know how she got here. She'd been missing about a week. My client had refused police assistance. And so on.

The EMT broke in, saying that questions could wait, and I needed to get out of the worsening cold. A wind had kicked up, and in my distraction and distress, my power sparked, reaching to embrace the gust before I could yank it back.

One of the firefighters looked up, jerking as though she'd been slapped.

We stared at each other, frozen, until I realized my panic was mirrored in her face. I didn't smell any other Othersiders around, and if she had sensed me and was panicked, she couldn't be an elf.

Cautiously, I eased my shields down. Nobody else reacted except the firefighter. Her dark eyes widened under her choppy, chestnut-colored bangs, and shields I hadn't noticed around her dipped. Heat, the scorching kiss of contained fire, hid behind them, much like the playful swirl of a zephyr hid behind mine.

She was a dea, a fire elemental. I'd never met another elemental, but what else could she be? My world rocked so hard it dizzied me. *There are more of us here?*

The EMT was trying to hustle me back to the main trail, a hand under my elbow as he looked ahead. Reaching into an inner coat pocket, I fished out a business card, and casually dropped it along the side of the path. When I looked back, the dea was eyeing it. She glanced at me, nodded, and then went back to helping the others.

Another elemental had been in the Triangle all this time, and nobody had thought I needed to know. I had no idea whether she would be friend or foe, but at least I wasn't alone in the world. There were others like me.

Betrayal curled in my gut, thick and acidic, nestling alongside the guilt at failing to find Sybil Sequoyah alive, and pushing out any regret I'd felt about involving humans in Otherside business. It stayed with me all the way back down the trail, twisting bitterly as I sat in a squad car and spoke to the police.

They didn't want me to call Leith. I argued with them—even if I didn't like the ass, he was *my* client—but they pointed out that we didn't know how Sybil had gotten down there yet. They did agree to keep it quiet and that I could call him tomorrow, after they'd had twenty-four hours to figure out what might have happened. I made them all the promises they wanted that I wouldn't interfere, and then got into my car. Leaving the parking lot was a pain, and I exited at a crawl, driving on the grass to get around the emergency vehicles blocking the exit.

The ice in my core emanated to my skin. It had nothing to do with being cold; I was hardier in all climates than humans, and the EMTs hadn't released me until they were sure I didn't have hypothermia. No, it had much more to do with ending a case so grimly. The police detective had assured me Sybil had been dead for days, possibly a week, with decomposition slowed by the cold snap.

If it had been a week, she'd already been dead when I started the case. Nothing I could have done would have let me find her in time.

I still felt like I should have.

Scrubbing at my face, I used the car's voice commands to call Roman and asked if he was free. He was, in his words, "always free for a certain pretty lady," so I went to his place.

Concern pinched his brow when he opened the door. "Not that kind of visit, then, is it?"

"No. Sorry. I just didn't want to be alone, and I don't know who I can talk to anymore."

"Oh, Arie. Come on in." His arm settled over my shoulders and he steered me inside. "Make yourself comfortable."

I tugged the tatty wool blanket hanging off the arm of the couch over me, curling up and wondering if I'd ever feel warm again. Was this Duke's vision? It certainly felt like I was surrounded by cold and dark.

Roman went and set a pot of water to boil on the stove, pulled out a chipped mug and one of the boxes of tea he'd gotten when I'd told him I didn't drink coffee, and leaned against the counter. "It's about that lady in the video, isn't it?"

"Yeah," I said in a small voice. Now that I was here, my chest and throat were tight, and I didn't really want to talk about it, despite what I'd said when I came in.

He waited, saying nothing, patient as a wolf outside a hare's burrow. I picked at a loose strand of blue yarn in the blanket as thoughts tumbled over each other.

The mug of tea appeared under my nose, and the comforting scent of rooibos with honey wafted up. "Mmm," I hummed appreciatively, taking it and hunching over it. Roman sat next to me, not touching, just there.

"Can you hold me?" I whispered after a minute of waiting for the tea to cool. Maybe that would chase away the feeling of failure and the humming fear of the punishment that awaited when Callista found out that I'd called human police on an Otherside matter.

He shifted over, being careful of the hot beverage as he wrapped his arms around me.

Another few minutes passed before I said, "I found her. She's dead."

He kissed the top of my head. I took a ginger sip of tea, hissing when it burnt my tongue, before continuing. "I really thought…I mean, I've always found missing people alive. Always. And I know I did everything I could, but there's a little voice that keeps telling me I should have worked harder. That I could have saved her if I'd taken the case sooner, or…I dunno. Something."

"Do you want my take, or just my ears?"

"Take. Ears. Fuck it, just tell me."

With gentle fingers, he nudged my chin to turn my face toward him. "I know you well enough to know that you would have told him to go to the police. You did what you could anyway, and you found her. She wasn't left alone in the cold."

"Thanks." The churning guilt in my stomach didn't lessen, but he meant well.

"And you're not a bad person, or a bad PI, for not finding her alive. You did your job as best as you were able."

That hit home and I inhaled sharply, then gritted my teeth as my eyes prickled. *I'm not going to cry. Shit. What happened to being a tough private investigator?*

Perhaps sensing that he'd said enough, Roman stopped talking and tucked my head under his chin. I hid in my mug of tea, which was still slightly too hot to drink but almost as comforting as strong arms and soothing words. Warmth started to thaw the chill in my middle. We sat in companionable silence until I was halfway done with the mug.

"Stay here tonight," Roman said suddenly.

"Ummm…"

"I know, you don't spend the night. Make an exception. We don't even have to do anything." He took a deep inhale, let it out in a subtle *whuff*, then inhaled again. "I'm just worried about you." What did he smell under the scent of lake water and rotting leaves to make him say that? "At least stay long enough to watch a movie or something. You looked shook when you got here, Arie."

"We're not…dating…though."

He pulled back, hurt darkening his eyes. "Oh, so I have to be dating you to give a damn? Why'd you come over here, then, if you think this is just about fucking?"

I flinched, covering it by setting the mug aside. "I know, I'm sorry. Wrong thing to say. I just…I don't want you to think you have to…I dunno."

"Arie…" He sighed, and closed his eyes, visibly gathering himself. "If I don't want to do something, I won't do it. My family learned that the hard way, and you probably will too one day if you keep up that nonsense."

"Sorry." I felt awful all over again, but he was mollified by the apology.

"Fine. We're watching *The Shape of Water.*"

"Okay." Was that the one about the woman who fell in love with the fish man? Was he dropping hints or something?

If only he knew what I was. If only I could have told him.

Chapter 13

Whether Roman was dropping hints or not, Netflix and chill turned out to be exactly what I needed. I cuddled against him as we lay on the couch, a big, hairy arm draped over me with the scents of cedar, musk, and man surrounding me. I missed the last half hour of the movie, the long hours and stress of the last few days finally catching up and dragging me into a doze.

Lips against my neck and a susurration of breath pulled me closer to consciousness, but I didn't open my eyes as Roman sighed. "I wish you'd tell me what you're so afraid of all the time," he whispered, so quiet that I was sure he was talking to himself. "I wish you'd let me in."

I didn't react, or tried not to. Maybe he heard a hitch in my breathing because the next thing he said was, "Arden? Movie's over."

"'Kay," I mumbled, reluctant to end the moment, and throw myself back into the reality of what had happened.

Roman tweaked one of my curls, stretching it out to its full length before letting it go to bounce back against my head. Anyone else would have gotten an earful for touching my hair, but I made exceptions for him. He was good with his hands, and having them move against my scalp soothed me.

"Arden?"

"Hmm?"

"Where did you find her?"

I huddled up tighter. "I don't want to talk about it."

"Hear me out. Where did you find her?"

With a sigh, I pushed up out of the circle of his arms, and hugged my knees to my chest. "Jordan Lake. New Hope Overlook."

"Where were the bodies of the drowning victims recovered?"

I frowned and bit my lip. "One from Reedy Creek Lake at Umstead. Another in Lake Crabtree. One at Falls Lake, and the rest at Jordan. All over the Triangle, all in state or local parks, or state recreation areas."

"But none here at Eno, even with the quarry there."

"No." I suspected that was because the deep quarry lake was rumored to have a protective beastie living in it but didn't mention that.

"Hmm. Okay. Which was first?"

Where is he going with this? "Jordan Lake. All of the first three. And now Sybil." It clicked. "Are you saying Sybil is tied to the drownings?"

He looked at me, eyebrows raised.

"That would mean they're not accidents," I said.

"Assuming Sybil wasn't. Maybe I'm just drunk." He toasted me with a glass of bourbon he must have poured while I napped.

"Roman, she…" I swallowed, remembering the dead-fish eyes. "She was wrapped in a blanket and propped in a hollow. Like someone wanted her to look out over her favorite spot. I think it's pretty safe to say she didn't have an accident."

"…Shit."

I winced. I shouldn't have shared the details of what was now an ongoing police investigation, but maybe sharing that little bit would let me sleep tonight. "It was someone who knew her, knew her favorite spot. But that could have been…a huge number of people." She'd had who knew how many bodyguards, and if her hairdresser knew that she liked to go and watch the eagles, lots of people could have.

"Could the same person have known the others?"

"I don't know," I said, hesitating to say *yes* because if he happened to know they were all elves then it might tip him off that I was something other than human myself. Paranoid, me? "Damn. You could be right. I have to get back to the office."

Nobody was paying me to look into the six drowning deaths. Nobody had connected those dots. Usually that meant I wouldn't have touched it. If the police needed help, they'd ask. This time, though…this time, intuition and my own broken past drove me to do something. Nobody should have to hear that someone they loved had drowned—as I had, growing up to hear about my parents. The ache was dull now, but it was there.

Still, I didn't know why I was so bothered by the death of an old woman who probably would have had me killed if she'd known I was an elemental. It made no sense. I told myself that it didn't need to make sense, that I was facing my fears and my past, and being the bigger person. Oh, and doing what it took to secure my own future, one where I didn't have to be so goddamn scared all the time. Whatever it took to shut up the little voice that was creating cognitive dissonance so I could focus on pulling together the facts of each case. Bidding Roman goodbye with a quick kiss, I left for the coworking space.

The big whiteboard in my office was soon filled with pieces of paper. Printouts of news articles, my own scrawled notes, photos of the victims, a map of the Triangle that I'd had to tape together from six pieces of printer paper to make. An army of colorful magnets shaped like push pins held everything in place. String or lines in red whiteboard marker linked individuals to each other, to the map, or to a news article. Cliché, but it worked for me.

When I'd finished throwing everything I knew onto the wall, I stood back and studied it, willing a pattern to jump out. House tattoos linked some, bites linked one of those and others. The only overlap for all of them remained elves and water.

After driving me all day, my intuition was silent. I needed more to go on. I needed to get myself invited onto the investigations. Only problem was, unless Doc Mike had convinced Chapel Hill PD that the house tattoos and the vampire bites were a connection, nobody would be looking at them as a bigger picture—and he didn't know they were house tattoos and vampire bites. That assumed, of course, that his report hadn't already been buried.

Vampire bites. What had Maria said about Leith? He had to be a piece of the puzzle somehow, or he knew someone who was.

I flipped through my notes. He'd been trying to recruit people into a group. Maria had said the name involved the color red. Palming my callstone, I focused a mental call to Duke. I'd pushed the limits negotiating with Grimm, so she wouldn't help further, but if Duke had come to me with a vision, he might. "I need to ask you something about elves. Please. I'll trade for it."

"Busy," he sent back, before slamming a mental block on his stone that sent a pulsing wave of pressure through my head.

"Ass," I muttered as I massaged my forehead, knowing he wouldn't hear it but unable to resist. *Now what?*

I could talk to Doc Mike in the morning, before checking in with the police about Sybil. There was nothing more to do tonight. It was late and my burst of inspired energy was spent, leaving me drained in every way possible. Stress knotted my shoulders, my lower back ached, and my head throbbed. Time to go home. I took a picture of the board with my phone to show Doc Mike and gathered my things.

A glimpse of emerald through frosted glass was all the warning I had to halt my next step when I opened the door.

"Maria," I said, backpedaling, all my aches forgotten. "What are you—" I took a breath and gathered myself. *Don't be rude.* "How can I help you?"

She looked me up and down, slowly enough to set my heart racing, and stepped past me into my office.

"It's late. I was just on my way out," I said, caution overridden by annoyance at the presumption.

"I won't take long." She planted her feet, and cocked a hip, making it clear that she had no intention of leaving before I'd heard what she had to say. When I grimaced, and waved for her to continue, she glanced at the door.

"Talk, or don't. I'm on a case."

"I liked you better at Claret. You were more…humble."

"Claret was your turf. This is mine."

Her pout vanished in a pleased smirk when I glanced at her lips. "Fine. I have a message from Torsten."

"He can't use a phone? If you found my office, you found a phone number."

"He preferred that I make this request in person." Another long look told me I might be her next hunt. If she'd been punished for biting more than her allotted quota of elves, she wasn't showing any sign of it now.

Crossing my arms, I said, "And?"

"We don't want to go down for this."

"For…"

She raised her eyebrows. "You know."

"Remind me, for clarity's sake. I like to know exactly what I'm being asked to do."

With an angry look that came off sultry, she stepped closer and leaned close to my ear. Her cool breath raised the small hairs on the back of my neck as she said, "The others in the morgue. And the queen. It wasn't us."

So, Sybil was a queen. *Shit. How'd they find out about her already? Does Callista know?* I forced myself to focus. "You're saying nobody bit the others?"

"They were bitten. But they were a snack, not a meal. You understand?"

"You think you're being framed."

"Does it not look so to you?" Maria leaned back to study me, folding her arms to mirror my stance.

"What aren't you telling me?" I asked.

She glanced at the door again, and I shut it with slow reluctance. I'd already done too much to bring supernaturals to public attention when I called the police. The risk of an overheard comment that could corroborate any odd findings outweighed the relative safety of the open door.

"Thank you." Maria's eyes were a warm chocolate brown, matching her undyed brows. She studied me, hunger turning to interest. "You were working for the elves."

"Not really my choice." If she knew that, she'd know if I lied outright. A half-truth would do.

Her smile was twisted, somehow both bitter and mocking. "And yet you came to Raleigh at their bidding."

I bit my tongue. Needing to hide the ineffectiveness of Leith's spell, or wanting to get something to use to secure my independence, wasn't her business. Nor was the fact that my visit had been on my own initiative. "What of it?"

"Torsten wants to hire you." She rolled her eyes when I darted backward at her reach into her purse. "*Hire* you. Not kill you. Rumors are circulating that we were sloppy, that we've been killing elves and dumping them in the lakes." She scoffed. "As if we'd be caught dead playing in the forest with all that mud."

"No, nuh-uh. I work only for mundanes for a reason."

"A rule you seem willing to break for enough money." She fixed me with a cocky smile. "Besides, what reason could be good enough to walk away from double whatever the elves paid you?"

Double? Ten thousand would cover a concealed carry permit, the associated update to my PI license, and the extra insurance rider I'd need to be a gun-carrying private investigator. If I was going to be pulled into a turf war between the Triangle's two dominant supernatural species, it was time to up my personal protection. I had the shotgun at home for personal and property protection, but the lead knife I'd commissioned wouldn't keep me safe from vampires or weres. I was out of practice with my powers, and couldn't risk putting myself in a situation where relying on them was my only recourse.

But taking the money would mean getting into bed with the vampires. I didn't want to continue being caught up in Otherside politics, not until I was better prepared. All secrets come out eventually, but there was no need to rush mine becoming known. Certainly not before I'd explored the limits of my control of Air, and had a chance to find out what that dea at the crime scene knew. "No."

"Don't do this," Maria hissed, anger flashing into her gaze. I felt the beginnings of the pressure Torsten had used when he tried to get me to tell him what I was. Glamour, but reduced. She was too young to catch me like he had. "You're useful, for now. Do you really want to change that?"

"What aren't you telling me?" I asked again.

She stamped her foot, the motion so childish it made me blink. "You will do this," she said.

"Or what?" The foot stamping displayed a loss of control I hadn't seen at Claret, even when Torsten was pissed. She was too desperate.

That should have been a warning.

The breath whooshed out of me as Maria lunged, stopping with a clockwork-jerky motion just inside my space. I jumped back, losing my spatial sense in my surprise, and hit the wall next to the door. The lights clicked off as my back hit the fancy panel that served as a light switch, leaving us in the dim light making it through the privacy glass from the street. For the second time in a week, a vampire had invaded my personal space. This time it didn't scare me, it just made me angry.

"Goddess *damn* you!" I said, pushing away and going nose-to-nose with her—or nose to forehead. She had so much presence I hadn't realized how tiny she was.

It proved to be the second mistake in dealing with her this evening. She didn't budge from her spot, but her jaw dropped to expose her fangs and her pupils blew to full black. Two points pricked over my left carotid artery. *Fuck*, I thought, going very still.

"Keep fighting me. Please, keep fighting me." Her voice wound through me, silk and smoke as she inhaled at my throat. "It sweetens the blood, and he's promised I can have you if you won't work for us to balance the scales."

I fisted my hands as she settled a hand on my shoulder, wanting to get the fuck away but not wanting to be prey. That's what she hadn't been telling me, that there was a stick if the carrot didn't work. That's why she'd been sent in person. Then again, using the stick tonight meant they wouldn't have my services.

We stood there, both fighting instincts that would take this to a bloody end. "I want triple," I said, my heart still thudding.

"Bitch. I should drain you, and tell Torsten you refused."

"But I bet you'll be punished again if you do, won't you?"

Her grip tightened before she let me go and stepped back with a grotesque slowness that screamed *undead*. I didn't move as she started pulling stacks of cash out of her purse. "How much?"

"Twenty," I said, teeth clenched.

"You're lying."

"I'm including an asshole tax." This shit was pissing me off enough that I wasn't scared enough to be smart anymore. "Or do you want to go back and tell Torsten that you weren't convincing enough?"

"When you fuck up, I'm going to turn you into my personal plaything," she snarled, stalking to my desk to drop two stacks of crisp bills on it. "We want to be cleared. You get half now and the rest on completion." Her challenging stare dared me to object.

"Great. Nice doing business with you. Now get the hell out," I snapped, staying wide of her as she made her way back to the door.

Maria left with a toss of her emerald mane, slamming the door behind her.

I went behind the desk and unlocked the drawer. Her ten thousand went in the drawer with Leith's five. I had no idea how I was going to get away with depositing that much cash at my credit union. I'd probably just have to use it a few hundred dollars at a time. Or pay Roman with it. He preferred cash, living off the grid as he did. I slumped into my desk chair, holding up a hand in the semidarkness to watch it shake as the adrenaline caught up with me, and wondering how my life had gotten so complicated in one week.

I made one stop on my way home, to pick up the carton of cigarettes I'd promised Nils in return for bumping my order to the top of the list. By the time I got home, the shaking had stopped. The anger had only grown into a banked rage warming both my heart and my temper.

Was I just a tool for every other power in the Triangle? Kept ignorant and ignored until someone had a use for me, and the strength to bully me into it?

No. Fuck that.

I practiced again in the backyard that night, until sweat poured over me despite standing still. I tried to think up new tricks, focusing on how air moved through my lungs and into my bloodstream. So much inward focus made me dizzy again, so I stopped, but continued with things that could be used offensively or defensively. I worked on my control, seeking a finer point of finesse until I was ready to drop.

Only when I fumbled a chord and snapped the branch from one of the pines ringing the yard did I stop. Tomorrow morning would hurt, but it would be worth it. Every small step toward improvement was a step out of Callista's control. This power was *mine*, and I was done having other people's rules dictate how, when, and if I used it.

Chapter 14

The morning did pack a wallop, if not entirely for the reasons I'd foreseen.

"Arden."

The smooth voice wound through my subconscious, tripping me into a dream from my childhood. I was lost, so lost, and so very alone. The voice called me home, but I couldn't reach it through the tangle of brambles that had sprung up all around me. Thorns as long as my hand, curved and hungry, stretched from the canes as they reached toward me. They sought blood, mine above all others, and if they caught me, I would die. I edged back, shaking, trying to find a way out.

"Arden."

I'd have to use Air to get to the voice. I didn't have Fire to burn it back, or Earth to uproot it, or Water to wash it away. Only Air, in whispering trickles whistling through the labyrinth surrounding me. Air, which slipped and teased, caressed and sighed, and affected the bramble not one bit. I pulled more to myself, then more still. I had to clear a path, I had to get out…

"Arden!"

With a gasp and a jarring thump, I woke at the same time I fell off the couch, my cheek stinging. Delicate slippers in Tyrian purple, peeking from under a richly embroidered robe of the same color, met my gaze, and a whole new shock rattled through me. "Duke?" I addressed the shoes.

"I hope you don't have sleepovers with your wolf if you still haven't gotten over casting in your sleep. Ishtar above, I thought we'd cured you of that."

My face flamed from more than the slap he must have dealt me to wake me up. Being caught at a failing I hadn't had since puberty was mortifying. From the disheveled state of my room the last few mornings, I suspected this wasn't the first time since I'd started practicing again. I was lucky a slap was all I'd gotten; they used to be much more aggressive in their efforts to stop me drawing on Air in my dreams.

When in a corner, go on the defensive.

"What the hell are you doing here? It's—" I looked at the clock over the fireplace. "It's seven in the friggin' morning! You know I'm not—"

"A morning person. I think the neighborhood must know by now."

Scowling, I swallowed the rest of my harangue. The neighborhood, such as it was, was spaced far enough away that nobody had ever complained about my rare moonlit dancing and the music that accompanied it, so they wouldn't have heard my shout, but embarrassment held my tongue.

"And might I remind you that *you* called *me*. Now that you're up—"

"Asshole," I muttered, unable to help it.

"Now that you're *up*," Duke repeated, "You can tell me what you wanted. I'll take a favor as an IOU." He grinned at the idea of me owing him, a thing I very much did not want. Djinn always seemed to call in their favors when it was least convenient.

But will it get you a clue? I'd already crossed a line calling the police. How much did I want my independence?

"Callstones, Duke," I said, deflecting to avoid looking desperate or eager. "Or doorbell charms. Didn't we just have this discussion? I'm not a child anymore, and boundaries matter."

"When you're old enough to have watched the fall of Ur, everyone is a child. And adults can control their casting."

I glared at the pointed lift of his brows, and hauled myself back up onto the couch. The Air hangover had been delayed as my body tried to figure out if we were dying, but now that it knew we were simply awake, the headache and nausea pounded forward. My glare lost its effectiveness with my closed eyes, and the hunch of pain that I couldn't hide from the djinni.

"You've been practicing. Is that wise, Arden?"

"I wanted to ask you about the elves."

When he didn't answer, I cracked an eyelid, and peered up to see him standing with arms crossed and lips pursed in clear disapproval. My stomach churned as I held his gaze, unwilling to fall back into old patterns of automatic compliance.

"On your head be it," he snapped, eyes flashing carnelian before he brought them back to sparkling dravite. "Your query?"

"Do you know anything about elven extremist groups? Nationalists, species supremacy, anything like that? Might give significance to the color red?"

"Mmm. Yes. It sounds like a certain cult. One we thought the matriarchy had eradicated in the Old World."

"A cult."

He nodded, and sat on the other end of the couch. A ripple of magic around his head resolved into a red baseball cap that was completely incongruous with the rest of his outfit. I hated when he made me guess; it usually meant he was under some kind of geas. Geasa could be tricky to get around, having more power even than a sworn word, but they were also oddly specific. My bet was that he'd been cursed not to *speak* of this cult, possibly to particular people or at particular times, on pain of death. It was always death with a geas, don't ask me why.

"Twenty questions," I muttered, trying to figure out how to get around it. "I wonder if it has to do with hats?"

"It did once," Duke said, his posture easing slightly at this sign that I was willing to play along.

"Hats. Red hats."

"Something like that."

I studied the hat, frowning at it. He wouldn't have chosen something so out of keeping with his usual style without a reason. *Not a hat. A cap. Red cap?*

"Red cap. Redcap." When I blended it into one word, Duke relaxed all the way back on the couch. I'd gotten it, but I still had no idea what he was talking about. I searched my memory, recalling all the old books I'd peeked into, or pored over in Callista's library. Running through lessons and conversations, recordings and cases. "Don't think I've ever heard of anything to do with Redcaps."

"You wouldn't have," Duke said, picking invisible specks of lint from his robes. He only did that when he really shouldn't be doing something…or when he wanted me to think that. Geas or not, Callista could have ordered him here. Or someone else. It took a deity, or someone nearly as strong, to set a geas.

Damn, it was tough not being able to trust your friends.

As he settled against the cushions, he said, "They're an old cult. The human tales have them as sprites or house boggles, some benevolent, some murderous."

"Let me guess. You think it's the murderous sort."

"Indeed. But not fae, not anymore."

"So, what, the elves took up the fairytale?"

"Isn't it always the way? Stories are symbols, and symbols breed yet more stories."

Chewing on my lip, I rolled it over. Were they acting alone, or had they pulled in allies? The weres were the ultimate survivalists and largely stuck to their own kind, with the occasional treaty—the leopards and jaguars, for example, to balance the more numerous and more powerful wolves. The witches believed too much in the three-fold law to risk being murderous. Hell, they were one of the best-behaved communities in Otherside. Most of them were vegetarian, even. I would have heard by now had a faction strayed so far as to be named a cult. There weren't enough of the fae, and Callista controlled the few in the area too tightly for them to act out. The vampires hiring me could be for misdirection, but that didn't fit with what I knew.

I sighed. "The elves are determined to be a pain in my ass." This rogue group had to be working alone. Everyone else was happy with the status quo, or if not happy, then more unwilling to cross Callista in an effort to unbalance the Triangle.

"They are certainly an ambitious sort," Duke agreed, which could have had everything to do with Redcaps, or nothing.

"A murderous elven cult, then. What do they want? Why now? And what does my client have to do with it?" This had to play into the buzz setting the Triangle's Othersiders on edge. *Not solstice fever, after all. Damn it.* Another question occurred to me. "Are the drownings related? Or are the Redcaps in response to them? Some kind of, I don't know, elf nationalist defense corps?"

My thoughts and tongue froze. Duke had gone rigid, a golden film clouding his eyes. I watched, breath caught, as he rode it out. Something I'd said had triggered it.

"The same vision you warned me about before?" I asked when he blinked the last of the Sight away.

He looked at me so blankly that it was like I wasn't even there, then vanished to leave my skin crawling and cold, like someone had just walked over my grave. In all likelihood, he simply didn't know whether his most recent vision touched on what he'd foreseen, and preferred to keep up the appearance of the all-seeing, all-knowing djinni. Visions were like that—and so were the djinn. Especially those with the Sight.

While I sat in my PJs with a mug of peppermint tea and tried mind-mapping the possibilities on a scratch pad, someone tripped over the block of Air out front and hit the door with a growling curse. Adrenaline flooded me, sharpening my senses, and I went for the shotgun on top of the kitchen cabinet.

As I loaded it with trembling fingers, a gruff voice with a thick Southern accent called, "Finch? I don't know what in Sam Hill is wrong with your front porch, but I have your order."

Nils.

I didn't put the shotgun up as I twitched the curtains aside to check. The grey-haired tomtar waited with a scowl that could crack stone, a paper-wrapped bundle tied with twine under his arm. I closed my eyes and gathered myself before leaning the gun next to the door and opening it. "Sorry about that, Nils."

He harrumphed, glaring up at me. He could probably pass for human even as short and slight as he was, except for the permanent crackle of magic hovering around him.

I grabbed the carton of cigarettes and extended it. "Thanks for the rush job. Much obliged. I'll put in a good word with Callista."

Taking it, he sniffed along the edge. A flash of pleasure lit him before he buried it under another glower and shoved his parcel at me. "Here. I don't reckon I wanna know what a Watcher wants a lead blade for."

"I reckon you don't." We stared at each other, both of us knowing that elves were the only species permanently harmed— poisoned, really—by lead.

"It's enchanted to hold its edge. Mind you don't cut yourself shaving." With a last nod, he left, grimacing at the block of Air he couldn't see and taking an exaggerated step around it. I was wondering where his car was, and why I hadn't heard one come up my gravel drive, when a shimmering slice of light split my front yard. Nils stepped through the portal, and was gone.

I shifted, uncomfortable with real fae magic. Those who could do more than petty illusions with glamour drew on a source that wasn't elemental or Aether. Before heading back in, I moved the block with a quick chord of Air that wrenched my headache up another notch.

At the kitchen table, I carefully unwrapped the parcel. I'd seen Nils' work before—Callista had a silver-edged sword hanging in her office—but here, he had outdone himself. The ornate wooden box held an eight-inch lead and steel knife, like a boning knife with the top half its edge smooth and the lower half serrated. It was accompanied by an ornately tooled leather sheath, the edge-side reinforced with blackened steel. I couldn't help my sound of appreciation. I'd never actually used Nils' services before, despite it being my right as a Watcher, and I regretted that now.

It would fit in one of my looser pair of boots, the fleece-lined ones, for the winter. I'd have to figure something out for the summer, but for now, this would do nicely.

New confidence put a spring in my step as I headed for the shower. I had a clue, I had a knife, and now I needed to see if my gamble with calling in human help had paid off. It was time to see Doc Mike.

Chapter 15

Despite it being Sunday, Doc Mike was more than happy to see me. He might have been an old Southern gentleman, but that just meant he went to church before heading to work for half a day. And I thought I was a workaholic.

"Nobody will listen to me about the cases being connected," he said, clapping me on one shoulder to jar my headache up a notch before accepting the coffee I offered. Relieved despite the splitting pain in my forehead, I didn't tell him that saved both of us a great deal of trouble. I'd have to tell Callista something eventually, but disbelief bought time. For now.

"Do you have her here as well?" I held up Sybil's picture. His eyebrows went up. When he nodded, I said, "I think she's part of it. And I don't think they were accidents."

"A serial killer? They're rare, Arden."

"I know, but…humor me. Is there anything about the deaths that links all of them, other than drowning?"

"Other than the tattoos? And the families insisting on the bodies being cremated, and all of the medical records destroyed on privacy grounds? No."

Blood drained from my face. "Their families had them cremated?"

"Every last one of them."

"Shit." I rubbed my temples, trying to get the throb of the headache to abate. There went my clues.

Doc Mike sipped the coffee I'd brought him, watching me with concern. I'd been hoping to take another look at the bodies, and see if anything other than the vampire bites and elven house tattoos hinted at Otherside, something the human doctor might have missed.

"I thought it was weird, but with no evidence of foul play the deaths were ruled an accident. I had no legal reason to keep them. Going to have to wait for more to come in to test those weird injection marks." He winced as he heard the insensitivity in his own remark and added, "There are always more, God rest them."

"No evidence of foul play," I said, not as bothered by the comment as perhaps I should have been. Maybe my own prejudices were showing. *It's the case getting to me.*

I thought through the facts and Duke's warning about the Redcaps. "Wait, let me get this straight. No foul play, yet nobody thought it was weird that six people—seven, with Sybil Sequoyah—have turned up dead in or near bodies of water within weeks of each other? When has that ever happened?"

He shrugged. "Like I said, we figured it was another YouTube challenge gone wrong, for the younger ones, at least. The rest lived in or frequented the areas where they were found, and had a history of spending time at the water. I don't know, Arden. Now that you mention it, it is pretty unusual, but the order to comply with the families' wishes came from the top."

Of course it did. The elves have people in law enforcement. That had to be it, not that it was a surprise. They had people in place in every elected office in the Triangle, some even at the state and national level. They might also have done some mindwork, a maze of Aether to make every mundane involved overlook, misunderstand, or forget. Doc Mike was usually sharper than this; I'd expected him to dig deeper on the water connection.

With a sickening jolt, I realized that probably meant Callista knew I'd been holding out on her. I wasn't her only Watcher. That she hadn't called me in was either an endorsement or a trap waiting to be sprung.

I forced myself to breathe and focus on the case. I could worry about punishment later. "So, the only victim left is Ms. Sequoyah."

Doc Mike narrowed his eyes at me. "I can't tell you anything about her, Arden. Not until it's cleared."

"Come on, Doc, throw me a bone. I found her."

"No. If—"

"Please." I let the misery of my magical hangover and my failure to find her alive spill onto my face. "I've never not found someone in time. This is all too weird to be a coincidence. I might be the only one who can put all the pieces together."

He sighed. "I could get in a lot of trouble for this." I didn't respond, and after another minute of thinking about it, he said, "There was no water in her respiratory system and no evidence of a fall. We didn't find any evidence in her lungs, but the best theory I have is that she was smothered. They're going to open a murder investigation."

"Shit. My client isn't going to be happy." Doc Mike gave me an odd look, and I added, "He hired me because he didn't want police involvement."

"You found her dead under suspicious circumstances. How were the police not supposed to be involved?"

I winced, suddenly seeing the big upfront payment and the attempt at magical suggestion in a new light. "I think I was supposed to have been bought off." *And nobody would have dreamed that I'd bring in the police before Callista's cleaners.*

The lines of his face fell into a concerned look. "I don't like the sound of that, Arden."

"I don't, either. Don't worry, I'm off to get the process started on a concealed carry permit after this." Hesitating, I weighed my loyalties to the Otherside communities against what had become a friendship with the medical examiner. "Be careful, Doc. I've been jumped twice in the last week and the only thing that's changed is that I started looking into the Sequoyah case. If they're all connected…"

"I could be next. Got it. I'll be careful."

I squeezed his arm to stop myself from playing with my pendant as worry bit deep. "Thanks for the tip. I really hope it doesn't come back to bite you in the ass."

He nodded, still frowning, and I left. It was time to see Callista.

* * *

The warmth and chatter of the bar blew out in a wave of familiar sensation as I opened the door and stepped inside. A dangerous glint shone in Callista's green eyes when they fell on me, and she tilted her head to the back.

I couldn't stop a wince. *Not good.* I bypassed the bar, and tapped in the code to the little room she used as an office.

I hadn't been back here in a while and was somehow surprised to find it completely unchanged. With so much going on in my life, it seemed like more should have changed everywhere else, too. But no; the rustic wood-and-leather chairs were still there, creased and cracked in the seams. The sturdy walnut desk had a new scratch, pale against the older wood, yet still the same desk. The silver sword still hung on the wall. She hadn't upgraded her computer, and the aging desktop was as free of dust as it always was. That was Callista, as immaculate as she was unchanging, unless something happened to put a scratch in her carefully presented exterior.

She kept me waiting, a predictable power move, and I used the time to cast my mind back over the years, trying to figure out how this might play out, and how much trouble I was in.

I had no memory of my parents. Humans had found my mother breathing her last with me clutched in her arms. All I had of my father was the onyx pendant I wore on a gold chain around my neck. And my life, I guess. His arms had been wrapped around my mother in such a way that he must have drowned trying to keep our heads above water. At least, that's what the social worker had said, her eyes going misty as she imagined the romanticism in the gesture and ignored the ugly reality of the broken child sitting in front of her.

I'd grown up in foster care, overlooked for adoption despite my robust good health and attempts at a pleasant manner. Even before puberty had kicked in and brought my powers with it, mundanes had sensed something *other* about me. I hadn't understood why until Duke had found me.

By the time Callista had gotten custody of me, I'd grown used to not belonging. Her coldness hadn't seemed unusual, and I'd learned that telling her what she wanted to hear was the key to unlocking hints of warmth. Not that I'd trusted it, but what kid didn't want to be loved? It was only when I'd become a private investigator and worked a few cases involving children that I saw how deeply a child could be wanted and cared for.

I never knew Callista's motivations for taking me—she'd deflected every time I'd asked—but she'd given me a stable home as I grew up. That was enough for me to forgive her emotional neglect. Not everyone was capable of love.

With a sigh, I decided this was probably one of those times where telling her everything was more likely to keep me out of trouble. I'd learned how to lie to her, but there were too many other people involved in this case for me to get away with it for long. When she caught me in a lie, I always paid in pain. Nothing that would be visible, of course. No matter how much it hurt.

I pulled my notebook from my backpack, flipping through the notes I'd taken to make sure I had my thoughts and the timeline in order. My memory was good, but good was rarely good enough when dealing with Callista.

Predictable or not, the failure of my attempts to brush the wait aside was evidenced by a jiggling foot when she walked in and settled herself behind her desk.

"I wondered when I'd be seeing you, my dear." The cool tone combined with the pleasant mask she used to cover her fury made me sit up, and hold myself very still. "I've been hearing some interesting stories."

"Interesting is one word for it," I said, striving to act normal even as my stomach churned from more than my hangover. Mob bosses had nothing on an angry Callista, especially now that I no longer had youth and ignorance as a shield. "We're about to have a turf war."

Her face blanked. "Explain."

I recounted the events that had occurred since my last check-in, ending with, "I can't turn down the vampires without triggering something."

"No, I suppose you can't." She steepled her fingers and eyed me over them. "I give you my blessing to dig into this. I want to know who's screwing who and why. That little health start-up you so helpfully bugged is on the brink of developing a technology that will make it even easier to see that *we*—" she gestured between us, "—are not *them*. I need the peace kept until we have finalized a plan for coming out."

My jaw dropped, and I stared stupidly. Maybe I had misunderstood. "Coming out? Like…tell them—tell mundanes—about us? About Otherside?"

Callista nodded, only a faint twist to her mouth ruining the perfect blankness. "Your little stunt with the mundane police accelerated my timeline. I'd prefer a managed reveal rather than an unplanned exposure."

Her eyes glittered as she reached into her desk and withdrew a flat bronze nail the length of my middle finger, then a second, and a third. They pinged as she laid them on the desk.

I recoiled as bile rose in my throat. "No," I said, clutching the arms of my chair. I'd seen her use those before. They were driven under the skin like subdermal implants. Bronze under my skin, mixing with my bloodstream, would poison me and dull my powers, as silver would for weres, and lead for elves. She wanted me to investigate the case, but if I did with those nails in me, I'd be human-weak, sick as a dog, and completely reliant on my new lead knife if anything went wrong. "Callista—"

"You didn't think you could just sidestep all of our laws, did you? Whatever possessed you to call the police, Arden?"

"I—"

"Yes?"

"Leith couldn't know that I'm Otherside," I said in a rush, not knowing what I said as words tumbled free. "If—I couldn't have called you without tipping him off." I couldn't pull my eyes away from the nails. My mouth was tacky with dry saliva as I stammered my excuses.

"You could have called him. He would have called me."

"I did what a human would have done. He's up to something. You know I'm right, or you wouldn't have given your blessing. If I'd called him, it would have been too easy to get rid of me." I dragged my gaze to hers, pleaded for understanding. "You always said they'd—if they found me—"

"Enough." She studied me with a hard, emerald gaze. "I accept your reasoning. This time. Don't try me again."

I relaxed my grip on the chair, swallowed hard, and tried to calm the whirlwind of my thoughts. "And this reveal?"

Callista leaned back in her chair. "You and a few others with low populations and other complications will remain protected, although…" I shied as she reached out, and ran a hand over me, an inch above the skin of my cheek, and then licked it. "Your aura tastes as though you've been practicing, darling one. Taking my advice?"

"You and Duke both creeped me the fuck out," I muttered, struggling to pull my composure back into place. The feeling of being misled and betrayed rose again, combining with my narrow avoidance of punishment to make me sullen. "And I'm tired of hiding so much that I put myself in a different kind of danger when elves and vampires start popping into my office and demanding my services."

"What does Nebuchadnezzar have to do with it?"

I flinched at her intensity. "You're not going to lecture me on the dangers again?"

The smile she turned on me then was not one I liked, at all. "Darling, I've been waiting *years* for you to find the spine to reject what you'd been taught and embrace your powers. I'm delighted that you've finally decided to move beyond being a simple tool, though I wish you'd found a way not to involve mundanes in Otherside business."

Her smile became condescending. "You've been useful as a tool, to be sure, but you could be so much more, and now you will be. Yes, it is dangerous and the elves will be more of a threat than ever, but you're beginning to prove yourself worthy of greater things. Just in time, I might add. Now, what does Nebuchadnezzar have to do with anything?"

Bitterness rose to choke me. It had all been a test? Decades of manipulation? The threats? The fucking nails? I'd known growing up that she was a guardian, not a parent, but I hadn't understood how cold she was until that moment.

I rose. "He had a vision," I said over my shoulder as I left her office, slamming the door behind me in a rare show of temper.

If she wanted a spine, I'd shove it up her ass. I was *done* with being used.

Chapter 16

Between finding Sybil, checking in with Doc Mike, and standing up to Callista, I'd forgotten all about Grimm.

"Do you have any idea how much I'd like to flay you right now, Arden Finch?"

Wincing, I juggled the callstone as her anger manifested in a flash of heat, and tried to keep my hands on the steering wheel. "Where are you?"

"Watching your damned elf go into yet another building warded against djinn. Some office park near the airport. I have learned *nothing* that could *possibly* make this worth the aggravation."

Ah. That was what she was really mad about. Not that I hadn't checked in before now, but that she'd been unable to gather elven secrets under the auspices of assisting a Watcher. The Détente meant she wouldn't have been able to use the secrets for anything offensive, but that never stopped djinn from gathering information which might one day be useful in a war that everyone else hoped would never happen.

"Meet me at my office. I want to know where he's been."

"Why should I?" she snarled petulantly. "All you said was to watch him, not tell you anything."

"Seriously, Grimm?" I rubbed my temples, so not in the mood for this shit.

"You set the terms, not me. I watched him and didn't harm him. Exactly as I promised."

Petty bitch. "I'm on task for Callista now, not the elves." She didn't need to know about the vampires. Nobody told me anything, and it was time for me to stop being so goddamn helpful. "Meet me at the office and mark on a map where he's been, and I'll tell her you helped."

"What do I care about Callista?"

My headache was coming back. Bargaining with a djinni was the biggest pain in the ass. "Because things might change soon, and you'll want to be in her good graces if they do."

"What do you know?"

I hung up, tired of playing games. She'd be there or she wouldn't.

A vision of red rage awaited me at the door to my office. Grimm, in her Lana Del Rey lookalike face, hair falling in cherry waves over a merlot-colored pencil dress, glowered at everyone passing by. Her eyes flicked to ruby at my approach.

"Eyes, Grimm," I murmured, brushing lightly past her to unlock the door. Acknowledging her further would only feed her little fit of pique.

"Eyes, Grimm," she repeated in a mocking singsong behind me. I ignored her and went to my whiteboard.

"You little—oh, now this is interesting." She stepped up beside me, and peered at the map, going closer to read the notes. "The drowned were all elves?"

"Yes."

Her savage grin transformed her from recalcitrant child to avenging spirit. "And vampire bites. Oooh, my. Torsten, you have been naughty."

"Maria has been naughty," I corrected, giving her that one for free in the hope that it'd make her cooperative.

She snapped around to face me. "Since when do you know so much about Torsten's coterie? First the rakshasa, now his number three?" Her expression turned sly. "What have you been up to, you naughty thing?"

I smiled blandly, pleased with the confirmation that Torsten was indeed the head vamp, and wondering who his number two was if not Maria. "You were going to tell me where Monteague has been the last couple of days."

She pursed her lips, considering. I scooped up a green push pin magnet and extended it to her.

"If there is elf hunting to do, I want in," she said.

"That's a whole new bargain." I tried to keep my face neutral. If she found out a serial killer was going after elves, she'd probably start her own copycat killings just for the hell of it. As in, raining hell on elves. "Right now, it's just information. I've shown you why I asked you to watch him. You show me where he's been."

"Something's changed in you."

"Being threatened by both elves and Callista in the same week tends to do that to you," I said with a snarl, shaking the magnet she still hadn't taken.

"Touchy." Soft fingers brushed mine as she took it, and her smile mimicked Mona Lisa's. She placed it in RTP. "The office park."

I made a note, and handed her another magnet. When she'd finished putting one everywhere Monteague had spent more than ten minutes in the last two days, there was a tighter cluster within the wide red circle indicating where bodies had been found. Most of them fell within elven territory, with a few in the neutral zone near the airport. Of those in elven territory, the majority were between Chapel Hill and Jordan Lake, on the opposite side of the lake from the Sequoyah family home. *What would he be doing there? Whose territory is that?*

"Talk to me about elven houses," I said.

"I want in on the hunt."

"I'll tell you what I learned from Callista today," I countered.

"Done. Speak."

"That healthtech start-up might be a problem."

"You hinted at that before. What kind of problem?" She'd gone still as a leopard in a tree, wondering if the approaching rustle was an antelope or a larger lioness.

"The kind that forces some of us to reveal ourselves to the humans."

Her eyes went ruby again. Had she not known, or not expected me to know? How much did Callista tell her these days?

"I see."

In the event she hadn't known, I gave her a few seconds to process the tsunami that would make in the supernatural community before pressing her. "Elven houses? I need symbols and territories."

Without a word, Grimm snatched a whiteboard marker, and started sketching symbols in the last bit of free space on the board. "High-blood take the name of their house," she said, pointing to the first three symbols. "Sequoyah, Monteague, and Luna are the main players in this area, but there are lesser high-blood houses, all just waiting for their chance to elevate themselves through marriage or murder." She noted the names in careful block letters.

I studied the symbols. The ones found drowned were all from high-blood houses. No human-blended low-bloods. Accident, or design? Is that why Leith went for outside help in hiring me?

"You're thinking about something," Grimm said from where she was scrawling rough lines on my map.

"Yep."

"Ugh. Spoilsport," she complained when I didn't elaborate. "Sequoyah." A slim finger landed in an area that spanned from Jordan Lake to Apex. "Monteague." A tap at an area encompassing most of Chapel Hill. "Luna." The area south of Durham, largely made up of RTP and Morrisville. "The rest have smaller patches adjacent to the bigger houses."

So, is Troy spending his time on family land, or Sequoyah land? I frowned, studying the map. "And the low-bloods?"

Grimm waved a hand to encompass the Triangle. "Vassals. Nobody cares who they are or where they live, as long as they don't make trouble. The high-blood houses do enough maneuvering for all of them, and the low-bloods are too busy trying to attract the notice of the second sons of high-blood houses to bother anyone else."

I studied the map with its new information, suspecting that people cared more about the low-bloods than Grimm thought, and chalking her dismissal up to either ignorance or disdain. Troy Monteague was still my best lead, but an uncomfortable itch reminded me that nothing had ruled out Leith Sequoyah's involvement. *Why would he have hired me if he was involved?* The simplest answer was usually the correct one. That was: he wasn't involved, and I was just being paranoid.

Of course, there was the knowledge that elves tended to do things in threes to consider. Monteague made one, so I was missing at least two other players.

"Did you happen to notice Monteague talking to any of the same people?"

Grimm looked at her nails and smirked. "You asked me to watch him, not who he was talking to. It seems to have slipped my mind. There's so much to remember when you're three thousand years old."

"Fine," I said, kicking myself for being so narrow with what I'd asked. "Thank you for your assistance, Grimm. I'll see you later."

"Ta." Aether warped the space around her, and she blew me a kiss before she vanished.

"Looks like I'm trailing elves this weekend," I muttered when the disturbance had settled, and I was sure she was gone. "Fan-fucking-tastic."

First, though, I needed to talk to Leith.

As I was mentally composing that difficult conversation, my phone rang with an unidentified number. I answered with a quick prayer that this wouldn't be yet another complication.

"Hawkeye Investigations, Arden speaking."

"Hey…hi. Um…my name is Val. You…I think you dropped a card the other day at the lake."

The lake—the other elemental! Maybe? "Right. Yeah, that was me." I hesitated. Had I misread what I sensed? Maybe I was wrong.

"If I'm not mistaken, you had an interesting talent. I have a similar one."

"I wasn't sure. I didn't know there were others in the area."

"What? How…never mind. Look, are you free to meet for coffee or something?"

"Sure. Anywhere but Callista's."

Val snorted. "Oh, don't worry. We steer clear of her."

"You do?" Heat flushed through me, and I rubbed my forearm, where one of the nails would have gone in had Callista forced the issue of her punishment. I hadn't heard of trouble from other elementals—hadn't heard of any other elementals at all—so what was their beef? "Why?"

"If you don't know, it's not my place to tell you. Look, there's a little cafe set back in the woods on Franklin Street, around the corner from the University Place mall."

"Okay...I think I know it." I'd driven past it often enough, even if I'd never been in. It was tucked way back in the trees, behind an art studio or something. She confirmed the address anyway, and we agreed to meet at eleven o'clock on Wednesday.

The thought that I might finally start getting some real answers buoyed me, even if I'd have to wait a few days—until I remembered the other call I needed to make. Leith. While I'd been making arrangements with Val, an email had come in from the police department confirming that I was free to speak with him. Couldn't put it off any longer.

When I reached him, he said, "The police just called, and told me they're opening an investigation. What the hell happened to no police involvement?" His growled, dangerous tone put me on edge as he asked, "Does there really need to be an official investigation?"

"Yes, I'm afraid so." *What kind of stupid-ass question is that?* "The circumstances were odd. Please accept my deepest condolences and my apology. I did pass on your request for privacy, and asked that it be kept out of the press."

"Not good enough. This isn't what I wanted at all—"

I held the phone away from my ear and let him rant. He was grieving. He was shocked at the outcome—nobody really expected that their loved one wouldn't come home alive. Hell, even I had held out hope that I could find her before the worst happened. I always had before.

I told myself all of that as I stood there waiting for him to wind down. It didn't make being shouted at any easier. Sometimes that was just part of the job, though. A shitty part.

"Mr. Sequoyah, as I said, I am truly sorry for your loss," I broke in when he started repeating himself. I'd learned over the years that for my own self-care, allowing myself to be abused beyond a single shocked reaction was not going to happen. I had to raise my voice to be heard over a new litany starting with "how dare you."

"I wish the outcome had been better. I will send a final invoice for your records in the next few days."

Biting my tongue to stop the automatic habit to invite new business, I hung up. Guilt started to tighten my chest, and I rejected it, forced it out with a burst of rage. I hadn't asked him to hire me. I'd only taken the job to hide the fact that his magic didn't affect me, and to try to one-up Callista, neither of which were things I should have had to do. If I'd been human and unable to shield against Aether, I'd probably still feel a compulsion to help him, unable to walk away despite the case having definitive closure—at least for my involvement.

Maybe demanding payment from, and then hanging up on, a person whose grandmother was just found dead in a lake was cruel. Fuck it. No amount of business was worth my physical, mental, and emotional well-being. I got enough shit from my friends these days.

This has to stop. All of it. All the fear that I'd been carrying around, of elves, of Callista and her demands and punishments…I was done with it. I'd thought I was done before, after the unpaid, unexplained Verve job, but then I'd been threatened by just about everyone. I didn't deserve to be bullied, intimidated, belittled, and used.

It was my own fault. I'd allowed it. I'd always allowed it, just like Callista said. I'd been a tool, and if I didn't find some self-respect, she'd just use me as a sledgehammer. My blood simmered. I'd never set boundaries, never pushed back with more than a token argument, was always too wrapped up in uneasy gratitude. And now I'd allowed myself to be pushed into a corner where even my effort to get free of Callista's control depended on her good graces.

Fuck. This. After twenty-five years, I was done with what I was "allowed" to do. I had to reach out and grab it.

I hadn't taken a day off in too long, but I needed to wrap up this case, and find unassailable leverage to wrest back control over my own life. It might mean never learning more about my background, but maybe Val could help with that. Callista had to have known that there were other elementals in the Triangle. Grimm and Duke too, for that matter. Not telling me, keeping me ignorant of *my people*, was just another form of control.

No more.

I spent Monday and Tuesday tailing Monteague. This was the boring side of being a PI, sitting in the car waiting for something to happen, making notes, and taking photos. The confrontation in Durham made me more cautious than usual, and I rented a car so he wouldn't get suspicious about seeing the same gunmetal grey hatchback all over town.

Determined to strengthen myself, I also made time to practice with Air, and got back into the hapkido class I'd dropped out of the last time my workload had spiked. I might be stronger than a human, but the people I was facing were as strong as or stronger than I. Social engineering couldn't do much against vampire glamour or elven tricks with Aether, so I needed to be prepared with a Plan B. Or C, or D, since fighting would mean I'd lost control of the situation, and hadn't been able to salvage it with reason or emotional appeals.

Hapkido was one of those martial arts that was more about leverage than size, so it worked for me. It also had some softer techniques that would let me protect myself without necessarily harming the other person—important for when verbally de-escalating a confrontation with a husband caught cheating didn't work.

Even with Air practice and martial arts, most of those two days were spent driving around the Triangle, taking photos of who Monteague met with. After comparing my observations with what Grimm had established of his patterns, I headed back to Callista's. A lump in my throat choked me as I reached the bar, though whether it was rage or some twisted sense of mourning for what had passed as normal, I couldn't figure out.

"I need to know if any of these people are part of the community," I said, pushing past it and opening the Drive folder with the photos I'd taken before setting my phone on the bar. Personal issues couldn't get in the way of my job, and I couldn't let Callista see my feelings. When I broke free, I didn't want her to see it coming.

Callista filled a glass with cola and dropped a lime in, sliding it to me before casually looking at the device. She smiled as though I were showing her cats or beaches.

"This one," she said in a voice I could barely hear over the rollicking folk music that was the bar's music playlist du jour. She tapped to zoom in on a man who looked vaguely Hispanic. "He's a Luna." She swiped a few more times, pausing at a blond man. "A Sequoyah, but a lesser branch. Another Sequoyah."

By the time she reached the end of the folder, Callista had identified seven people, all men, all of the high-blood elven houses. "You're tailing a Monteague?"

"Troy. I have a video of him arguing with Sybil Sequoyah."

"Oh, ho." She zoomed in on a photo of Monteague, and stared at it hard, like she was memorizing it. "So that's their prince. He's stayed off the radar until now. Hmm…he's gotten handsome, though a bit of a sourpuss from the looks of it. Shame."

"Prince?" I hissed.

Callista glanced at me and smiled. "Didn't you know?" she said mockingly before striding away to serve someone who'd been waving a five-dollar bill at her for at least the last minute or two.

Of course I didn't fucking know, because you keep me in the dark! I clenched my drink, willing the icy glass to cool my temper so I could see the big picture. An elven prince. A dead queen. And vampires out for my blood. Could the new year have kicked off any better?

When she shuffled back to me, I was still trying to wrap my head around the mess my life had become—and the growing feeling of exhilaration that for the first time in years, I was growing. I was a good PI, but people should be more than their jobs.

"Welcome to the high-stakes table," Callista said. "Be careful not to lose your head."

"Nobody is taking my head." I gulped down some cola to cover the disquiet the reminder caused, coughing when the bubbles caught in my nose. Her look told me she wasn't fooled, and I decided I'd had enough of her. "Thanks for the IDs," I said as I threw a couple of bucks on the bar, and stood to leave.

"Keep me posted," she replied.

I waved over my shoulder, already lost in thought. If the situation was delicate before, it was potentially explosive now.

Chapter 17

The meeting with Val had slipped my mind while I was working. Running surveillance on Troy Monteague without being spotted had taken all of my brain power. Practicing with Air at night and working on fine control sapped my physical reserves. The dinging notification about the coffee date on my phone was a much-needed reminder that there was more to life than this case. The vampires were paying for my agreement and their convenience; that didn't mean I should feel obliged to work yet another seventy-hour week.

After a quick recon to make sure there weren't any nasty elven surprises waiting, I went inside. Val had snagged a corner table in a darker section of the small yet cozy coffee shop. She already had a steaming mug—more of a small bowl, really—in front of her. I waved just to be sure I still remembered who I was supposed to be talking to, then queued up for a press pot of Ceylon tea and a vegetarian quiche that I hoped would ease the Air hangover I had. They were getting better, each one less severe than when I'd started, and that plus allowing myself to sleep in offset today's misery.

"Thanks for the invite," I said as I settled at the tiny table. She'd taken the seat with her back to the wall. I hated having my back to an open area or a door, and there was just enough space for me to move. Val waited until I'd shifted my chair to see more of the room before replying.

"I wasn't sure you were the real deal until you sat down, to be honest." Her voice lowered. "Nobody has seen a sylph in decades. You've been practicing though, from the smell of you."

"Nobody? Wait, there's more like us?"

Val gave me a strange look. "Where have you been that you thought you were the only one?"

"In hiding." My lips twisted, and I poured my tea, blowing on it to buy a few seconds. "They never told me there were others. All these years and—"

"They?"

I shrugged one shoulder. "The djinn. Callista." My tea was still too hot, but I took a sip to stop from saying more. Being able to speak freely about being an elemental was making me foolishly loose with my tongue. Something about Val made it easy to talk to her as well. I'd never understood the phrase *kindred spirit* until now.

"Ah." Val sipped from her bowl, which appeared to be full of coffee. Don't ask me what kind, I didn't drink the stuff.

Her wary expression frustrated me, kindred spirit or not. "What?" I snapped.

"It's like I said. We steer clear of Callista."

"I wish you'd tell me why, but to be honest, I don't blame you," I murmured, still frustrated and pissed about the threat with the nails. "If she hadn't raised me, I'd probably do the same."

A startled twitch spilled coffee over Val's hands. She didn't react as the scalding liquid splashed. "Oh, my stars," she breathed. "You're her."

"Huh?"

A flush tinged the terra-cotta brown of her skin. She looked down at her hands, noticed the hot coffee all over them, and grabbed a napkin. "Sorry, that was rude."

"I don't even know what you're talking about." The hangover headache was coming back. A barista set the reheated quiche in front of me, and I leaned away from the smell of it, appetite fled. "You make it sound like I'm some kind of urban legend."

"You're the trueborn, you have to be. So yeah, you kind of are a legend."

None of this made any sense, and I didn't like it one bit. I resettled in my chair, easing to the edge in case I needed to get out of here. "You've lost me. Trueborn? What does that even mean?"

Val peered at me, searching my face as though it would tell her something important. "Who were your parents?" she asked when I stared back at her.

I frowned. "My parents? Who cares?"

"Please. It matters. Were they like us?"

"My mother was—" I glanced around. The coffee house was packed, the hum of conversation rising with each new arrival, but I still lowered my voice. "She was a djinni, or at least that's what they told me." My stomach turned over, and my heart clenched as I realized that up until now, I'd always *assumed* my father was, too, but nobody had ever actually said that. My pendant—my father's pendant—seemed to burn where it hung under my shirt. "Isn't—I mean, what's…" I didn't know what to say to Val's suddenly blank expression.

"You *are* her. Shit. After twenty-five years you start to think it's just stories."

"Well, weren't your parents…?"

"No, of course not. My family has been wild since Atlantis. Mostly Fire, but my sister is Water. Air is the rarest, and there haven't been any elementals trueborn since—"

"Okay, wait. I don't know what you mean by 'wild,' and that's the second time you've said 'trueborn.' What are you talking about?" My stomach roiled from more than the Air hangover. How much had Callista and the djinn hidden from me?

Her expression became pitying. "Goddess. You don't even know our history."

I pressed my lips together and glared, hating to be ignorant, hating even more that she saw it.

She winced and whispered, "You know your father will have been an elf, right?"

Heat washed over me, chased by cold, and the room spun.

"Arden," Val said, reaching over the table to grab my wrist. The firm press of two unusually warm fingers told me she was taking my pulse. "Breathe, Arden. Breathe. Shit, you really didn't know. Shit."

"That's impossible." I couldn't wrap my head around it, and my mind reeled away from considering the idea. "I thought I was just a weird, I don't know, some kind of stunted djinn. They said…they told me the—you know—would kill me—"

"Oh, they will. No doubts there."

I stared at her, uncomprehending.

"You gonna eat that?" Val pointed with her chin at my quiche. I slid it across the table. My stomach was too full of acidic betrayal to tolerate food. She picked at it, peeling off the crust to nibble first. "You know about Atlantis?"

"Everyone knows about that," I said. My voice didn't sound like my own.

"Right. That's why it's forbidden for people like your parents to have children together."

Okay, maybe I don't know about Atlantis, then. "I don't get it."

She huffed a sigh and finished off the crust. "Our powers weaken with each generation. Only people with your background—" she raised her eyebrows to make the point, and I nodded "—or close to one side or the other, have the full strength of their element. It's something to do with blending the two halves of Aether."

"Okay…I thought that just created Chaos. What does it have to do with Atlantis?"

"The djinn wanted to take revenge on elves who kept their children's elemental power for themselves. Both sides used elementals as pawns, but the djinn tricked us, and got the last jab in. Atlantis was an elven city, drowned by a coalition of undines and oreads—water and earth elementals, you know? They made the waves rise and the earth sink. Rescue ships were held back by sylphs turning the winds against them, and deas burning their decks. The elves nearly went extinct."

I blinked, feeling stupid all over again as I tried to follow that.

"I'm not explaining this very well. I do action, not storytelling." Val put the fork down, and propped her chin in her hands, looking up at the ceiling to think. "We're at our most powerful when we're like you. If it's diluted too far from one or the other side, we're almost human weak. Nobody cares about that; we're not a threat. I'm heat resistant, but I can still be burnt.

"We don't have the strength of the ancient ones to drown Atlantis or pull down mountains, even in a collective. *You* though, you're a threat. You're undiluted, *and* you represent the fallen virtue of some elf. Do you see?"

"So…you're not in hiding?"

She smiled sadly. "Not really. I have enough strength to be a very lucky firefighter, but I will never have anywhere near your potential if that peek behind your shields is any indication. I try not to draw attention, though, just in case."

I looked out the window. The trees hugged the patio outside, and the sun peeped out for the first time in days. Steps led down to a trail running alongside a small creek. The walls pressed in. "I need to take a walk."

"Sure. Want company?"

"If you're quiet." I was being rude and didn't care. Neither Duke, nor Grimm, nor Callista had so much as hinted at my true heritage. They'd let me think that there was a death warrant out for *all* elementals, when really it was just me, just the one *trueborn* elemental. I'd thought myself alone in the world, a strange genetic fluke that required me to live apart as a dirty secret.

I wasn't sure if the truth was better or worse.

Val didn't say anything until we reached the paved trail at the bottom of the stairs. "I figured you were just new in town." She glanced at me, tucking a short strand of chocolate-colored hair behind her ear before shoving her hands in her pockets. When I didn't tell her off for talking, she added, "It's happened before. Most of us aren't strong enough to be worth hunting anymore, but we still keep a low profile. Especially those who've had to move. Usually they're running from something. Are you?"

"Not running so much as avoiding."

Nodding, Val ambled along in silence, letting me think without being alone. I found myself relaxing again, and was inexplicably irritated. "Why do I feel like telling you things?" I grumped, crossing my arms to hug myself. The sun might be out but it was still chilly.

"Because you're a sylph and I'm a dea. Air and Fire are sympathetic elements. And if you aren't used to it…"

"Oh." I hadn't expected her to have an answer. We moved to the side when a cyclist hollered, "On your left!" I waited for him to disappear around a curve before asking, "Why would they lie to me?"

"They didn't exactly lie, from what you've said." She wrinkled her nose when I turned to glare at her, and shrugged. "They're djinn, right? A lie of omission isn't the same as a true falsehood. And Callista is…Callista."

That was annoyingly true, and I sighed. "It's still not right. I *knew* they were hiding something, but I was just…"

"Scared."

"Yeah. Well, that and obedient." I didn't want to admit it, but the words came out anyway. We quietened again as a pair of joggers passed, wearing UNC t-shirts. Low-blood elves, from the faint sweet-burnt scent as they passed.

"Damn, girl, no wonder nobody found you. I've never seen anyone lock down so tight. You could pass for human."

"I was told my life depended on it," I said bitterly. "I guess it still does."

Val reached for my arm, pulling us to a halt. "It does. But you're not alone." She caught sight of the watch sticking out of her coat on her upraised arm and swore. "I need to get going."

"Sure. And thanks. It's…nice to know there are others."

She grinned and started back along the path. We made our way back up to the cafe in companionable silence and headed for our cars.

"I'll tell the collective about you, okay? Not everyone is as comfortable being known as I am, but you don't have to be so alone. It's hard for us, not having others of our kind around." That last drew a deep sadness into her voice, as though some tragedy had occurred because of loneliness. Maybe that was why I was always drawn to spend time with Roman, Grimm, or Duke.

Grimm and Duke. I had words for them. "Maybe hold off, if you can. I need to handle some business first."

After thanking Val and saying goodbye, I headed for the hapkido gym. Exercise was just the thing to focus my mind on what I'd learned while doing something to keep in shape.

Maybe it would help me find the words to express how betrayed I felt.

* * *

Two hours later, I had a solid ache in my thighs, a sore hip, and zero reduction in anger. I debated going to Roman's to work it out with a different kind of physical activity, and decided against it. The shift in his behavior lately suggested he was edging toward something more serious, something I had neither the energy nor the inclination to encourage just now.

Telling myself that space would help cool things down, I headed home, and jumped in the shower. What I really wanted was to uncork a bottle of wine, but I needed to talk to Duke and Grimm without the complications of alcohol. A cup of chamomile and catnip tea would have to do for now.

When I was as calm as I was going to be, I dug the callstone out of its inner pocket in my backpack. Concentrating hard, I reached for both of them at once. "I need to talk to you," I said.

Duke's reply whispered in my mind. "What about?"

I threw the stone across the room. They'd feel the anger behind the intent, even if the stone would disconnect when it left my hand. It hit the decorative river stone flanking the fireplace and cracked in two. Callstones weren't meant to be handled roughly.

I'd finished my cup of tea and had a fire crackling in the hearth by the time they popped into my living room, already bickering.

"I *told* you, you shouldn't have—" Duke was saying.

"Don't tell me what I should or shouldn't—"

"Shut. Up!" Tonight was not one of those times when I'd sit by and wait for them to get to the bottom of it. They stopped mid-sentence, Grimm's jaw snapping shut while Duke's dropped open.

"Someone's tetchy tonight," Grimm said with a small sneer. She sniffed. "And you've been practicing, naughty girl. Wherever did you get the idea that was a smart thing to do?"

Duke seemed to have caught my mood, his eyes flickering to carnelian as he spotted the broken callstone. "Grimm," he said, his gaze back on me. "She knows."

"What do you mean she—" Grimm looked at me, really looked, for the first time since they arrived. Maybe for the first time in years. "Well. It was bound to come out sooner or later. I just want to know how."

"Exactly what is it that you think I know," I said in a soft voice, the one that came out when I needed not to scream.

"Let's not—"

"Stop." I wasn't going to let Duke smooth it over this time. "Say it."

"Arden."

"Say. It."

The two djinn exchanged a long look. "Callista won't be happy," Grimm said, hedging. "And in any case, this is a very stupid idea."

"I don't care about Callista!" I shouted. Duke raised his hands in a placating gesture, which only stoked my anger into rage. "Tell me! Tell me, I want to hear you say it!"

"Your father!" Grimm shouted back, her voice ugly. Duke flinched, and the muscles in his jaw bunched as he ground his teeth. "Your father was a bloody elf! There, is that what you wanted to hear? You are *elf spawn*!"

I recoiled at the hatred in her voice, feeling it like a slap, and clutched my pendant.

"Grimm!" Duke barked. "Arden, it's not like that," he said, trying, as ever, to smooth things over.

"What's it like, then?" My voice didn't crack with the emotions threatening to overwhelm me. I was proud of that.

"Your mother was our cousin."

I stared, confused. "We're…related?"

"That elf *ruined* her!" Grimm broke in. "He drove her to—"

"For the love of the lamassu, Grimm. Stop. Talking." Duke glared at her until she crossed her arms and turned her back on us. "She hates what happened, not you, Arden. You can't help…what you are."

"*What* I *am*? Fuck you both."

"I meant who your parents were, Ishtar damn it all. Don't be like this."

"And you couldn't help lying to me. Telling me every possible way *my father's* people would kill me, but never why. Never that I was some kind of freak special case!"

"They would have killed you, and they still will," Grimm said, dark and nasty, without turning around. "That danger is very real. Maybe if they had been more practical and less proud, Atlantis would still stand above the waves. But no. They need a scapegoat even now. You'll do." Her voice became even nastier. "The elves aren't even the worst of those who would hunt you."

Duke reached out to squeeze Grimm's shoulder, and she shifted away. He sighed. "We never hid the danger from you. Only the full reason for it. Or the real reason for it."

"But why? You kept me isolated, let me think I was the only one left—"

"Ah. You found a wild elemental." Duke nodded as I answered Grimm's earlier question. I didn't confirm it, not wanting Val or her collective to be drawn into this drama, and furious that I'd given them the hint. He shrugged as though it didn't matter.

"Why, Duke?" I repeated.

"For the Hunt."

"The what?"

Duke glanced at Grimm, who crossed her arms, and kept looking at my fire. "The old gods are waking, Arden," he said in a hard, quiet voice. "That means the Wild Hunt is coming. And here you are, the most powerful elemental in generations, practicing without wards, and wielding the powers of creation. Drawing the attention of anyone who knows what to look for."

"What does any of that even mean?" I stood with fists clenched, trembling in a sickening blend of anger and confusion. "You know what, fuck it. If some old gods or whoever are coming, that's not on me. Maybe if you'd told me—"

"Maybe you should have bloody well minded your business and stayed in your box!"

I recoiled at the sudden anger in Duke's voice, then spat back, bitterly unleashing my own. "So, you admit it. You two, and Callista, were keeping me stupid on purpose. To use me."

"And you allowed it," he said.

"Just like the tool you are." Grimm turned around and glared at Duke, cutting off my reply. "We can't be sure she's on our side anymore. Let's go."

"On your—" I spluttered. "On your *side?* What the actual— you know what, forget that. Who's on *my* side? Two of my only friends have been hiding things about me—my heritage!—for my entire life, and if that isn't enough, you were planning to use me in some hunt as well?"

"We only wanted what was best for all of us," Duke said. "Including you. We were going to tell you when the time was right."

"Stop it. Just…stop." I held up a hand to halt the flow of bullshit. Something Duke had said niggled. "Before I tell you to get the fuck out, what did my father drive my mother to do?"

"That's a story for another day." Duke's voice made me shiver with the tired sadness woven through it.

"Tell me. I'm not sure there will be another day for us and you owe me that much."

"No."

"Then tell me about the fucking vision."

"Learn to swim."

And with that, he disappeared in a twist of Aether, so sudden that a pop tickled my ears as air rushed to fill the space where he'd been. Grimm followed without another word.

Chapter 18

Their words crashed around in my head until I finally opened the bottle of wine I'd denied myself earlier. Some things needed help to be processed, and it wasn't like I could go talk to anyone about it. Even if there was an Otherside therapist specializing in fucked-up family situations, from what Val said, elementals kept a low profile.

That hit me as well, a sudden deep loneliness settling in my heart like a stone. The rift created by decades of secrets and manipulation was too deep to be mended with simple apologies—not that djinn offered apologies even when warranted. Survival and personal power were the twin drivers of all the djinn I'd met. Neither was something to apologize for, as far as they were concerned. The used were tools. Nobody felt remorse over using a tool.

Even when those tools are their relatives. That merited a refill of my glass of wine. Never in a million years would I have guessed that. I should have known there'd be a reason for why they were my constant companions. My usefulness to them, this Hunt, whatever it was, and the apparent rarity of a trueborn elemental meant that of course the djinn would have found a way to stay close.

Duke and Grimm, though? They'd been extra close. Family close, in the smothering way tight-knit families headed by parents with bad childhoods sometimes were. I'd been sheltered and protected, aware of other djinn, meeting them occasionally, but never left alone with one, or any Othersider outside the two of them or Callista.

Alcohol simmered with anger in my blood as I remembered little things. How they popped up everywhere, and always seemed to be watching. A violent confrontation with a witch, one of the few Otherside species that could read auras with a touch. There'd always been a paranoid watchfulness that I'd taken for love, or at least care. Now that I knew more of their motives, I saw it for what it was: an effort to protect an asset and a source of power they could claim by blood ties.

I swirled the wine, willing myself to be soothed by the whirl of rich red spinning around the glass as I thought through the other implications. If the djinn knew, Callista certainly did. She may even have masterminded the whole idea. At the very least, she'd signed off on it. What did that mean for me? And what the hell did swimming have to do with anything?

The fire cracked, and a rush of sparks danced up the chimney. I got up to light some incense, copal this time, before going back and curling up tighter in my armchair. Staring into the flames, I tried to center myself, and find my way through this mess.

After another top off, it came to me. Freedom, that's what it meant for me, and wasn't that what I'd wanted to begin with? All the rules I lived by had been instilled by Duke, Grimm, or Callista. That some of them nominally kept me safe meant nothing; they wanted to protect their asset. Whatever this Hunt was, they needed to keep me alive and cooperative, and to give me reasons to trust their instructions. Fear of elves had kept me in line, and after being forced to work the Sequoyah case, a lingering respect—or fear?—for those who had raised me had continued guiding my actions.

Nope. No more.

"They didn't do it for you. You owe them nothing," I whispered to the fire. "And that means you're free. So, what do you want now?" Freedom was just the start. What would I do with it? How would I maintain it? It wasn't like they'd just let me go, and so far, the Sequoyah case hadn't delivered my Hail Mary against Callista. Nails under the skin were the gentlest of her punishments. I'd get worse if I half-assed my breakaway.

Would the gods Duke had mentioned help? Did I want them to? Or was that trading Callista for a bigger, badder wolf?

A difficult question that would not be answered this evening. The wine started to burn in my veins with more intensity as it drew my power forward. I focused inward, trying to tame it, separate it, set it aside. It wouldn't heed me, so I heeded it.

* * *

My place was trashed when I woke late the next morning, with the random destruction usually indicative of a small windstorm. It might well have been; I was probably lucky I hadn't lost control, and created a tornado or pulled the fire out of the fireplace and burnt the house down.

A plant pot lay on its side, spilling dirt among scattered leaves, and only a single air plant still hung in place. It swung alone from the ceiling, the ionantha bulb tipped half out of its holder of spiraled silver, hanging on by a few stiff leaves. It looked forlorn and out of place without its fellows. Some picture frames had fallen, the shattered glass making a dangerous glitter across the hallway. Everything that had been on any flat surface no longer sat there.

I felt the same way the house looked: disheveled, in disarray, with jagged, broken edges. The air plant drove home the point that I, too, was alone, swinging from a thread of fishing line and holding on for dear life.

No. I shoved self-pity aside, reaching for derision. "Great. Good going, dumbass," I muttered to myself as I went for a pair of flip-flops and the broom. "Note to self, don't practice indoors anymore."

The only upside was that the booze had staved off the usual Air hangover. By some miracle, I'd found the balance between magical and chemical overindulgence, without having drunk so much that my secondary powers kicked in.

I shuddered. That would have been even more of a disaster than my trashed house. I had no interest in discovering what *that* magic would have called to me.

Cleaning put my mood in order as well as my house. By the time I'd swept up the glass and dirt, put everything right side up and in its proper place, restrung my hanging garden of air plants, and thrown out anything irreparably broken, I had a plan.

If I wanted to maintain my independence, I needed to prove that I could stand alone in the supernatural community. The elves needed to know that I wasn't easy prey, the vamps needed to know I wasn't fast food, and the weres, Callista, and everyone else unaffiliated needed to know I was a power unto myself. That I had power and would use it. Could use it. Forcefully, if I needed to.

That meant solving the elf drownings and bringing any guilty parties—elf, vamp, or otherwise—to justice. To do that, I'd need to figure out who the hell was drowning elves in the Triangle, and why they'd risk outing the vampires to do it.

My one, only, and best source of information was Troy Monteague. *Is it stupider to run toward a death sentence in an effort to avert it, or to run away from it thinking you can hide forever?* I didn't have the answer. All I knew was that I was tired of this shit. Tired of hiding. Tired of limiting myself. And utterly exhausted by the idea that this would be the rest of my life if I didn't grow a pair right now.

The feeling had been growing over the last ten days, and every time I thought I'd hit a breaking point, the Goddess sent a new one. It'd keep getting worse until I stopped reacting and took control for myself. Finding leverage against Callista wasn't the be-all and end-all. Finding my own strength was. I needed to face the elves head-on.

When the house was tidy enough that I wouldn't cut myself on broken glass, or track dirt all over, I threw on a clean-ish pair of dark-wash jeans, a hoodie, and a UNC scarf, then wrangled my curls under a matching UNC cap.

The new lead knife I sheathed at my belt, and hid under my sweatshirt and coat. North Carolina was an open-carry state, so it was illegal to carry a knife like mine concealed, but I wasn't confronting an elf with nothing. My mark would be near the university today if he stuck to his usual schedule, so it would be easier to blend in by masquerading as a student, but being on or close to campus meant carrying a weapon was also illegal. With all the campus shootings around the country, and one locally at a Barnes & Noble bookstore in Cary, campus police would be unforgiving. I'd take a risk and carry, but not be stupid enough to taunt the police or frighten students.

I already had a pretty solid idea of Monteague's day-to-day, barring one-off trips or unplanned needs. It wasn't hard to pick him up in a trendy part of Chapel Hill, past the university and closer to Carrboro. Staying in line with the habits Grimm and I had observed, he met up with a few of the elves I'd photographed. I waited as he got back into his Acura and pulled away, then followed him into town as the sun was setting.

This is not where he usually goes. What's going on? I shifted in my seat, glad I'd brought the knife even if it would be asking for trouble from human law enforcement.

Early evening brought out university students ready to party in trendy, hipster bars and restaurants. Driving through this part of town was bad enough when most people were sober; add in hordes of drunk students and you had a disaster waiting to happen. I slammed on my brakes as one dashed out into the street against the light, my faster-than-human reflexes the only thing standing between him and a broken skull.

The number of people who drove, with all the bus lines connecting this area, astounded me. All the curbside parking was taken, and several of the street lots had signs proclaiming them full. I tapped my fingers in a wave across the steering wheel, and mentally cursed the throngs of barhoppers.

Troy turned into one of the few multi-tier parking garages. I followed, parking in a space reserved for monthly pass holders so that I wouldn't lose him, and taking the stairs when he got into the elevator. When we hit the street, I pulled up my hood and kept my head down, sticking to the edge of a crowd of chattering youths in university sweatshirts as I followed my target.

I almost lost him when he wove through the little courtyard outside the Weaver Street Market. A bad feeling settled in the pit of my stomach when he angled for the train tracks. Not just because I'd gotten jumped the last time I'd crossed some tracks. He hadn't done this before in all the time I'd spent watching him. Pattern changes were a bad sign.

Troy knew he was being followed. How, I didn't know. I was good at following people undetected. But he knew, I'd bet anything on it. If stealth was out, I'd have to go with…what? Guile? Charm? My cute nose?

I hitched my backpack up on my shoulders and shoved my hands in my pockets, taking a slightly different path over the tracks, and trying to look like someone coincidentally going in the same direction for a different purpose. He stopped and peered into a window—that trick, I knew. I kept walking, and turned a corner, hoping he'd bought it and was coming this way.

We'd made almost a full circle to the parking garage, and he didn't strike me as the type to ride the bus. I needed to make a move.

Lounging against a wall, I pulled out my phone, and pretended to type out a text message. I didn't want to draw the knife and risk arrest unless I had to; my environmental needs meant I wouldn't do well in a human jail. Less than a minute later, a tall, well-built figure in black strode by at a fast clip.

This is it. "Mr. Monteague?" He didn't react, not a look or a change in his pace. "Hey! I'm talking to you!"

Clutching my backpack, I started to hustle after him, ignoring the small voice in my head screaming that this was a terrible idea. When he turned a corner to duck into the narrow space between two buildings, partially blocked by industrial-sized waste bins, I hesitated, then darted after. He was mixed up in this somehow. That made him my ticket to independent standing. Dangerous or not, I had to follow.

I was so intent on catching up that I forgot situational awareness, missed the cue from the stalled, swirling air patterns, and passed him, a rookie mistake I hadn't made since one of my first cases as a private investigator.

A strong hand gripped my right bicep and pulled. Adrenaline spiked, and my senses sharpened. Reflex kicked in, and I levered my arm free, glad for the hapkido classes. Before I could do anything else, he gripped both my arms, and hauled me around.

My back hit gritty brick as he swung me. I caught the scent of burnt marshmallow and whatever of him was underneath it, herbal and male. It tickled something in the back of my mind, but I was too busy catching lost breath to place it as I stared up into hazel eyes, the gold in them sparking with his anger.

The setup was perfect, I had to give him that. He'd tucked in behind one of those stupid bins, holding himself so that his shadow under the lone light was lost in that of the building. A trellis, twined with dead vines and framing the other end of the pedestrian way, shielded him from view on the other side. He had me trapped, with no space to go for my knife.

Chapter 19

The way Monteague pushed me against the wall was familiar. The movement combined with the scent finally clicked, and my original purpose for tailing him fled. A flicker of fear tried to push its way forward, and I forced it to the side. I was half-elven, whether anyone wanted that or not. I'd stood up to Callista and the djinn; I had no more time and no more room in my soul for fear. I was *owed*.

The deepening pit of smoldering anger at the betrayals and mistreatments I'd suffered gusted into a hurricane. "You! You're the one who threatened me in Durham!"

"I don't know what you're talking about."

The same all-business, no-emotion tone from before. "Yes, you do! You moved the same, and I fucking smelled you!"

His eyes narrowed. "You smelled me."

Whoops. Way to let him know you're not human. I tilted my chin up and shut my mouth, though I could tell by the glint in his eyes that it was far too late for that.

"What are you, then, to scent me and yet not smell of human, elf, were, vampire, or witch yourself?" He sniffed. "Fae?"

"None of your fucking business," I said, staring hard at him. The look didn't faze him, and the words just seemed to irritate him.

"I'm making it my business."

"What, you gonna kill me, like you did Sybil?"

That got a reaction, a jerk that could have been an aborted jump, and a pinch at the corners of his eyes. "Sybil Sequoyah? Why would you—never mind. I didn't kill her."

"You expect me to believe that? I have a video that suggests you did." Okay, so I was grasping at straws, but I needed *something*.

"You…what?" His fist tightened in my coat. When I tensed to try breaking free, he shook me a little. "Don't. Where did you get the video?"

"Like I'm going to tell you that," I scoffed.

"Leith Sequoyah gave it to you. After telling you he wasn't able to descramble it."

It sounded like I wasn't the only one who was good at taking shots in the dark. I stared at him, a sick feeling making my stomach roil. I'd been played. Given Leith's strange behavior, especially when I insisted on visiting the house, it made sense.

"I thought so," Troy said, seeing the answer in my face. "He's a rogue. Do you think we don't have the tech to descramble videos? Or scramble them, for that matter?" His gaze went distant, and his next words were spoken more to himself than to me. "I knew he'd been there that night. Damn."

"How was I supposed to know? He brought me the case, for fuck's sake!" I tried to get a rein on my anger before I made another stupid mistake. I was in over my head, and I didn't like it. I was used to dealing with humans on simple cases, not this kind of convoluted plotting.

Focus. "Why were you there if you weren't going to hurt her?" From the whirl of thoughts, one danced to the front like a sirocco. "Wait. *We* don't have? Who the hell are you? Who's we?"

His eyes flicked back to me, picking up golden flecks again when a cloud moved away from the waxing gibbous moon, and his lips compressed. I swallowed, realizing that I should have let that little tidbit go quietly to be filed in the back of my brain, not voiced aloud.

"Um…I mean…shit." I tensed again. "I won't go easy."

Troy continued weighing me on mental scales. A muscle in his cheek jumped, then he eased his grip on my coat, and took a half step back, running fingers through thick, dark hair to resettle a stray lock. I stayed where I was, not taken in by the casual movement. He'd already proven he was fast, and he was too close for me to get away without using Air. The situation wasn't that desperate. Yet.

"Why are you still on this case?" he asked in a measured tone. "I told you to stop digging."

"So, you're admitting it was you."

He stared at me, but his bad mood had nothing on Callista. A tendril of Aether probed at me.

"Stop that," I snarled without thinking.

He blinked. "Well, Ms. Finch of species unknown, who can apparently sense magic, if you won't quit looking, I'll have to do something with you. I can't have random Othersiders meddling in my business."

Double fuck. I glanced around, looking for an exit, a path to freedom whether physical or metaphorical. Where were all the people from the street? *Stall.* "Something like what?"

"To start, I'm going to need you to turn over everything you've got on Leith. And on me."

"Not gonna happen."

He didn't move except to shrug. "It's that, or I can kill you, take what I need anyway, and not worry about a nosy private investigator at my back anymore. More work, but I'll get what I want. Your choice."

"Callista would have a problem with me turning up dead." My face burned with shame as the words left my tongue. Here I was trying to gain my independence, yet still leaning on that bitch's name.

Troy's tight smile sent chills over me. "I don't answer to Callista. Besides, 'turning up dead' would require them to find you. They wouldn't." Of course, I had gotten tangled up with the one Othersider in the Triangle who didn't give a damn about Callista's authority. If he wouldn't be intimidated, I'd have to try talking him down.

"Come on, Monteague. You expect me to believe that you didn't kill Sybil Sequoyah, yet you can casually stand there and threaten to kill me? Talk to me. If it wasn't you, who did it?"

"If you won't work for me, I won't leave you as a loose tool to be picked up by someone else. I don't leave threats unaddressed."

There was that word again. *Tool.* "You wouldn't d—"

Before I finished the word *dare*, he moved. In another blink, a short punch blade was under my chin, and he cupped the base of my skull, ready to drive me onto it. His eyes had gone cold and dead, like there was nobody home. Against every instinct that screamed at me to get away, I stood very, very still as my heart thumped so hard I thought it would choke me.

"You're boring me, Finch, and delaying me. I don't care what you believe, but I need to root out the rogue agents following Sequoyah and bring them all to justice. You'll be my tool, or you'll be dead. Decide."

My stomach twisted. Had he guessed what I was? And agents of what? Either way, I didn't want to work for another elf. Then again, I wanted to be dead even less. I hadn't survived twenty-five years only to be done in by an elf in an alley, and I hadn't stood up to Callista and her damned nails to leave here as yet another person's tool—especially not that of an elf. They didn't even know what I was. There had to be a way out of this, a way to salvage it.

I glared at Troy, trying to get a read on him. Frustration came off him in waves, though that could be at dealing with me. He didn't have the icky-oily feel that Leith had though, a feeling I'd chalked up to dealing with an elf for the first time. Had I been wrong? Time to find out. "Let go of me. You want to make a deal? Don't touch me again."

After three pounds of my heart, he released me.

I stumbled, thinking fast. Go for my knife? No. This was my one chance to wrest some control back to myself. Back? Who was I fooling? To take control for the first time. "If you'd asked *nicely*, we could have made an arrangement sooner," I bluffed. "I'll help, but for my own reasons."

"Those are…?"

I almost told him that my reasons weren't his business, but I had a feeling that wasn't going to fly. "If you're not the liar here, then Leith screwed me. I found Sybil at Jordan Lake, but she'd been suffocated, not drowned, around the time he'd come to hire me. If he's the killer, I was supposed to take a fall, but I called the mundane cops instead of a cleanup crew. I'm not his patsy, and I *won't* be used." I glared to make the point.

"Jordan Lake. There's an old boathouse Leith uses there," he said. "I haven't been able to access it. It's warded to alert them of other elves."

"Only elves?"

"Nobody else would dare enter Sequoyah territory."

"Fair enough. Fine. I'll go. I can get a few photos, and set up camera traps." It was a bad fucking plan, but I couldn't figure out how else I was going to get something that would both help me and incentivize Troy and everyone else to back off.

I stepped back and flinched toward my knife when he reached into his jacket, but it was only his phone. A few taps and mine buzzed in my pocket.

"That's the location," he said.

Frowning, I got my phone out. It was my actual number, not the dummy number routed through my Google Voice account. "Where did you get my private number?"

"Please." The condescending expression made me want to slap him. Having just had a knife to my chin, I reined in my desire to punch him with a fist of Air, and settled for a dirty look before checking my phone. A screenshot of a map had been texted to me, the little red pin giving its coordinates.

"Something is going on there. The other two of my team went to bring Leith in and died before they could report back. I need something good to get into the inner circle. I need answers, Finch. Don't mess this up. Whatever you are, you don't want to cross me."

"I'll head over tonight." I wanted this entire fucking mess done with, wrapped up, and behind me.

The only answer I got was him stepping back. I forced myself to walk away without turning to see if he was following.

The confrontation bothered me enough that I blew a stop sign on the way home. No cops around, luckily, but I needed to calm down and figure out why Troy Monteague got so deeply under my skin.

Thinking back, he'd never actually denied hurting Sybil Sequoyah, only killing her. For all I knew it was normal or expected as part of the political machinations between high elven houses, but I didn't give a monkey's ass about that. Proving *someone* was responsible and handing them over to the vampires as their scapegoat would buy my freedom.

Snow started falling while I was getting my kit together. I swore at the heavy white flakes, hoping they wouldn't stick. Snow meant tracks and dangerous roads that would hamper a quick getaway. My hatchback had anti-slip technology, but it wasn't built for driving at speed over rough roads coated with ice. I stood in the doorway and hedged, tasting the crisp cold and knowing this would be a proper snowfall even before I checked the weather app to confirm. We only got a couple of these each winter. Of course, it would be my luck that one would come now.

A cloud as heavy as the one overhead dampened my mood as I stomped to my car and loaded everything in the cargo space. This couldn't wait, not if I wanted to get something Troy couldn't take away from me while Leith was still unsuspecting. "Get in, get some photos or something as evidence for Torsten, set up cams for Monteague to get him off my ass, get out. Simple." Saying it out loud did nothing to make me feel like it actually would be simple, and my mood worsened as I headed out onto the slick roads.

A forty-five-minute drive and two wrong turns later, my headlights fell on the weathered and defaced sign announcing the road to the old boathouse. As it had been at the New Hope Overlook boat ramp, this was another dead zone for mobile data. Fortunately, I'd downloaded directions to be used offline, and looked for a spot to hide the car. Driving all the way up to the front door would be stupid, but so would trying to walk several miles in the woods when I didn't know how fast I'd need to get out.

The trees hemmed the road closely on either side, the distance between them and the side of the narrowing track growing smaller as I hit the four-mile mark. I slammed on the brakes when I spotted a gap wide enough to hide the Honda, maybe an old parking area reclaimed by the forest.

The sudden stop sent me skidding off the road, and I resisted the urge to fight the wheel, breathing hard as I stopped inches short of a tree.

Shifting into a lower gear, I turned around and backed into the small clearing. Getting it back under the pines without scratching the paint all to hell was a challenge, but finally, I had it where I wanted it. The gunmetal grey car would be lost in the dark and forested gloom.

The hike to the clearing with the boathouse took longer than it should have because I had to drag a branch behind me to hide the tracks that were obviously no deer. Fortunately, there were already tire tracks down the road, so I didn't have to cover that up as well, although I did brush away the tracks into my hiding spot.

By the time I made to the clearing, I was cold, grouchy, and had a damp ass from where I'd slipped and missed the tree I'd reached for to save me. I crouched at the edge of the tree line, taking advantage of a stand of American holly and its evergreen leaves. As I settled onto my haunches, I pulled out my binoculars and took a look at what I was getting myself into.

This had to be the place. It was far too stereotypical, a battered warehouse-looking building with broken windows showing jagged glass like the bared teeth of a werewolf. Aether, a heavy casting, created a pressure similar to that I'd felt approaching Claret and Torsten's influence—the magical equivalent of a dog pissing on a fire hydrant. Other than a few small sheds off to the side, it was the only building in the area, and there was something rightly wrong about it to my sixth sense.

Its enormous dimensions probably could have housed a dozen boats, and what looked like a small, makeshift living area jutted out from one side. A bare window showed bunk beds crammed in tight. A tiny kitchen connected to it. People were living out here judging by the unmade beds. I affixed a small motion-activated camera to a tall pine just outside the reach of the boundary of Aether before taking out my camera, propping it on a monopod, and snapping a few photos on a slow shutter and a high ISO, grateful for the almost-full moon. I might find something better later, but there was no use passing up what I could see now.

When I didn't see any movement, I tucked the camera and monopod back in the backpack and crept around the edges to the other side, sticking to the trees and cursing the wet mess underfoot. It didn't snow often in this part of North Carolina, but when it did, a few inches of heavy white slush coated the ground, and turned the earth to mud where people had stepped in it. Yellowed grass peeked out in a few places and upped the risk of slipping.

Another check through the binoculars showed that the ground leading to the door was thoroughly churned up, disturbed by dozens of footprints going toward and away from the building. That made my task easier. I could focus on getting close while staying in cover, without having to be careful to step in the same tracks.

Even if tracks weren't a concern, being spotted was. As much as I wanted to push forward to the warehouse, I had to remember the likelihood that there would be cameras or lookouts. I wasn't supposed to be here, and the knowledge weighed on me.

Time to put on your big girl boots. This was my last shot to make the Sequoyah case pay out for me—and to make Leith answer for his deception.

Of course, then I'd have to figure out Troy's angle.

Chapter 20

Taking a deep breath, I forced myself to step out of the trees and dash to the cover of the closest shed, before I could lose my courage. With luck, there would be something worth using as evidence in there, and I could leave without having to dare the boathouse.

Clouds scudded over the moon. The smell of wet vegetation from the lake hovered under the scent of gasoline coming from the shed, both cut by the cold. Something told me I was not going to be lucky with the shed. Not that I had been particularly lucky this month anyway; why would that change now?

A small snap came from the woods as I leaned to peer through the jutting glass in a shattered window and froze. Nothing moved to disturb the evening's stillness. *A raccoon, or a deer. I hope.* My skin prickled into goosebumps as I went up on tiptoes to get a better look.

Red gas cans lined one wall of the shed. A few scattered tools, an old lawnmower, and a coil of rope made up the rest of the contents. *Okay…I guess they wouldn't have the good stuff out on the edge where a sneaky PI could find it.* I'd have to get closer.

Another shed stood between this one and the huge boathouse. I took a step toward it, then another, staying low and moving as carefully as I could.

Movement in the corner of my eye, from the woods. Not delicate enough for a deer. That meant human—or elf.

Shit. I backtracked, and slipped in the snowy mud. My fingers squelched, muck squeezing between every digit as I scrambled to push myself to my feet. By the time I made it upright, a hand at my neck kept me there as much as the concrete wall scraping against my gloves.

I didn't bother protesting my innocence. There was no reason to be out here except for the crimes being committed, as agent, victim, or, in my case, witness.

"Easy, Finch," Troy Monteague growled in a low tone, between clenched teeth. "Damn. I'd really hoped it wouldn't come to this."

"Fu–"

His hand tightened around my throat and cut off the curse. The inane thought, *What is it with him and walls?*, flitted through my head before disappearing under a wash of panic. I didn't know what the hell he was doing here, but I was caught. This was his game now, one I had no say in. I'd have to be smarter than I had been to date if I wanted to walk away.

"Monteague? What the blazes are you doing here?"

I froze, not having realized that Troy wasn't the only elf patrolling the woods.

He glared at me before calling back to the new voice, "Keeping an eye on that private investigator. As ordered."

"She's here? You were supposed to scare her off!"

I shook my head and tried to break free as he pulled me away from the wall. He kept his grip and held me close, my back to his front, my arms trapped, his hand over my mouth.

Playing along and following my impulses both amounted to the same thing just now: struggling. I cut off Troy's reply with a sharp elbow to his ribs, ineffective given his embrace but satisfying all the same when he grunted. That grunt became an angry cry when I bit the palm over my mouth, and I screamed before he could clap it back. The likelihood of anyone else being out here was slim to none. I still had to try.

"Feisty little bitch," the other elf said as he approached. I kicked out, trying to get him to stay back, but he turned my ankle aside with an easy block. "Cute, too. Let her go. The feisty ones are fun."

I stumbled as Troy's grasp disappeared, and barely managed to dodge a kick at my head from the other elf. When I tried to turn the dodge into flight, Troy hemmed me in, his stony expression suggesting he didn't like this—not that he put a stop to it. With escape not an option, I drew the lead knife and squared up, determined to go down fighting.

My opponent grinned. "Nice knife." He pulled his first few strikes, teasing me into betraying a reaction. By the time I figured out what he was doing, he had my style figured out. "Hapkido, with a touch of MMA," he said, sounding surprised. "Interesting choice."

"Stop playing with her, Callum," Troy grumbled behind me.

"You got a problem with how I do things, new boy?"

"I have a problem with standing in the snow with a storm blowing in."

I shuffled away from a low kick. Losing my footing was the only reason my head wasn't where he expected it to be for the open-handed slap that followed.

"You can always leave," Callum said, his attention on me as he spoke to Troy.

"I want in."

"Do you now? Huh. I suppose you've earned it." Callum moved like a switch had been flipped before he'd finished speaking. All of a sudden he was everywhere, fists and feet flying to deal blows that would leave me black and blue.

A few martial arts classes didn't give me the skills to deal with this. I tried blocking and, when I could, slashing with my knife, but my inexpert attempts only made him laugh.

"Dumb bitch."

He got through my guard, and his swinging fist knocked me stupid. I was too dazed to do anything effective as he wrestled me back to my feet, knocked the knife from my hand, and half-dragged me to the second shed. A hard shove sent me sprawling to the floor, and I knocked my head again when I couldn't quite catch myself in time. Rough hands tugged things from my pockets while I struggled ineffectively and tried not to throw up. Callum left with my backpack and keys, and I gave myself a minute to lay still.

When I could see things normally and not in doubles, I made out a boundary of chain-link fence secured with a chain and padlock. The walls pressed close. Boarded-up windows kept out the moon's glow; it was replaced by the harsh glare of a bare bulb hanging from the ceiling. Discarded equipment lined the space outside the cage, and I guessed I'd found out what was in the other shed. I forced myself to focus, and pushed away the panic rising to close my throat. I could still get out of this without using my powers, but losing my shit would not help.

A dark stain under my outstretched hand flaked when I clenched my fingers. I brought them close and sniffed. My stomach clenched at the scent of old, dried blood. I was not the first person to be held here. Groaning, I pushed up until I was able to fall onto my back. The fencing extended overhead, so there would be no climbing out.

Time to take stock of the situation. Anything useful had been taken. They had my keys, which meant they'd find my car, since all they had to do was trigger the alarm. My gloves and hat were gone, but at least I had the coat. With tentative fingers, I probed my face. A warm puffiness told me I'd have a black eye, my lip was split, and my jaw ached.

Callum hadn't used magic once. Unlike the djinn, elves could manipulate Aether to affect others, so the fact that he hadn't bothered suggested that he liked hurting people in more primitive ways. His gendered insults had me thinking he probably liked hurting women in particular.

That confused me. Elves were matriarchal, and supposedly revered and respected the role of women in society. What had happened with this group? On reflection, Troy hadn't interacted with women during any of my surveillance, unless harassing me counted. An ugly idea started to form in my mind, one for which I didn't have nearly enough hard information to take back to the vampires but felt right in my gut.

The elves were splintering, and I must have stumbled—or been pulled into—some kind of related conspiracy.

Where the drownings and vampire bites played into it, or this little boys' club, for that matter, I had no idea. Finding the answers to all of that would be my ticket to independence, if I could get out alive.

I'd get out. I just needed to be smart.

Footsteps stopping at the shed door and the rattle of an old lock drew my attention. My breath caught. I considered rolling back over and pretending I'd passed out. A man—another elf, from the roil of Aether surrounding him with the choking scent of burnt marshmallow—was standing outside my cage before I could decide.

"All things in threes," I mumbled, tonguing a new bead of blood as my lip cracked. Leith, Callum, and now this guy. There would likely be at least two more to balance Troy. Five on two was not good odds, and that assumed Troy was on my side.

Spitting blood in the general direction of the new guy, I said, "You guys have no sense of fair play."

"Can it, bitch." The elf started to unlock the cage, and I forced myself upright, scooting back as far from his reach as I could. Everything ached, and the chill, hard floor did nothing to help with stiff, beaten muscles. Using the fencing of my cage, I dragged myself upright. I'd met men like this before. They wanted you to cower, but if you did, they lost whatever hair-thin thread of restraint they might have had and things went from bad to worse.

Callum lurked in the shadows, his thumbs hooked through his belt loops and a predatory look in his eyes. "Cuffs," he prompted the new elf. New guy loosened the chain enough to crack the gate and toss a pair of handcuffs through. "Here. Put those on."

When I hesitated, Callum called, "Put them on, or we drug you and put them on for you." Something in his face told me I would not like what else they would do if they drugged me, and I flashed back on his comment that I was cute.

"Shit," I muttered with feeling, taking the cuffs. *Play along, and pray Troy isn't the biggest lying bullshitter of all time.* I had no reason to trust him, and yet he was my main hope. Me. Relying on an elf. The Goddess' sense of humor sucked. What had Troy even been doing in the woods? Checking on me? Or triggering the ward to make sure I got caught?

Either way, my knife was gone, and I was running out of options. I'd practiced enough that I knew I could wall them off with Air and break free, but I had no idea where my car keys were, and I hadn't seen other vehicles on my way in. Even my cold resistance wouldn't help me if I had to wander the woods at night in a snowstorm with half my winter gear taken. I had to play along until I could find a way out. Then my powers might have to be my big play to get free.

My heart hiccupped at that; after hiding so well for twenty-five years, my own ambition was what would expose me. Grinding my teeth in frustration, I snapped the cuffs on.

"Make 'em nice and tight," Callum ordered. I glared and did as he said, hating him even more when he added, "There's a good little wench."

As soon as the second cuff clicked shut the new elf stepped into the light beaming down on the cage. He looked enough like Leith that I stared. "What are you looking at?" he snapped, grabbing for my arm when I glanced away.

Callum got the door, and they pushed me ahead of them. When I slipped on the icy ground, he caught me by the back of my coat and kept walking, practically dragging me along. As I twisted, trying to find my feet again, I glimpsed my car at the edge of the clearing.

The tree line was achingly close. There were only two elves here, now. If I could make it to the car…I still couldn't get away without the fob. As though he'd read my mind, Callum shook me and said, "Don't even think about it, bitch." Whether he was goading me or simply an ass, I was real tired of the insults.

The boathouse was warmer, at least, if not by much thanks to one of the walls being corrugated metal and the rest bare brick. A few derelict boats and a single pristine one took up one side, near a hinged door that looked like it should be in a garage. Tall, oxidized pillars, painted a bright shade of safety yellow around the bottom, held up a high roof. Darkened windows over a loft area let in some moonlight, although most of the lighting was provided by industrial-sized overhead lamps. Random odds and ends that I assumed would have been used to repair boats littered the floor where nobody had bothered to tidy up.

And tucked away in one corner next to a space heater was a long collapsible table with folding chairs, Leith Sequoyah seated at its head with the air of a king. Troy stood at his right shoulder, and two more elves lounged against the wall where they could watch both Troy and Leith.

"The douchebag himself," I said, earning a cuff from Callum that made me hiss as it rattled my already aching head.

"The PI, as ordered," Troy said to Leith in clipped tones. I couldn't read his expressionless look as he met my eyes. I looked away first, too pissed off by Leith's apparent status as the leader of this shitshow and my own gullibility to focus on Troy.

"I see," Leith said, rising and coming around the table. He extended a finger toward my cheek, and I jerked my head away.

"What the fuck is going on here?" I asked. That finger came close again, and I snapped at it.

Rage—at being defied?—and something else, something more dangerous, made Leith's ice blue eyes even colder. He casually backhanded me. I couldn't help the whimper that escaped as my bruised cheekbone split. A trickle of blood oozed, spilling faster when an unbidden tear mingled with it.

"Arden, Arden." The disappointment in his voice confused me. "You haven't done any of what I needed you to do."

"Ms. Sequoyah—"

"No." He leaned forward to whisper. "You weren't supposed to find her at all. And if you did, you were supposed to follow my breadcrumbs, and give my boys enough to pin it on Monteague."

My breath caught. My eyes darted to Troy, but Leith's broad shoulder blocked my line of sight.

"I set everything up for you, just right. It was the perfect distraction for the conclave of queens, and you fucked it up." He started to circle like a shark. My skin crawled as he passed behind me, and I tried to turn around to keep sight of him. Callum wore a wide grin, and he tightened his grip on my arm to keep me where I was.

A terrible twisting in my guts accompanied a sickening thought. Then a long, intimate sniff along the back of my neck made me shudder.

"That's interesting," Leith murmured, coming back around to consider my face. "I'd assumed the ozone was all the electronics in your office, but it's you."

"You killed Sybil," I blurted, unable to keep the confirmation of my earlier guess in my head in the panic of needing him to stop thinking about what I was. "You killed your own grandmother?"

The spark of rage he'd mostly hidden before flared to a full-blown inferno. "She deserved it!" he roared. "That meddling *bitch* took everything from me!"

I shook like a leaf in the face of such unhinged fury, and his hand came up again. "What was it supposed to be a distraction for?" I asked, trying to sidetrack him. The woozy weight in my head told me another hit would knock me out. I'd taken some solid knocks in hapkido, but that was training. This was pure, unrestrained violence. Adrenaline made my heart gallop.

Leith paused. Dropped his hand, and cocked his head, smiled a creepy little smile. "I think you know."

I thought fast. It couldn't just be his disagreement with the vampires, or with elves spending time in vampire establishments. There was more to all this. The boathouse, the lake…I darted a look at the one boat in good condition and ready to launch, and played his game, praying it would be enough. "The drownings."

"The drownings," he agreed. "And if you know why the drownings are connected, you know a good deal more than you should if you were only human." The last word was scarcely more than a breath, and a sweet ashy smell rose an instant before he lashed out with Aether.

My shields barely held. I quivered as my mouth went dry, only upright because of the elves gripping my arms.

His gaze sharpened, and bore into mine. "Not very human at all, to resist that."

Chapter 21

"I don't know what you're talking about," I breathed around a throat closed in terror. I'd fucked up, and now my worst nightmare was coming true. "I don't know what you think I am, or what you think I'm resisting."

"Oh, I think you do." He lashed out again, and my shields trembled harder than my body. A groan slipped out, and I sagged, panting as I focused on a chip in the concrete floor.

Black boots entered my field of vision. "Let me," Troy said.

"I'm not very sure of you right now." Leith's voice dripped venom, more than could be accounted for in the short time I'd seen them together. "You never mentioned she wasn't human."

"I didn't realize. You know shieldbreaking is one of my family's talents; it didn't even register that I'd slipped one when I tagged her."

"You tagged her?" Acid shifted to suspicion.

Troy brushed it off. "She's a private investigator. Tough, used to people not being happy with her. A little roughing up wasn't going to keep her off the case. How do you think I knew to follow her here?"

This would all be so much more interesting if I wasn't on the verge of having my metaphysical shields shattered. Grimm had done it once in training, and it hurt more than breaking a bone and grinding the pieces together.

Leith stepped back, and Troy cupped my chin to tilt my head up.

"Don't do this," I said.

His lips thinned, and he didn't reply.

If he slipped past my shields and broke them open, I'd react on instinct from the pain of it, lashing out with Air in a blunt, brute-force attack before passing out. One way or another, my secret was about to be discovered.

Years of hiding, of fear, distilled down to this instant. Clarity bloomed as fear faded. My heartbeat gave a last walloping thump, and then faded into the background as my natural sense of the air around me grew painfully sharp. This was it. There was only one way forward. If I had to go out, I'd go down fighting, not by having everything torn from me while I sat there and waited for it.

Troy froze when I stopped shielding and reached for Air. I knew my eyes were glowing gold when he said, "Elemental. She's a damned elemental!" His face twisted, and his hand jerked away as though burned in the instant before I compressed some of the air in the room to make a thunderclap.

Chaos exploded along with the boom. The elves reeled away, hands over their ears. Adrenaline pushed me into a scramble. My hands were still cuffed in front of me; I needed a key, or something to pick the cuffs open. My car fob would help, too.

Drawing on more Air, I made a massive fist, and sucker punched first Callum, then Troy. Leith found his feet, and I pushed a wall of Air at him, blocking him into the corner with the two bodyguards who'd barely made it away from their positions. The elf who'd come with Callum got my fisted hands cracked on the crown of his head. He went out cold. Elves weren't the only ones with greater-than-human strength.

Callum tried to grab me as I scrabbled in his pockets. I found a bulge in his jacket, and snapped my forehead down to break his nose. He forgot me as he screamed, and his hands flew to his face. The bulge was the key fob for my car. I could sort out the cuffs later, after I was out of this deathtrap. I didn't have enough fine motor control to manage a handcuff key in the moment, anyway, with adrenaline making my hands shake.

Movement in the corner of my eye. I created a whirlwind, knocking Troy off his feet and the tables on their sides—and in so doing, lost track of the chord of magic keeping Leith and his bodyguards pinned behind the wall of Air in the corner.

They stumbled out as it fell, then surged toward me. I ran, awkward with my keys clutched to my chest. Hitting the heavy door stunned me, and I jostled the doorknob with stars in my vision. My fingers wouldn't work, clenched tight around my car keys, but the knob was the kind you just needed to push down on. Screaming in frustration, I leaned on it with an elbow.

The door opened so suddenly that I tripped over my own feet and fell, causing the elf who'd leapt for me to overshoot. I pushed at him with Air to clear the way, and had just lurched into a run when arms tangled around my legs, bringing me down.

"No! *No!*" I tried to summon another whirlwind but whoever was on my back tucked low and close. I couldn't shake him off. I tried another Air punch. An arm slipped around my throat, and flexed into a chokehold. I lost all reason, lashing out with Air, bucking and struggling, fighting to get my fingers between solid muscle and my neck.

Darkness threatened. I couldn't keep this up for much longer.

Didn't matter. I wouldn't go easy.

Someone dragged my wrists in front of me. Pressure weighed on my left forearm, and the cuff on that wrist clicked open before three stacked metal bands were shoved over my hand. The sharp bite of a scrape on my knuckles accompanied the loss of Air, so sudden and shocking that I forgot to keep fighting for freedom.

"What the hell did you do?" an elf asked from my back.

"Bronze." Troy's voice was cold as he snapped the cuff back on. "Some of the grommets in the boathouse are made of bronze."

Fuck. Callista's nails were small enough, and targeted enough, that they'd only weaken her victim's powers. Heavy bands of thick, solid metal would sever it.

"So?"

"So, it's like putting a charm of silver and lead on one of us. She's cut off from her element. From her magic."

As black stars spread in my vision, Leith crouched in front of me. "Sleep," he said with a forceful push of Aether. With my shields open and my mind addled, I had nothing left to defend myself. So I did.

* * *

I woke on my face. *Woke* was a bit of a strong term for what had happened, given that I'd blearily found my way to consciousness in increments. Every one of those increments ground rough, cold concrete another millimeter into my face. No chain link fencing this time, just metal walls that leaked winter's chill. I was back in the boat warehouse.

A burning itch on my left arm and around my neck drew my attention. I sucked a breath in, hissing at the sight of the bronze grommets pushed up around my forearm. Feeling at my neck, I discovered a crude collar, made of a single strip of metal forced into a circlet, and held shut with a small padlock. From the itch, it was probably bronze as well. A chain clinked, and I looked up to see it secured to a ring in the wall.

"I think our new pet is awake." Leith sounded gleeful. I didn't want to roll over, but I did. Sitting up made my stiff muscles tighten and my bruised face throb, but I'd face my enemies upright, not as a coward curled into a ball against the wall.

All six elves were gathered around the table, their anticipation almost touchable. A few beer bottles and some takeaway boxes now rested on it, reminding me that I hadn't eaten in most of a day. Thinking of food made me hungry for a minute before it made me feel sick.

"Aw, you guys started a party without me," I croaked. My throat hurt, probably from the chokehold. Maybe I was catching a cold from being left on an icy, bare floor in the winter. "You're terrible hosts."

"Brennan, go show the elemental how terrible we can be if we put a little effort into it," Leith said. Callum's sidekick from before smiled, grabbing a thick stick of wood from the floor as he approached.

"Me and my big fucking mouth." I forced myself into a crouch. Even if the chain would keep me from going far, I wasn't just going to sit and take it.

I barely blocked Brennan's first swing, falling back on my ass with a hiss as my arm went numb. The wood clanged against the metal with a resonating *bong* that hurt my ears. He wound up for another swing and paused, looking over his shoulder when the main door opened. I took advantage of his distraction and kicked out hard with both feet.

Brennan screamed as I dislocated his knee. The two bodyguard elves, who looked like more Sequoyah cousins now that I was getting a good look at them, started to rush toward me.

"Leave it," Leith said. "If Brennan can't hold his own against that trash, he deserves what he got. We have company."

Three more elves were pushing a fourth in front of them. His arms were bound behind him, and he looked as badly beaten as I felt. The newcomers were, again, all male. Two of the three were blonde and pale—more Sequoyahs?—and the third was black.

"You were supposed to bring a little queen," Leith said. "What's this?"

"We can go back for the wench. This one we found with a vampire," one of the blonde ones said. Anger thickened his voice, and his fists clenched at his sides.

Leith's lips twisted in a sneer, and he surged forward. "Another traitor giving our blood to our enemies. It's not enough that the bitches we're forced to call queens hold our people back, hobble our ambitions, and cripple our power. No, blood whores like you *have to go and give it to the vampires!*"

My jaw dropped as Leith fell on the prisoner in an absolute fury, smashing him in the face with a fist, and then kicking him over and over once he fell. None of the others moved to stop him.

I'd had a feeling that Leith was disturbed, and had written it off as a man worried for his grandmother. Then, when I'd learned about his recruitment efforts at Claret, I'd figured him for some sort of low-level species supremacist, but still never dreamed that this level of unhinged rage lived within him. I'd been exactly the kind of foolish that humans were when they thought words wouldn't incite violence. This depth of hatred stemmed from something ugly and personal, a loss or an injury, perceived or real, that he'd never processed, and had the privilege to act out on.

My stomach curdled as I watched the beating. I was in more danger than I'd realized. Leith had a mission. Probably a manifesto. Something that fed his fear and hatred, justifying his sickening actions. If the other blond elves were more high-blood Sequoyahs, I had to wonder how deep the rot in the House went.

This was my ticket to independence from Callista. I just had to get out. I tugged at the collar again, studying the eye bolt linking me to the wall. It was rusted into place, but I might be able to work it free. Everyone's attention was on Leith.

I had just started getting the bolt to turn when the heavy, vicious thuds of fists hitting flesh stopped. I stopped working at the bolt and looked back over my shoulder. The prisoner had stopped protesting, and lay still.

Leith pulled himself up, straightening his jacket, and smoothing his hair back from his eyes. He glanced at me, and grinned. "Now it understands its place," he said, reading my expression. "Not so cocky now." He stalked over to me with the slow steps of a hunting lion.

I looked at Troy's blank face, heart racing.

"What, do you think he's going to save you? Monteague?" Leith scoffed, and crouched in front of me, a wide, evil smile making his handsome features nasty. "Oh, no, pet. You're going to be his final test before we fully initiate him into my Redcaps." He gave me that long, slow look again, the look a man gave a woman when he wanted her to know that he could do what he pleased, regardless of what she wanted.

Redcaps. I stopped breathing. Duke's vision. His warning: "Arden…something is coming. In the vision, everything around you is cold and dark. Colder than ice. Darker than death."

This was it. It had to be. What else had he said?

"Learn to swim."

I'd misunderstood what Leith had said earlier. The Redcaps weren't a vigilante response to the elven drownings. They were the cause. My stomach plummeted. *Fuck.*

"What's this?" Leith said as his gaze fell on my chest. His hand flashed out and caught my pendant. It must have fallen out of my shirt.

"Where did you get this?" he said, reddening as he tugged it. I couldn't help a small cry of dismay as it snapped free. He stared at it, then at me. "This can't be yours. And if it is, you're even more of an abomination than I thought."

With a last leer, he stood and pocketed my pendant. Its loss was a blow; I hadn't even begun to understand what it symbolized, only that my elven father had owned it. That Leith considered it important bothered me. Did everyone know more than I?

Leith glared at me once more before pulling Brennan out of my reach, strolling back over to the heap of a man on the floor, and kneeling in front of him to slap him awake. Aether rose, prickling my skin despite my being unable to reach for my own magic. I squinted, trying to get the sense of it until Leith said, "Stop breathing."

A hard knot settled in my stomach as the prisoner did what he was told. "A good healer is also an excellent weapon," Leith said casually to the room at large. "And yet the queens and mothers would deny me my full potential." He gazed emotionlessly at the man in front of him. When he started turning blue, Leith said, "Breathe."

A wracking gasp shook him as he did, and an awful possibility tightened my chest. Troy had mentioned talents that his ran in his family. Did healing run in the Sequoyah family? Were there more killer healers with a grudge of hatred?

Leith watched him writhe a while longer before standing. "Monteague. Take this one and the elemental. Throw them in the lake, somewhere they won't be found."

"Who's going with me?"

Leith shrugged. "Nobody will be there forcing you. If you can manage these two on your own, you have what it takes to be a Redcap. Fuck it up, and we'll hunt you down. You'll be taking the long drink with them. The boat's out and fueled. Go." He turned to point at two elves. "You and you. Get this out to the boat while Monteague gets the elemental."

With a last sneer at the gasping prisoner, he went for the door. "I'm going hunting for that little queen. Oh, and Monteague? Record it. I want proof that your house can produce a real man."

Troy nodded, and came for me.

"You stay away from me!" I said as I pushed as far away from him as the chain would allow. It wasn't long enough for me to get far, and was too short to give me something to strangle him with. I faced him, heart pounding, as he studied me, head tilted and squinting as though he could see something I couldn't, ignoring the jeers of the others.

"There," he murmured. Goosebumps raced over me, and the scent of marshmallow filled my nose the instant before something slid between an infinitesimal crack in what remained of my natural shields to touch my mind. He said, "Be still," and I dropped. The heckling stopped, replaced by silence.

He put my mind in a maze. Locked behind a foreign wall in my own mind, I tried to find the shape of what he'd done, what he'd woven from Aether to put me in such stillness.

"How did he do that?" someone asked. He didn't reply as he leaned down, opened the padlock holding the chain to my collar, slid his hands under my armpits, and hoisted me up and over his shoulder.

Winter air scented by the lake slapped me. We'd moved outside in the time that I was trying to find the end of the thread. My ass thumped against something metallic. The boat. The elven prisoner was there as well, bruised and bloody, bound hand and foot, gagged, and hyperventilating. Troy watched me as he pushed the boat farther out, hopping off the end of the dock when he reached the end to land lightly in the stern. In the haze he'd put me in, all I could do was close my eyes as he settled on the bench and fired up the small outboard motor.

The other prisoner was not so lucky. A few fragments broke through my concentration. "You're a Monteague, I'm a— Houses are allies—what—"

I tuned him out, determined to find a way out of the maze. I was half-elven myself. I could do this. Had to do it, even if I couldn't use Aether. Troy had betrayed me. I was going to break free and kick his fucking ass for it.

Time slipped by again. The boat was slowing. I was almost there…almost…I had it. Gasping as though coming out of a nightmare, I arched up as the will to move, to *fight* came flooding back. The world sharpened and cleared as triumph lit a flame in my heart. Not that it did very much good; at some point between putting me down and now, Troy had bound me as the other prisoner was bound.

"That's interesting," Troy said, turning to glance at me from where he'd attached his phone to a gorilla-grip tripod on the edge of the boat. The phone dinged when he tapped it, and without a word, he hefted the other elf over the side. Splashing and muffled howls cut off as he threw a concrete block on a rope in after.

"We—"

A slap cut off my reminder of our deal, and he gave me a fierce look. "You weren't supposed to be awake for this. Shame I won't be able to find out how you broke that enchantment." He threw another concrete block over the side. A rope hissed and tugged at my ankles, jerking them over the side.

"No no no no—no!"

Strong arms hefted me up and into the air. Freefall to the soundtrack of my heart beating in my ears. I scrabbled for Air, finding nothing as the bronze around my arm interfered. And then I hit the water.

The world was cold, so cold. Shockingly cold. Warmth fled, leaving me in the clutches of icy water. There was no air, and not enough light. Darkness closed in around me, pressed against me, taunted me. The elf whose name I'd missed jerked violently as bubbles rose, then went still. A gentle movement caught my eye, and I turned my head.

We weren't the only two. We were in the midst of a small graveyard. Some of the corpses were bones on the bed of the lake. One, a woman, looked almost like she was asleep, much as Sybil had. The bodies that had been found weren't the first Leith had doomed.

I blinked, eyelids scraping, and tried to scream.

Icy water poured down my throat, stopped by another cough-choked howl. My muscles begged for oxygen as I struggled, but I couldn't free myself from the ropes.

Darkness edged in. I fought the ropes, fought the water, and cursed the world. My body tried to take a breath. I fought that too, until I couldn't. My lungs betrayed me. Lake water thick with the taste of algae and death flooded me.

Something splashed overhead.

Didn't matter. Everything was cold and dark. Colder than ice and darker than death. Just as Duke had said.

Chapter 22

I found consciousness by degrees, through pieces of sensory data. The almost blinding glare of light through my closed eyelids. The stale smell of a room that nobody lived in. The caress of quality fabric wrapped around me, so intimate that I knew I was naked. The heap of a heavy duvet, blessedly trapping heat around me.

The headache slammed into my temples with a nauseating sharpness worse than any hangover I'd ever had, and a groan clawed its way out of my throat. My breath came in the fast-shallow cadence of someone trying not to vomit until I couldn't hold back. I managed to drop my head over the side of the bed before heaving. Nothing came up, but my stomach still insisted on clenching mercilessly. Once more, and again, before I hung over the side, limp and wrung out.

"Done?"

I tried to sit up and see who was talking, but my muscles spasmed. I fell back against the pillow and ground the heels of both hands into my eyes, just trying to breathe. The lamp clicked off, and the absence of artificial light helped somewhat.

Magic rose.

"No!" I spared one hand from my forehead to slap at the invisible coils. They dissipated.

"You'd rather suffer?"

The voice was cold. It didn't really worry about whether I suffered or not. Only one person needed me enough to try, but hated me enough not to care. I cracked my eyes again, finding a tall form with tousled dark hair framing a tawny face. Hazel eyes glared at me from the door.

"Monteague?"

"Finch."

Somehow, he managed to sound both bored and annoyed as the magic pulled back. It had to have been him who'd fished me from the frozen lake, resuscitated me, and kept me from dying of hypothermia. My headache worsened as I considered the implication that he'd played Leith. How important was ending this conspiracy that he'd do all that for an elemental?

I groaned. My bones had the all-over ache of a fever, and I shivered despite being swaddled in blankets. My lungs tickled, and I rolled to the side, hacking wet coughs into the pillows.

"So. Elementals are hard to kill. Good to know."

I swallowed and pushed up on my elbows. Troy stared, face blank and gaze hard. He was clothed all in black, and looked utterly uncompromising.

"You know what I am," I said before pressing my lips together. Talking hurt, and I was stating the obvious. Of course he knew what I was.

He pursed his lips. "You're not going to deny it?"

"Why bother?" He'd seen my eyes, felt the gust of Air as it knocked the Redcaps off their feet, seen the effect of bronze on me. "The real question is, what are you doing?"

Troy narrowed his eyes. "If you think I'm going to explain myself to you, you're mistaken." He took a step closer, hand falling to the long-bladed knife at his hip. "You're the one with an automatic death sentence, one I haven't carried out—yet. I think I'll ask the questions."

I tried to remind myself that he wouldn't have hauled me out of the lake and treated me for hypothermia only to kill me now. It didn't stop my reflexive movement to push myself upright.

He didn't even glance at my breasts as the sheets fell, and I didn't waste energy covering myself. If it had been him who'd gotten me out of my wet clothes, he'd seen everything anyway. Even if it hadn't been him, I didn't care. He was here now, and there were bigger issues.

"What do you want?" I rasped before coughing again. He hadn't risked his life to keep me alive for nothing.

The corner of his lips flickered in a hint of a smile. "Leith and the Redcaps, of course. I thought I'd made that clear."

I blinked. Opened my mouth. Shut it. Then let the words out despite the high odds of a bad reaction. "You know what? Fuck you. I literally died to get you in with them. Information my ass, I bet you followed me hoping to instigate everything that happened."

"You didn't die."

"Fuck you, anyway." I crossed my arms and turned onto my side. Giving him my back was stupid, but I was about as strong as a wet tissue until my elevated healing abilities kicked in. Back or front wouldn't make much difference right now if he wanted to finish what he'd started with throwing me in the lake.

"Finch."

Lifting one hand, I gave him the finger. "I don't owe you anything."

"I'm giving you your life."

Rage spurred me upright again. "Like hell you are! *You people* might think you have a reason to have this massive fucking grudge against elementals, but newsflash: that reason is so far in the past that it doesn't even matter. *I am a person* and you *will* treat me as such. That means no murder or dehumanization!"

"Hard to dehumanize you when you're not human."

With a growl of pissed-off frustration, I pushed myself out of the bed, falling to my knees when they refused to hold me up. As my hands hit the floor, I noticed that the damned bronze grommets were gone. I checked my neck to find a raw patch, but no collar. Air still wouldn't stay in my grasp when I reached for it, though. I'd pushed too hard, too desperately, and probably had residual contact poisoning from the bronze.

Troy came around the bed. "Where are you trying to go?"

"Anywhere that's not here."

He leaned over and reached for me. I wasn't strong enough for a proper punch, so I clawed my fingers and swiped at him.

He dodged, and we glared at each other, at an impasse, until he crouched. "How did you break the enchantment?"

"You're unbelievable."

"How?"

"What's in it for me?"

"What do you want?"

This was like dealing with the djinn. I sat down hard, tangled in the sheets and unable to stay in a ready crouch, then closed my eyes as I leaned back against the side of the bed. Not out of trust. I just felt that crappy. "I want not to be hunted. I want a normal fucking life where I can practice my magic in peace and…just be." I held back wanting to be free of Callista. I had House Sequoyah's secret, but so did Troy. I didn't need him stealing my thunder—and my golden ticket to independence.

Shifting fabric made me open my eyes. Troy was just out of my reach. "I can't give you that. You're asking too much."

"Then you can go to hell."

"I'm already there," he snapped. The gold flecks in his eyes flared. "I let an elf from an allied House die and saved you instead. I couldn't save you both. I chose you. Do you understand what that means if I don't return to the Darkwatch and my grandmother—my *queen*—with Leith in chains?"

"No," I whispered, dropping my head to my upraised knees as my mouth dried. *He's fucking Darkwatch?* I shifted to keep an eye on him as I said, "And I don't care."

His eyes narrowed. "I could make you do it."

"And I could shake off your stupid enchantment again," I said with more confidence than I felt.

"Leith had me take a video."

"I remember that much."

"He didn't want proof, he wanted blackmail."

"None of this is telling me why I should give a flying fuck when you're acting like my life is an actual negotiating position."

"Elven law says—"

I lifted my head, and snarled, "Does it say something about leaving another elf to die? I assume you got that on video as well. One that was also sent to Leith."

His mouth snapped shut. If looks could kill, he'd have finished me off with his scowl alone.

"Give me what I want, or go hang yourself," I said.

His eyes deadened by degrees until there was no personality left. It didn't scare me anymore. I'd drunk death in, swallowed it, and vomited it back up. I knew its taste, its clasp as it dragged me into the depths.

"Goddess damn you," he said when I wouldn't budge. "Fine. I will do what I can. But only if you help me take down Leith and eliminate the Redcaps."

"Why me? Go get another one of your precious Darkwatch agents."

"Leith is Darkwatch. And in case you hadn't noticed, all of the major Houses, plus some of the minor, were in the boathouse. I don't know how far the conspiracy goes. The rest of my team is dead. There's only you." A resentful growl pulled the last words down an octave.

Shock slapped me. *Jackpot.* It wasn't just a scion of House Sequoyah who was a twisted serial killer. Even the Darkwatch, always touted as above reproach, had been corrupted. This would be worth my life, and my near death. A thrill raced through me, and I suppressed the laughter that threatened to bubble out of my chest to join the savage grin on my face. That was Callista covered.

I didn't have to agree to help Troy, but I would. Leith had played me, reduced me to being less than an animal, and appointed himself judge, jury, and executioner in absentia. I was an elemental. It was past time that I owned that, and stood up for myself. Nobody would do it for me, not even those who claimed to be my guardians and allies. Breaking free of Callista would only make it worse, signaling open season on sylphs unless I claimed my own strength and made it clear that I wasn't to be fucked with.

I also wanted justice—Otherside-style.

Extending a trembling hand, I said, "We go in as partners, or you go in alone."

Too many emotions to read raced across his face. "As partners, then." His hand engulfed mine, and we shook. A spark leapt between our palms and we both jumped away, startled and untrusting.

With the most immediate danger averted, my fight-or-flight energy crashed. The fever hovering behind the adrenaline made itself known in uncontrollable shaking. My teeth clattered as I hauled myself back into the bed, and curled into a ball, dragging the duvet over my head in a desperate search for warmth.

"You're not in any condition to go hunting, are you," Troy said flatly.

"Is it that obvious?"

"Goddess burn it," he swore half under his breath. "Stay here. I'll go to the pharmacy."

"What, don't have Leith's healing power?"

"Would you let me use it if I did?"

When I didn't answer, he stormed out.

Even when my accelerated healing kicked in, it took a day for me to recover enough to handle Air without having it slip through my fingers or blow down everything in the room. Two for me to stop coughing every other minute, and about that long to get over the fact that Troy was a Darkwatch agent now embedded with an elven terrorist group. No wonder it was so important to him to bring Leith in.

Troy had recovered my backpack and my knife, though not my camera. That would be expensive to replace, but at least most of the photos were backed up in a cloud storage drive. He claimed to have my car hidden away somewhere, having been tasked with disposing of it. The keys he kept.

My pendant was still missing as well, and its loss bothered me. Its negligible weight had hung around my neck and between my breasts my entire life. Now it was gone. I wanted it back from Leith, and I had a feeling I'd only get it if I took it off his dead body.

As far as I knew, neither Duke, nor Grimm, nor Callista had checked to see where I was. None of the vampires followed up, either. That surprised me; I would have thought they'd want to keep an eye on their investment. Maybe they just had that much money. Or maybe Troy had staged a scene to look like I'd left town.

A sullen elf prince who hated me was my only companion, and I was trapped in his safehouse. He'd woven some kind of ward over the entire one-bedroom apartment that would ignore elves, allowing him to come and go freely, but discouraged other beings from looking too closely. My attempt to leave while he was at the pharmacy had put me in muscle cramps that had me writhing on the floor when he'd walked in.

When I demanded my phone back, Troy snorted. "You're supposed to be dead. I didn't risk everything keeping you alive to have you give it away by calling someone."

"Guess I shouldn't have posted that status update to Facebook," I said saucily, never mind I stayed off social media as a general rule. He blanched before remembering that he still had my phone.

I hated him for it. I had my life, sure. My freedom…that stayed within his grasp, along with everything else. Deal or not, he didn't trust me. I sure as hell wasn't going to explain that going back for my necklace and my vengeance mattered more to me than our deal. The lack of trust was mutual.

The walls grew stifling. Elementals didn't do well for long periods indoors, and even two days was too much for me. I needed the trees, the fresh air, the sun. It was why my little house backed up to the woods, and was full of live plants bathed by sunlight streaming in the windows, which were always cracked at least a little even in winter.

My body might have been recovering from its ordeal. My spirit suffered.

After three days languishing in Troy Monteague's possession, I'd had enough.

Chapter 23

"I need to get out of here," I said the moment he returned from whatever the day's errand was. He bristled, casting a critical eye over me. I crossed my arms. "Don't look at me like that. Keeping me here is going to make me worse, not better."

"You've barely regained control of your…power," he said, lip twisting. "I'll have one chance to bring Sequoyah and his cousins down. One. I will not blow it on an impatient…" He trailed off, as though the word *elemental* would sully his tongue.

"I need fresh air, Monteague. The whole elemental thing? I need to be in the *elements*." Shoving that in his face drew a scowl that barely concealed disgust and loathing. The look put my back up, and I lifted my chin. "What? Are you afraid of Leith?"

"No," Troy snapped.

I smirked. "Looks to me like you are. You can't tell me that you didn't get everything you needed to convict him or whatever when he spelled out what he was doing before *ordering you to murder me*." I emphasized the last to see how he'd react. My gut twisted when he didn't flinch, not even the flicker of an eyelid or a twitch in his cheek. He felt nothing about dropping me into a lake with a concrete block tied to my ankles.

"You're a real fucking piece of work," I said with a shudder.

"I do what the law says. I complete my missions. And I don't give explanations to elementals." He spat the last word.

"Fine. What-the-fuck-ever. If you want me to help bring him down, I need out of here. I'm a *sylph*. I need *fresh air*."

We stared at each other. I was done talking, and he had nothing to say. If he was the lone surviving Darkwatch agent out of a triad, he'd have been conditioned to find a consensus before acting. I, on the other hand, had had the questionable support of the djinn but otherwise been alone my whole life. I had no need for a consensus.

All I needed to do was convince him…or break the spell on the flat.

His gaze sharpened. "You just thought of something."

"Did I?"

"I need you to—"

"Fuck what you need. All of this, even you doing the decent damn thing and not leaving me to drown, has been about what *you* need. *I* need out. I need *trust*." When he said nothing, I gave him my back, and stormed back to the bedroom. I had a jailbreak to plan. "Fine. Good luck hunting your renegade on your own."

"Finch!"

I kept walking.

"Fine!"

Pausing in the doorway, I glanced back. Now we were getting somewhere.

Troy's initial solution was his family's main property in Chapel Hill. I refused that flat-out, and we argued until agreeing on a vineyard the Monteagues owned southeast of the Southpoint mall. What they were doing so close to the neutral area of Durham and the Luna properties in Research Triangle Park, I didn't know, nor did it seem wise to ask.

All I cared about was the open land and trees whispering in the wind, rather than closed walls. I could have left, but some part of me hoped this bizarre arrangement would work out. I wanted my necklace, my revenge, and my freedom. Leith dead meant one less reason to be looking over my shoulder.

Fresh air hastened my recovery. I spent the rest of the day gleefully pulling up an old plot of vines with tornadoes and blowing earth into the sky by exploding compressed pockets of air. Pushing so hard at the boathouse had expanded my powers, though my fine control still needed work.

In retrospect, it wasn't the best idea as far as alleviating elven fears of powerful elementals. I didn't give a shit. Troy didn't respect asking nicely, and I was tired of being less so that others could be more.

He got back from his errands in time to catch me at it. When I faced him, panting with exertion and wild with power, he visibly steeled himself. A vicious smile tugged at my lips as I said, "Told you I just needed some fresh air. I'm ready whenever you are, Monteague."

Fists clenching and unclenching, he opened his mouth. Closed it. "Don't make me regret pulling you out of that lake and leaving Javier," he finally said. Darkness gathered close around him in the early evening, making him harder to see in the hazy light.

"Holy shit. You have control of shadows," I blurted. I hadn't clocked that the Darkwatch had their name for any particular reason.

As soon as I said it, they fled and he was just a man again. "I don't know what you're talking about."

A secret power. Good to know. "Sure," I said agreeably. "Trick of the light. So. Leith?"

Troy scowled before gesturing for me to walk with him. I dismissed the traitorous stray thought that he'd be attractive if he weren't so dour and hateful, and came up alongside him, careful to keep a healthy distance between us, though not so far that he'd think I was afraid of him. We'd reached a turning point, one where he might be as afraid of me as I was of him.

Mutual antagonism was so much fun. Not. All it did was make planning more difficult.

"What's your angle, anyway?" I asked after we got stuck on the ninth point in two hours. His plans had me playing the vanguard while my amendments had me as the ace up his sleeve as he confronted Leith. "Or I guess I should ask, what's going on in elf-land that you're fighting each other like this."

"Like I'd tell a Watcher." He pointedly avoided looking at me, and focused on the map in front of him.

"A what?"

"Don't play dumb. You wouldn't have mentioned Callista if you weren't one of her people."

"What people?"

Fists slammed on the table. I managed not to jump—barely—but the tension in me probably gave it away anyway. "Finch, we either go in as a team or I follow the law and kill you now."

"Again with the death threats. Where'd you learn how to be a team player?"

This time he pushed away from the table to pace the wine cellar he'd taken over for planning his attack. I forced myself to stay put, and kept my full attention on him. Going from being terrified of all elves to taunting the first one halfway inclined not to kill me might not have been the best strategy, but I guessed drowning had that effect.

Annoyance made me squirm. If I wanted my pendant back, not to mention my revenge and the safety it would offer, I'd have to manage myself and the situation better. Be the grown-up, so to speak, when I really just wanted to snark and bitch to cover up the residual fear.

I sighed. "Look, Monteague. I'm not happy with Callista just now. Working with you gets me a ticket to independence, okay? It's really not in my interest to fuck this up."

He looked me in the eye for what might have been the first time that day, a weighing, contemplative stare, as though he was trying to see into my soul.

Goosebumps prickled over my arms. "What?" I asked. "I'm serious."

"Yes, it seems you are. Or at least you believe what you're saying strongly enough that it tinges your aura."

"My aura? Is that an elf thing?"

"It's a me thing."

"What—"

"Stop. I am not answering questions." He squinted at me again, a frown flashing across his features as though he wasn't quite sure he liked what he saw. "Swear to me that you'll be my ally against Leith and his Redcaps."

"Sure."

"Swear it."

"Fine." I assumed he meant swear like the djinn would mean it. "I swear to stand at your side as ally against Leith and his Redcaps, until they are defeated."

"That will do."

"Bless your heart," I muttered, grouchy for the moment it took for me to remember that I was only half djinn, and oaths had never quite bound me like they did Grimm and Duke. If this went south, he couldn't trap me with it.

Troy ignored me, and turned back to the map, unaware of the loophole. "We can't go back to the boathouse. It's too hard to get in and out, and Leith has put new traps in place after your little excursion."

A knot in my gut loosened a little. I hadn't wanted to go back there. "So, where then?"

"The Sequoyah family home in Jordan Lake. He doesn't let anyone go there now."

"He let me go. And you were there."

"I was—" he bit down on the rest of his words.

I raised my eyebrows, willing him to remember that we were a team. It didn't help. "You were her bodyguard," I said. I'd figured that much out, at least, if not the rest. "What happened that night if you weren't there to hurt her?"

Muscles bunched in his jaw, and he glared at me. "I was trying to warn her."

"About Leith and his underwater graveyard?"

Troy looked surprised. "Yes."

"How long has he been doing this shit? And why are bodies being discovered now?"

"Years, and because he wants them to be." From the firm press of his lips, that was all I was getting as far as details. Yeah, this teamwork-partnership thing was off to a fantastic start.

"Fine. So, what changed?" I asked.

"What?"

"What changed? He's been doing this for years. He wants them discovered now. What changed?"

He threw himself back in his chair. "You're annoyingly perceptive."

"I'm a private investigator." I scoffed, insulted. "It's kind of part of the job. I've sworn your stupid oath, now work with me."

Another staring match commenced, and ended when he scrubbed his hands over his face to muffle a frustrated noise. "Allies. He has enough allies among the three highest houses and the Darkwatch."

"Okay. Do you need him alive? Or do you just need to end the threat?"

"Alive is preferable."

"But not required?"

"No."

Look at that. A little trust, a bit of maturity, and we're actually starting to get somewhere. I kept the thought to myself and allowed myself to relax. Troy mirrored me, and the tension dropped a notch. We'd never be friends, but maybe working together wasn't out of the question. For one mission, anyway. If I got what I wanted, and he didn't try complying with elven law again.

"And the other houses?" I asked.

"What about them?"

"Do you need a guilty party from each house or just Sequoyah?"

Leaning back in his seat, Troy steepled his fingers, and stretched his legs out to rest the heel of one foot on the toe of the other. "There are alternative resolutions if we can't get the highest-ranking Redcap from each house."

"Great. Let's make our lives easier and get Leith to the house alone. Then what do you need?"

"A recorded confession."

"You didn't record any of what he said before? He did that whole bad guy monologue and you missed it?"

Troy rolled his eyes to the ceiling in disgust. "He's Darkwatch-trained, and I wasn't fully trusted until I passed my test. No wires, no recording devices."

"Deep cover. Jeez. What if we can't get one recorded?"

"There's a very short list of admissible evidence or trusted witnesses. We need a recording."

"What, the sworn word of a Watcher isn't on the list?"

He started to throw back a reply, a snarl on his lips, and then paused, cheeks flushing. "Actually…it is."

I spread my arms wide. "Your witness. But I want immunity."

"I can't get you immunity from all of elfdom."

"But you can get me your House." I swept a sarcastic bow. "My prince."

He stiffened. "Don't call me that."

"Why? Aren't you one?"

"I'm Darkwatch."

"Fine. Can you get me immunity from House Monteague or not?" *And why are you so touchy about being a prince?* That was just a title. As I sat there negotiating for one less houseful of elves to be hunting me for something I couldn't change, I could only imagine having the option to pretend you weren't what you were, or to choose to be something else.

With an annoyed sigh, Troy said, "I can try."

"No immunity, no witness."

"I understand the deal, Finch."

"Do we have one, then?"

"Yes."

I grinned devilishly. "Swear it."

A dark look crossed his face as he did. Not like he could decline, after making me do the same. Drowning was a high price to pay for safety and freedom. I wasn't going to half-ass this.

"So. We get Leith to the house. We get a confession. We…?"

"Capture or kill him. Preferably capture but if we can't, I'm not leaving him alive and unpunished. I owe Javier that much."

Not to mention me. "And I come into this where?" I said instead of getting snarky. I needed to know why he'd picked me, now that we were being honest.

"I know you made walls. With…Air." His expression suggested he'd just eaten a crate of lemons. "I need you to box him in, distract him, and keep him off me for long enough to prepare a more complex aura spell that will compel him to confess. You saw what he can do if he's allowed to focus."

Working through that request told me something interesting: elementals might be the only beings capable of manipulating the physical world. Djinn could do any number of things to their person, and weres could shift. Elves could wield Aether to manipulate others, and vampires could pull you under with a personal glamour. Most fae magic was all illusion, no substance. Even the witches could only affect other life forms on a small scale, and were further self-limited by their personal beliefs.

Elementals? We could cause the wind to gust, fire to consume, the seas to rise, and the earth to move. With enough organization we could do more than drown a single ancient city. We could break the world, revert it to its primordial state, and reshape it.

It hit me like a lightning bolt. *That's* why we were considered so dangerous. The scale of everyone else's powers was limited to a few individuals at most. Elementals sat outside the self/other dichotomy that the rest of Otherside was so comfortable with. Having a reason for them to dislike me, something other than blind hatred or a grudge more than a thousand years old, somehow made me more comfortable.

Not that I would share any of that with Troy. He didn't seem to be in the mood for introspection.

"You need a defense. I can do that," I said.

"I also need him not to call in reinforcements."

"Right, because all things in threes or multiples of three. Okay, so we'll need a cell signal jammer." He looked at me blank-faced, and I smirked. "What's this? Something you don't have? Lucky for you that I know a guy."

My cheeky grin hid a spike of apprehension. This would mean going to see Roman and having to come up with a damn good reason why I'd been ignoring him.

The disquiet only got worse as Troy and I got further into planning. I wouldn't be able to hide from Roman anymore, and I didn't know how the werewolf would take it.

Chapter 24

I nearly found out why it wasn't wise to surprise a werewolf when I knocked on Roman's door.

"Not interested!" he shouted.

Forcing a smile, I waved at Troy, who pulled away and sped off. Pointing out that his presence would make it harder to convince Roman to help had given me just enough leverage to get my elf captor to set me loose in the woods for a little while.

Sweet freedom, I thought as I breathed deeply of the night air. I knew whatever Aether tag he'd put on me to follow me to the lake was probably still there. If I ran, he'd find me again, but I enjoyed the illusion.

I thunked the toe of each boot on the concrete slab, trying to whack some mud loose as I put off knocking again for a few more seconds. I wasn't looking forward to the conversation.

The flicker of light through the closed blinds and the thrill of action sequence music said Roman was watching a movie. I banged again, harder this time.

"I said, not interested!" His voice had deepened to a dangerous growl.

I slammed my fist against the door, and kept going until he pulled it open so violently I was surprised it stayed on its hinges.

"If you don't get the fuck—Arden?"

His eyes glowed silver in the dark. My breath caught as musk overbalanced cedar in his scent. Magical runt or not, he could still shift and tear me to pieces if my unannounced reappearance was a bad surprise. Eno was a big park; he could find somewhere to dispose of a body. "Um. Hey," I said sheepishly, trying to defuse the potential for hostility. "Sorry I—"

"Arden."

All of a sudden I was engulfed in warm werewolf as he bear-hugged me, picked me up, and whirled me around into his trailer. I fought off a sudden spike of panic. I was not underwater; his arms were not ropes. My brain had barely caught up to that when he put me down, and held me at arm's length with a grip on my shoulders that would fracture a bone if he pressed any harder.

"Ouch," I said, breathless.

He loosened his fingers but didn't let me go. "Where the fuck have you been?"

"Did ya miss me?" I couldn't help teasing him, even if it was just a cover for my dread at the idea of being confined again. Bad idea. He spun me around and propelled me toward the couch. "Hey! Enough of that!"

"We need to talk. Some dangerous people have been looking for you."

I winced, wondering how anyone who might be looking for me would have known to talk to him before remembering Duke's observation that I smelled of wolf. "Did they bother you?"

"Arie, these are not the kind of people you should be spending time with. I don't know what they have on you, or what kind of deals you've been making to solve this case, but it's not worth it." He paused his tirade to take a closer look at me. "Are you okay?"

"I had to go handle some shit." While it was good to be missed, his single-minded fixation was starting to grate, which in turn was refocusing me. I needed to distract him, calm him down before laying out the big ask. "Hey…any chance of some food?"

"Sure. Of course." He frowned, and strode toward the kitchen, his uncharacteristically heavy steps telling me he was still upset.

I took off my coat and hung it up before following him. He clattered around in cabinets, getting out the ingredients to make pasta. "Where ya been, Arie? You go incognito for more than a week, no response to my messages to see if you're okay after you tore outta here, and then out of nowhere you turn up at my door without your car," he said once the water was boiling in one pot and a thick Bolognese sauce was warming in another. "And then the—those people turn up at my door looking for you. I was worried as hell."

So much for getting him to drop it. Now that I was here, I knew none of the lies I'd rehearsed on the way over would be enough to answer for my radio silence. I could try them, of course, but then I'd be continually having to remember what I'd told him. He was a clever man. He'd figure it out, and then I'd lose both my best source of tech support and possibly the only friend I had left, one that I'd grown fond of.

I'd have to just go with the truth and hope for the best.

"I got mixed up with some elves."

Roman jerked as though he'd taken a jolt of electricity, and he tried to play it off as though he'd burnt himself at the stove. "Damn it. Some what, now?"

"Elves."

He kept stirring the sauce, movements growing stiff. "Is that a new thing the kids are saying these days?"

"A werewolf should know it's not."

Roman froze, the stillness of a predator calculating his next move. I held myself equally still and tried to breathe evenly, tried not to be prey as he slowly turned. Something wild lit his eyes, and they seemed to glow again. "Be careful, babe. Some things shouldn't be said lightly. There could be consequences."

In response, I embraced my power, knowing my eyes lit a brilliant gold as I sent a zephyr to play with the pots hanging from the overhead rack. His eyes widened as they clanged, then his nose wrinkled, and he *whuffed* before his nostrils flared again. "Thunderstorms. Or electronics. I thought I was imagining things before. What are you?"

"An elemental."

He blinked, then frowned as though remembering something from a long time ago. "Bullshit. They're myths. Or if they were real, the elves killed them all ages ago."

"A sylph, to be exact."

"Arie…"

"Roman."

Something in the pot on the stove popped, and he twitched, stirring it without taking his eyes off me. "Every time I messed up and let the wolf out a little, you barely reacted. I should have known it meant you were…*something*…and not just a complete magical null." He stared at me. "This whole time?"

"Yeah. I'm sorry, I should have said something. But—"

"Elves."

"Yeah."

"Well, shit." Biceps bunched as he crossed his arms. "An elemental. Why are the djinn looking for you?"

"Tall black man who looks like he's about to laugh at something? Slim, chesty redhead with a serious attitude problem?"

"Yeah. Both of them."

"They're my cousins. They say. Probably best they don't know I'm around for now. I'm just glad the vamps haven't caught up yet."

He stared. Opened his mouth, then shook his head, and threw his hands up. "I can't. This is too weird. Dammit, Arden, you should have told me!"

"I'm sorry." It came out in a whisper, guilt choking me at the echoes of my own feelings of betrayal in his voice. "I wanted to. I just…" Anything I said would sound like an excuse, and in a way, it would be. He was a wolf in exile. Of everyone in Otherside, he knew what it was to be hunted and alone.

I closed my eyes and hugged myself, hoping I hadn't broken this. Not just because I still needed his help. Because I knew what a hypocrite I'd been with him, being pissed off about the djinn and Callista hiding things from me while doing the same to Roman.

Regret stole the air from my lungs and weighed heavy on my shoulders. What had I been thinking, coming here? How could I have imagined it would be okay to waltz in and announce that I'd been hiding the biggest secret I had from the only person who'd continually had my back—and oh, by the way, I needed a favor?

I'd done him wrong. I'd done us both wrong. I didn't deserve his help. "I'll get out of your hair. Sorry."

For the first few steps toward the door, I was certain he was angry enough to let me go. When he growled, I walked faster, thinking I had overstayed my welcome. Without a car I couldn't go far, but I couldn't stay.

I screamed when his arms slipped around me, and he released me, jumping away. Trembling and suddenly short of breath, I steadied myself with a hand on the wall, and turned.

"Someone hurt you while you were away."

I swallowed hard, and nodded, determined not to let the tears fall.

"They hurt you bad."

I nodded again, a single sharp jerk, and tried to take a deep inhale. *Calm, I need to be calm, I don't need to trigger a shift and make this worse.* I could probably handle a shifted werewolf, but I didn't want to have to hurt him.

Roman took a step back, and I let out a shuddering exhale, grateful that he wasn't going to push. "You came to me first? Only me?"

Not sure if it would be safe to admit that, I didn't react.

"Arden. I need to know if I should be ready to defend against an elven attack. Or the djinn. Or vampires, or anything else, since apparently you're mixed up with half of Otherside." When I still didn't answer, he added, "Come on, babe. You're the closest thing I have to a pack. I'm here for you. You're mine to protect."

That did it. The tears I'd resisted started falling. *Why didn't I tell him before?*

"Aw, now, don't do that," he said softly, a hint of what must be his native mountain accent slipping out. I gave in to the heartbroken look on his face, and went to him, allowed him to slide strong arms around me, to rub a hand up and down my back. "I wish you'd have told me. I wish you'd have known you could trust me. That's all."

I couldn't explain that I'd been conditioned not to trust anyone outside a small circle, and that only in the last few weeks had I been forced into a position of expanding that circle. Guilt made me cry harder because I knew that if I didn't need his help, I still wouldn't have told him.

"Can I pick you up?" he asked against my ear when I started to wind down. I nodded against his chest, tired of being strong and holding my life together in the month's never-ending shitshow. Moving slowly, he dipped enough to get my legs, and then hefted me, lifting my weight easily, and carrying me to the bedroom. I stiffened, not in the mood for anything sexy.

"I'm not going to ravish you," he scolded. "You look like a rabbit that's been run half to death. Relax and I'll bring you some pasta."

"You eat in bed?"

"I'm a grown-ass man, I eat where I please."

It made me snort, and helped break through the leaden cloud that had hovered over me for the long days with Troy. For the first time this month, I felt safe.

I fell asleep a minute after my head hit his pillow, breathing in the pleasant, woodsy scent of werewolf.

* * *

The sound of arguing woke me.

"I know she's here!"

"And I know what you are. You're not going near her." Roman's bass growl rumbled deeper than I could ever remember hearing it.

Shit, I never got around to telling him what happened. I scrambled out of bed. Fortunately, I was still dressed and didn't need to waste time with that. Both men had seen me naked, and clothes were flimsy armor, but I'd take what I could get.

"Roman, no!" My stocking feet skidded on the linoleum as I saw the beginnings of the shift to wolfman in the claws that now tipped his fingers.

"Arden?" He kept the door braced against a furious Troy Monteague. "Stay back."

"No. He's—he's why I'm here. I'm sorry, I didn't get to tell you what happened before crashing out."

"You going to let me in now?" Troy asked in clipped, cold tones.

"No." Roman was in full-blown territorial mode, and hanging onto human form by a fingernail. Tremors shook him as he used all of his self-control to maintain the balance.

"Monteague, get out of here," I said. "I'll be back later. Nothing's wrong—"

"Yet," Roman threatened.

"—but your being here is not helping anything. We talked about this, dammit!"

Troy looked at me long enough that Roman growled again, long, and low, and dangerous. He looked at the werewolf as he replied to me. "Sequoyah will be at the house at six this evening. Be there with what I asked for or pray I don't survive the encounter." Backing away slowly to avoid antagonizing Roman further, he climbed into his truck, and drove off.

"Always with the threats," I muttered.

Roman slammed the door so hard the trailer shook. "What the fuck, Arden?" His glower was amplified by eyes shifted to wolf silver, and I held myself unmoving. "Does he know? What you are?"

"Yes. He drowned me for it," I said, unthinking in my bitterness.

"He—*what?*" That roar shook the walls as much as the door slamming had, and he grunted as the shift resumed. My jaw dropped as bones rearranged themselves under his skin, and clothes ripped. His knees reversed, his bare feet elongated and grew claws, a toothy snout protruded, long smoke-and-charcoal fur erupted…and then the change stopped.

He can't become a full wolf. That's what Grimm meant by magical runt. I stared at the half-and-half monster my sometime-lover had become. "Roman?"

"I'll kill him," the wolfman snarled in mangled words.

My mind raced. Were werewolves matriarchal or patriarchal? Who had dominance? Would I be safer if I claimed it or submitted? While I tried to figure it out, he took slow steps toward me, the tatters of his clothes hardly stirring.

"You're terrified. I can smell it."

I gasped and trembled as a single sharp claw traced down my cheek, so light that it was barely there.

"Don't be scared. It's harder to change back if you're scared, and I never…you should never have seen this."

Something in the hunch of his shoulder caught my attention. *He's ashamed. Is it the loss of control, or the shape, or both?*

Seeing this secret side of him, watching his usual steady confidence crumble with every second I didn't answer, made it easier not to be afraid. "It's—it's okay." I forced a smile. "Really. I always knew you could do this, remember?"

He heaved a sigh, and walked around me to the bedroom. "Give me a minute."

At least ten passed before he reemerged, clad in a new t-shirt that stretched tight over his muscular chest and grey sweatpants instead of jeans. I couldn't help but glance downward to appreciate the sight of him. Who doesn't enjoy checking out a well-built guy in grey sweatpants?

When he shoved his hands in his pockets and avoided my eyes, I shook off my admiration, and went to him, pulling him into a tentative hug.

He went rigid, and I started to let go, but at the hint that I might his arms captured me. "Thank you," he breathed to the top of my head.

I shrugged. "You were willing to fight an elf prince with some scary magic to keep me safe. Least I can do is not run away screaming, right?"

Roman didn't answer, only hugged me closer before letting go again. As he looked down at me, a new vulnerability hovered in his storm-grey gaze. I bit my lip, not sure what to say or if he wanted to talk about it.

"So." He rocked onto his toes, then to his heels and back. "Elf prince? Drowning?"

"Yeah." Scuffing a foot against the floor, I folded my arms tightly. "Long story short, the vamps hired me to clear them of blame for the drownings. I got caught going in for evidence, and had to out myself in my escape attempt. For all the good it did."

"Shit, Arie." He moved to the couch, and sat, propping his elbows on his knees, and burying his face in his hands. "And the guy at my door?"

"Um…"

"Don't worry, I have an idea of what to expect this time," he said from behind his palms.

"He threw me in Jordan Lake with a concrete block tied around my ankles, and recorded it to get an in with the elves responsible for the other drownings," I said in a rush. I'd sort of gotten used to Troy over the last couple of days, but having to say out loud what he'd done made my gut clench. A cold sweat covered me, and I wiped my damp palms on my jeans. *Is it smart to be making deals with him?*

For a minute, Roman looked like he was fixing to lose it again. He dropped his hands, and stared at them, shaking as a grim expression and silver eyes spoke to his anger. Then he breathed, clenched his hands into fists, and pushed himself to lean back on the couch.

"I figured you just wanted space," he said.

"I kind of did."

"Then I thought I'd done something."

"I would have told you."

A small smile quirked his lips as he said, "I figured." The smile vanished. "I want more for us, Arden. I know that wasn't the deal. Just ass and cash. But—"

"Roman."

"I know. You've always been a bird ready to fly away."

Feeling miserable, I went to sit next to him. "I'm sorry."

He shrugged, and tentatively wrapped an arm over my shoulders, pulling me into his side when I didn't try to get away.

"Don't be sorry. It's your nature, like needing to protect what's mine was bred into me. Just…let me be there for you next time."

"I don't want to get you killed," I whispered. "If I didn't die in that lake, it was a close thing. And only because that insufferable dick thinks I can be more useful alive. For now."

Roman flinched, then bristled. "I can take care of myself." His defensiveness had a note of stubbornness in it, as though he'd had to convince a lot of people.

I patted his thigh. "It's not that I don't think you can. It's that these elves frighten me that much. This is more than just a couple of bad guys, Roman. I think…I think they want to start a war."

Chapter 25

"A war." The flat look accompanying Roman's words made me wince. It did sound far-fetched. He leaned away from me and peered at my face. "Arden, who would possibly benefit from that?"

"Leith Sequoyah."

"Your client?!"

"Oh. Ummm. Yes. I forgot that part in the story. That case was a cover for a conspiracy."

"A conspiracy. Led by the man who hired you to find his grandmother."

"The man who killed his grandmother as a distraction to discredit a rival, yes."

Roman leaned even farther away. "Arden, all of this with you has gone from safely interesting to next-level fucked up."

Picking at a fingernail, I said, "It gets better. I want to tell you more, but all I was supposed to do was ask if you can build a cell signal jammer."

When he didn't answer, I looked up from the worsening fray in my hangnail. His crossed arms and belligerent, confused expression worried me. "Roman…if you don't want to get involved, we'll find another way."

"I'm just trying to figure out how we went from something human-normal to you being balls-deep in some wild elven conspiracy."

"You and me, both," I said tiredly. "It's okay. I'll find another way."

"No. I'll do it."

Relieved, I leaned in to give him a peck on the cheek. "Thanks. What's it gonna cost?"

"Dinner and a movie," he said without hesitation. "You give us a chance to see what we could be like as a real couple when I'm not hiding that I'm a werewolf and you're not hiding your entire life." His eyes pinched at the corners as I leaned back, folded my knees up, and wrapped my arms around them.

"Roman…" I didn't know what to say because I didn't know what I wanted. I remembered wondering what it would be like to be his girlfriend for real not so long ago, stopped by the realization that I'd have to tell him my secret. Now he knew it, so what was making me hesitate? Old habits?

"Okay," I said before I could mentally talk myself out of it. *Time to open a new chapter.*

His smile made it worth it. My heart paced a little faster at his bright smile as he squeezed my thigh, then leapt up off the couch. "Where are you going?"

"That elf bastard said six," he called over his shoulder as he strode to the second bedroom he'd converted into a workshop. "It's already ten, and it'll take a few hours for me to cobble something together."

If nothing else, Roman was a man of action. I could appreciate that, especially when it would benefit me.

While he tinkered, I took care of some work that'd piled up while I'd been incommunicado. Using one of the spare laptops Roman had laying around, I got some bills paid for both my business and my home, responded to some contact form queries, and ordered a new, unlocked phone. Troy could keep the other one. The last thing I did was check in with Maria.

"Our mysterious private investigator is alive," she said when she answered. "How fortuitous. We were about to start looking for a new one. Where have you been, little duck?"

Little duck? "Earning every last penny of your money."

"Sounds exciting."

"Maybe for those who get a life after death. Look, Maria," I rushed on before she could ask something that would get me in trouble with Troy, "I found the killer responsible for the drownings, and was present for a confession."

"Delicious. When can we collect them?"

"That wasn't part of the deal," I stammered.

"Yes. Well. In your absence, Callista took exception to the bites on the dead elves, and demanded recompense to restore the balance. We want our pound of flesh back. You owe us."

"How do you figure that?" Trying to get a rein on my temper was not working. "I practically *died* finding this information. I don't owe you shit!"

"You owe what we say you owe." The whisper of a threat in her voice gave me an idea. Maybe haughty elf princes didn't call in the cavalry, but I could.

After staying silent a few more seconds, I huffed a sigh, and put a note of desperation in my voice. "The elves are sending someone for him tonight. I don't know if—"

"When and where?"

Got ya. Now to make it look good. "Maria, you can have my testimony to Torsten, or Callista, or whoever but I can't—"

"You can and you will, if you like your blood in your body and not mine."

My breath hissed in; I didn't like being threatened. "Fine. I want the rest of the payment we agreed on, and for the vampires to leave me alone. I get you to the killer, and our contract is complete."

"Done. When and where?"

"Six-thirty," I said, before giving her the address. Twilight fell around that time, but I also assumed they'd get there early, and wanted to beat them there.

The phone clicked off, and I slumped against the worn fabric of Roman's sofa, closing my eyes and trying to get a grip. Troy would be furious. I tried to tell myself that I hadn't done anything wrong—on the contrary, giving the vamps a chance to play might do more to rebalance the situation than a few words. That I was becoming the community arbiter settled uncomfortably in the pit of my stomach. Wasn't this Callista's thing? What would she do when she found out what I'd done?

Do I care? The clench of my stomach told me that yes, I did, even if I had proof that House Sequoyah and the Darkwatch were rotten. At the same time, I resented the taunt about not having a backbone. What better way to stand up for myself than to stand up to everyone? It was a good way to get myself killed, but so what? I'd already died once, and it wasn't like I'd really been living up to now, running scared and hiding among the humans.

As an afterthought, I checked in with Val. Her number had been saved to my Google contacts and was easy enough to find in my account. Using my business' Voice number, I dialed her from the browser.

"Val, it's Arden," I said when she picked up.

"Arden! Holy shit, people are saying you skipped town to escape a death threat or something. Are you okay?"

"Left town? Nah, that would have been too smart. Look, I only have a minute, but I wanted to say it's probably a good idea to lay low for a bit. And to, you know, pass it on."

The line stayed silent as she worked through that. "You were discovered."

"My hand was forced, and a few people were reminded of what we used to be."

"Damn, girl. Sounds like you're lucky to be this side of the grass. Alright. Thanks for the heads-up."

I ended the call and looked up, sensing eyes on me. Roman was standing in the doorway to the second bedroom he used as a workroom, an odd expression on his face. "What?"

"I just listened to you call the vampires and a party I'm assuming is another elemental, invoke Torsten's and Callista's names in the same breath, and outmaneuver that elf bastard. In fifteen minutes, you hit all the power players in the Triangle except the djinn and the local were coordinator."

Wincing, I glanced away. I hadn't realized his hearing was that good, and had assumed that he'd be focused on the signal jammer.

"Arden." He waited until I looked at him to continue. "Is this what you really do? The human cases are just a cover?"

"No."

"No, but…?"

"But nothing, Roman. I didn't ask for any of this, and I'm sure as shit not able to explain it beyond what I've already told you." Annoyed more with the situation than with the fact that his question echoed my thoughts, I got up, and stomped to the small kitchen to make a cup of tea.

The werewolf followed me. "I want in."

"What?"

"I want in. Whatever is going down, I don't want the wolves left out of it."

Turning from the pot of water I'd just set to boiling, I took a long look at him. The vulnerability was back. "This is about your family."

Roman jerked, looking as sick as if I'd punched him in the gut. "You know nothing about my family."

"I know the Volkovs are a big name in the mountains. I know it's odd for a wolf to be on his own. And I might be persona non grata in Otherside, but I've still heard what happens to weres who can't shift fully."

Shock turned to outrage in his expression. "Where did you learn all of that?" he asked in the bass growl that said he was feeling emotional.

Great. How many times could I set off the werewolf today?

"I'm a PI," I replied. It seemed like I'd been reminding people of that a lot lately, and I was starting to feel like a broken record, not to mention more than a little resentful. What about having *investigator* as part of your job title made people think you wouldn't look into things? "I also noticed you said 'wolves,' and not 'weres'. You want back in, don't you? But you need something of value to bargain with."

Belligerence drew his brows down further. "That's none of your business."

"And yet you want all the details of mine." Our sort-of-relationship was off to a smashing start. We hadn't even gotten to lunch, and we were already squabbling. I held his stare and returned it with interest, unafraid and unwilling to back down. I didn't even know why I was so bothered, other than the fact that this was all moving too fast for me, I hadn't had time to process it, and Roman wanted to be involved. I'd kept my secrets so close my entire life that being asked about anything personal felt like an invasion.

He looked away first. *Does that mean I'm dominant?*

"Okay," he said as all the tension flowed out of him. "Sorry, Arie. Really." A quick glance up and then back to the side, a step back when I didn't ease down. "I just...it was easy to ignore it all when we were pretending to be human. And then now, all in a rush, there's an opportunity. Carpe fucking diem, right?"

"Is that why you want to date me?"

Flinching, Roman raised his hands. "No, hell no. I like you."

"But."

"But I was born and raised to be an alpha." His shoulders curled in and he hunched. "That—that *thing* you saw earlier? That's the best I can do. I can't become a real wolf. I'm not strong enough. Until now, I had nothing to offer my pack." Bitterness twisted his lips, and shame flushed his cheeks.

"And now, you realize you've been fucking an elemental with connections."

"That's crude."

"It's also true."

Crossing his arms, he said, "Okay, okay. Fine. Yes, if you insist on putting it that way." When he finally looked me in the eye again, his burned with something I couldn't read. "I was born to be *somebody*, Arden. Not…this." His waved hand encompassed the trailer, with its much-repaired fixtures and worn furnishings, making me wonder what lifestyle he'd grown up with.

My tea water was boiling. I rinsed a cup from the sink, and pulled an English tea bag out of the box on the counter before plonking the bag in and pouring water over it. Roman wasn't the only one getting emotional; my feelings roiled as much as the pot had. "Everyone wants to be someone, and I just want to be left alone," I muttered.

Roman didn't answer, watching me with a wary, hurt expression.

Exhaustion tugged at me. *I don't have the energy to fix everyone's problems right now. I'm barely keeping my own head above water.* Dropping my chin, I leaned against the counter, and tried to find some strength. Tried to think through the best way to get to the meet and get out alive against an elf healer-turned-serial-killer who could order you not to breathe.

At the boathouse I'd gone in alone. Troy hadn't been with me, not really, and that had gotten me drowned. I'd turned up on Roman's doorstep without warning, and he'd embraced me and put me to bed.

Guilt twined through me as I realized I was judging Roman too harshly. Troy had used me. Roman was just doing what he always did, jumping in with the enthusiasm of a puppy in an antiques shop. Only this time, he was overturning the artifacts of my carefully maintained past. That was what I was reacting to, not anything negative or malicious on his part.

"It's not just about me," Roman said in a soft, cautious tone as I came to that conclusion. "I want to help you. Yes, I want to mend things with my family, but that's such a long shot that I don't actually believe it'll happen. Whether it does or not, you're the pack I have here. Let me help you."

I'd already invited the vampires, knowing Maria was just there for business as well. All signs pointed to a group effort on this one. Why shouldn't Roman join, too, especially if being involved could help us both? Taking my frustrations with being exposed out on him wasn't fair.

"Do you have a gun?" I said quietly. I only had my lead knife, and was still waiting for my concealed carry permit to come through. After being strapped with bronze, I was not at all willing to go in without physical firepower.

"Yes."

The edge of hope in his voice slashed what resolve I had left. Closing my eyes, I lifted the mug of tea. Breathed deep of the soothing aroma while reminding myself that independence didn't have to mean shutting out people who cared about me, or turning down help when it was offered. "Okay."

"Okay?"

"You're in. Bring a gun and the signal jammer." I'd never used one of the damn things, and it would be difficult enough trying to manage defenses against Leith while keeping an eye on whoever the vampires sent. "Also, you're driving. The damn elf hid my car somewhere, and I'm not calling him back for a pickup." I took a sip of tea before setting the mug aside to hug myself, eyes still closed.

The scrape of a footstep on linoleum gave me warning as he lurched forward to pull me into an embrace. "Thank you, Arden. Thank you. You have no idea what this means to me, to have both a pack and a chance to reconnect with my family after fifteen years."

"I might," I murmured against his chest as I forced my muscles to relax from their automatic tensing.

A werewolf, a vampire, an elf, and an elemental go hunting. What could possibly go wrong?

Chapter 26

North Carolina, while not far enough south to avoid snow, was southern enough that the temps warmed up above freezing in winter. Having had my fill of being frozen, I appreciated the end of January's cold snap and the shift to more tolerable weather.

Twilight still reigned when Roman and I arrived at the road leading to the Sequoyah house. I'd called Troy from my Voice account to tell him I had a ride, and not to come back for me. He'd pitched a quiet, controlled fit laden with not-so-veiled threats, until I told him it would mean war with the Volkovs if he came back to Roman's house and pissed on his territory again. A full-blown lie—Roman's family didn't give a monkey's ass for their outcast son—but it kept the elf at bay, and gave me an excuse to have Roman at my side.

He switched off the headlights of his battered F-150 as we turned down the long dirt drive, relying on his superior night vision to keep us on the narrow path through the trees. The porch lights at the house shone like beacons. An image of one of those deep-sea anglerfish, the ones that use those little lights to lure in prey, came to me. I shuddered.

"You'll be fine," Roman murmured, sparing a hand from the wheel to squeeze my thigh. "You've got me this time."

I didn't answer, my mouth having gone dry. Doubts clattered through my mind. I was alone in the dark forest, near the lake that had nearly been my tomb. Though completely irrational, the thought that nobody would help me if it came down to it, that nobody was here for me, pounded at me. Grimm, Duke, and Callista had betrayed me. Why shouldn't everyone else? My breath rasped in my throat as I started to pant, and I gripped the door, then started clawing at the handle.

"Arden, what the—shit." Roman pulled to the edge of the road and unlocked the doors. I fell out, catching myself in the sandy mud and grunting as the points of sweetgum hulls pricked my hand. The interior lights went out behind me as I scrambled to put my back to the bark of a wide tree.

Heavy footsteps. "No, no, no, not again," I whimpered, turning to run. A hand caught me, and another covered my mouth to abort my scream. My wild struggles produced a grunt as my heel connected with a shin.

"Arden, stop, goddammit! It's me! What the hell is wrong with you?"

"Anxiety attack," a rich voice said from the darkness. The arm around my waist disappeared, and a gun was pointed toward the voice. No one was at the other end of it. I froze, tears dampening my cheeks, and the hand still over my mouth. The Darkwatch used shadows.

Roman sniffed. "Fucking elves."

A deeper patch of darkness melted away to reveal Troy Monteague, his hands held away from his body. "Easy, Volkov. We're all on the same side. For now." He took a step forward.

"Stop," Roman growled. My skin prickled as the scent of musk grew stronger behind me.

Troy obeyed, frustration flashing across his features. "I can get her to be still."

Be still.

The echo of the words he'd said at Jordan Lake sparked a renewed panic, and I clawed for my knife. The gun pointed at

Troy dropped as Roman's arm came around me again, trapping my arm before I could draw it. "Shhh, Arden," he hissed low in my ear. "Shhh, or Sequoyah will know we're here, and not just Monteague."

That cut through. Quivering, I held still as a mouse watching a cat pass. Drawing Leith's attention was the absolute last thing I wanted.

Troy had taken advantage of the distraction to approach close enough to touch us. When he extended a hand, I stiffened, and Roman snarled. "Don't."

"We don't have time for this." Troy grasped my shoulder, and a tendril of Aether slipped through my shields with a zap that made me gasp through my nose. "Calm," he said. "You're with allies."

A melodic female voice said, "Is she? Certainly doesn't look like it."

I tensed again as Maria stalked out of the forest, a tiny commando clad in functional black leather boots and a black bodysuit that hugged her considerable curves, her long emerald hair pulled up and covered in a black stocking cap. Twin sword hilts poked up over each shoulder, and pistols rode in black leather holsters on each thigh. She grinned to show sharp little fangs, and put her hands on her hips as Roman's gun swung back up. Troy moved to stand at his shoulder, drawing a wicked-looking, black long knife.

"What the hell is this?" the elf snapped.

"She invited me to come and play," Maria said, nodding to me. Whatever Troy had done with Aether started asserting itself, and tension eased from me. I embraced it this time instead of fighting to shake it off, letting it slide through my mind. When I stopped struggling, Roman peeled his hand away from my mouth, taking his gun in a two-handed grip when I didn't try to scream again.

Troy's face was hidden with the lights from the house behind him, but I could feel his glare like a physical weight. "Arden, this was *not* the plan."

"You're right. This is a better one," I countered once I'd worked the spit back into my mouth. A small corner of my mind still wanted to run screaming. Leaving Leith Sequoyah alive to hunt again, always at my back, was not an option, though. Holding onto that thought helped me claw my way back toward sanity and capability.

Resting a hand on Roman's arm, I said, "Put the gun down. She's not here for any of us."

"Well. Let's be honest, I'd love to sample the Otherside buffet going on here, but you're not on the menu today."

"Not helping, Maria," I hissed. She shrugged, not shifting out of the loose ready stance, or losing her predatory smile. Something occurred to me. "How are you here already, anyway? The sun can't have been down before you left Raleigh."

She waggled her eyebrows playfully. "A girl's gotta have some secrets."

"You're in a good mood."

"I'm hunting elves with Torsten's blessing. Of course I'm in a good mood."

Troy got in Maria's face, a choice I would not have made. "You're not hunting elves. You're hunting Leith Sequoyah."

"Does that mean you'll let me play?" she simpered, not intimidated in the slightest despite his greater height. Troy's hands fisted.

"Someone's gonna notice us if we don't get in there soon," Roman murmured. "I don't know what time you were supposed to meet Sequoyah, but it's getting on past six."

Troy grimaced. "Goddess save me from meddling—fine. Finch, you're coming with me. Stay hidden. You two stay on the perimeter until and unless you hear fighting."

Roman glanced at me, and I nodded. Better to have them as pocket aces than to show our hand too early. He shrugged and tucked his gun away, before pulling the signal jammer out of his pocket, flicking it on, and handing it to Troy. "See y'all on the flip side," he said, then loped into the woods to the south.

"Guess I'll take the north," Maria said. In a blur of speed, she was gone.

"We're going to talk about this later," Troy growled as he pocketed the jammer, sheathed his knife, and stalked toward the house.

I didn't bother answering as I followed him. We'd wasted enough time and stopping to argue again wouldn't help. Being the grown-up sucked. Keeping my clapbacks to myself was intensely dissatisfying.

My resolve got shaky again as we reached the edge of the trees. "Remind me why I can't just huff and puff, and blow the house down?" I whispered.

Troy's sharp glance made me wish I hadn't said it. "Could you? Blow the house down?"

"Dunno. Never tried. Kind of hard to practice much when you're under a standing death threat."

"I need a confession from Sequoyah." He flicked his eyes over me assessingly. "Are you up for this?"

Swallowing past the lump of fear in my throat, I nodded.

"After I go inside, count to sixty and then follow me in. Try not to be obvious about it." When he stepped out of the trees, I gave a one-fingered salute to his back.

"Arrogant jackhole," I muttered under my breath as Troy hopped up the wooden steps to the porch in one lithe leap, then knocked in a pattern.

Leith's appearance at the door gave me the shakes all over again, in rage rather than fear. This was the man ultimately responsible for what had happened to me, and I'd be damned if he walked away from this night. *Otherside justice is coming for you, Sequoyah, and then I'm coming for the rest of your House.*

The contrast between the two elves was striking. Leith was taller and broader than Troy, more heavily muscled, his hair and skin light where Troy was dark. A mocking smile showed perfect white teeth as he stepped back to sweep an arm inward.

Troy didn't look back as he stepped over the threshold, and I started counting down a minute. Leith gave a cursory glance around—useless, given that the house lights would ruin his night vision—then shut the door.

My last visit to this place provided me with a mental map as I reached sixty. I scuttled around the back, keeping low to the ground and sticking to the cover of decorative bushes where I could. Troy's plan might have been for me to come in the front door, but mine involved not being a complete sucker again. That, and finding an opening to use my new, unblooded knife. I'd let Troy and the rest weaken him, but I wanted the final shot.

The back porch had a normal door rather than sliding glass, and Roman had lent me his lockpicking kit. I eased up the stairs, skipping the one I'd thought had creaked before. A low screech of wood told me I'd remembered wrong, and I froze, wincing. When nobody stuck their head out to investigate, I kept going.

I was grateful for Troy's calming spell as I manipulated the tumblers in the lock. When your blood pounds with adrenaline, fine motor skills tend to go. My racing mind was oddly separate from my body, an alarm heard in the distance rather than something immediately distracting.

This lock was better than most and it took longer than it should have to hear the soft click of success. Pausing to press my ear against the door, I tried to gauge whether anyone was in the room. My hearing wasn't as good as a were's or a vamp's, though. The rush of blood in my own ears was the only sound.

One last deep breath, then I slowly pulled the handle down just enough to crack the door, listening for the elves. Nothing. I slipped inside.

The room was empty.

Heart pounding, I shut the door again, softly, so softly, and paused to listen. A rumble of male voices came from the kitchen. I crept in that direction, keeping to the rugs, and shielding as hard as I could. As I drew close, the distinctive sound of a knife being drawn from a butcher block slithered out.

"Finch, *now!*" came Troy's shout.

Abandoning any pretense of stealth, I dropped my shields, and drew on Air more strongly than I ever had as Troy stumbled back through the kitchen archway and away from a steel blade. He snarled as it kissed his cheek. A ribbon of blood splashed, and he raised his knife even as Leith crashed headlong into my wall of Air.

His disdainful sneer turned to incensed disbelief as his eyes fell on me, and he slammed his fists against my wall. "I'll kill you both!" he roared at Troy, who ignored him as the pressure of Aether grew.

I gasped as Leith looked at me. The first hints of fear started breaking through Troy's earlier spell. A cunning look replaced his rage, and he fixed me with an icy stare.

I'd miscalculated. Leith might not be able to pass the wall of Air, but Aether could.

The delicate slip of magic through shields was Troy's talent. Leith went for brute force as he had at the boathouse, battering at me until I dropped to my knees with a groan. The first chord in my wall went discordant and slipped from my control as I fought two fronts, one to hold my shields and one to keep Leith trapped in the kitchen.

"Hold him!" Troy shouted.

I tried, going to all fours as I focused on the magic and not on staying upright. "Hurry up, Monteague," I panted, lacking the energy to make it a shout. Sweat rolled from me. Another chord snapped, and the faint blue wall, visible only to my third eye, wavered as he pushed against it with his hands. Sparing one, he grabbed his phone, and stabbed his thumb at it three times before putting it to his ear. The hiss of static that greeted him made him hurl the device away.

"Damn you!"

Troy ignored him, muttering under his breath as he focused on building the Aether in the enchantment he was trying to cast on Leith.

"Monteague, whatever you're doing, fucking do it now!" I couldn't hold the last chord, and it wavered, wailing mentally as it rippled. Leith pushed once more, and it snapped as I pulled back to defend my mind.

Swearing, Troy stumbled away as the butcher knife again sought his throat. I crawled backward in a crabwalk, finding questionable shelter behind a sofa before leaning around it to throw a gust that knocked a deathblow aside.

"Is this all you've got? You sorry, sniveling excuse for an elf. For a man! No wonder you would prop up those puling queens." Leith swung again, blond hair plastered to his head by sweat. Troy dodged, his liquid grace mesmerizing. I forgot to cast, forgot to breathe watching them.

"Die!" Leith said, a push of Aether behind the words, and Troy stumbled. Leith's blade whispered with a second form of death as it slipped under his opponent's guard, and bit into his flank. Troy dropped, convulsing, and Leith turned to me.

"No. No!" He wouldn't win. He couldn't. I drew the lead knife, and started forward, summoning a gale to throw him away from me. Glass shattered as vases flew from tables and picture frames were ripped from the walls. An end table toppled over, creating a negligible barrier. He swatted at the wind as though it were a physical thing before refocusing on me.

"When I take your head to the queens, it will give me enough influence to overthrow them," he snarled. "You worthless bitch! You will die screaming and in pain after I've taken everything your body could possibly give!" Leith advanced on me, pummeling my shields. My attempts to keep him away weakened.

"No!" I cried as my opponent reached me. Agony lanced through me as my shields cracked, then fell. Needle-sharp splinters pierced my mind until all I could do was curl up in a ball and scream. Leith rolled me to my back and straddled me, dragging my wrists to the floor, and leaning forward to whisper viciously all the ways he'd ravage me before taking my head.

My pendant fell out of the neck of his shirt. Seeing it, I fought the pain of broken shields, barely managing to gather a fist of Air. "Like hell you will." Agony seared me as I aimed the fist at his jaw. He rocked back with a shout, his grip on my hands loosening enough that I got the one with the knife free and plunged it into his thigh. A spark scorched my palm, and the knife seemed to glow. Energy flared as my broken shields mended just enough to leave the pain as a throbbing ache rather than an assault. What magic had Nils put in the blade?

Glass burst from a window, and a savage snarling bark cut through Leith's scream. The elf staggered from me, dragging the knife free of both my hand and his leg and sending it spinning away. He whirled to meet the wolfman, dropping into a backward roll to avoid snapping jaws and kicking out to send Roman flying into a wall, following him over to lash out with another kick. Roman whined. The scent of fresh blood rose again, rotten cedar mixing with marshmallow in a sickly-sweet mélange.

"You useless pack of heathens! You think you can best me?"

"You haven't given me a shot yet, blondie." Maria's liquid voice swirled with invitation as she sauntered through the unlocked back door, swords drawn. Her hips swung as she stalked toward him, and her dark eyes were lit with an inner flame.

"Oh, this should be good," Leith said as he squared up to her, the recovered butcher knife in his grip held in a guard. He was favoring his left thigh. "A piece of shit Monteague, an elemental, the weakest werewolf I've ever seen, and now a bloodsucking hag. No wonder everything's going to hell." He rolled the knife over his knuckles, and Maria whirled her katanas in response.

They circled each other in complete silence until Leith lunged. Maria danced aside, one blade flicking out and missing him by a hairsbreadth. Closing my eyes, I clawed pieces of my fragmented shields back into place, then tried to gather even the faintest zephyr to me. When I caught one, it seared my mind, and my eyes flew open in shocked pain. It had never hurt like that before, but I'd never been forced to tame Air so soon after having my defenses broken. Even the burst of energy from the knife hadn't been able to restore them completely.

I pulled myself to my feet, not sure if Maria would need help, or what I could do other than get in the way. "Roman?" I called.

He groaned, but pushed to his feet, clutching his ribs and hunching over. "Bastard broke a rib," he said, spitting blood.

I winced. Weres healed fast, but a punctured lung was dangerous. Nothing we could do for it now, though.

A gurgling heave to one side turned into a harsh gasp as Troy broke free from the compulsion to die. Rolling to all fours, he shook his head and looked around, eyes glazed, as Leith advanced on Maria.

She fought him back with cool confidence and swift slashes of her swords. She was faster and by far the better fighter physically, and the stab wound in his thigh was slowing Leith significantly, but he had Aether on his side. A steady invocation of pain and injury fell from his lips as he ordered her body to shut down, to harm itself, to die.

Maria slowed, growing clumsier against a force she couldn't repel. If she was working her glamour, it wasn't effective. Roman and Troy were still down. I had to do something before Leith had us all so beaten that we would literally roll over and die when he said the word.

Magic scoured my mind as I poured everything I had left into another whirlwind. Someone was screaming, the cries hoarse, and ragged, and long, and I realized it was me. I kept pushing.

Leith flew back and smacked against the wall. His head hit it with a thick thud, and his deadly refrain stopped for a few seconds—enough time for Maria to shake her head and free herself of the Aether-driven commands.

"Let me have him!" she howled, hammering on the barrier I threw up between them. At the end of my strength, I obliged her, letting go of Air and hunching over as she pinned him to the wall.

She sank teeth into his neck, swords forgotten as she pulled the life from him, and swallowed it down.

"Maria, stop. Stop!" Troy had finally found his feet again. "I want him alive, there has to be a trial!"

She stiff-armed him, holding him away with one fist bunching his shirt around his neck as she glutted herself on Leith.

No. This is my kill. The elven terrorist was fading fast with the blood loss. I looked around for my knife, spotting it against the wall not far from Roman. I staggered over and scooped it up, gripping it hard enough that my hand hurt. "Maria," I said, approaching her.

Something in my voice made her stop and look up at me. She smiled, showing red-stained teeth. "You have a prior claim, too, baby doll? Yours, I'll honor. A gift."

Nodding, I hefted my knife. As Maria held Troy off, I smiled into the face of the man who'd ordered me killed. He pawed at me as he slid down the wall and crumpled, trying to push me away, to pull Aether to him and form more words to hurt me. Today, it was me who would have the last punishing word. I crouched, then leaned forward to whisper in his ear. "Die, knowing that your House will follow you into oblivion at the hands of an elemental."

His eyes widened. Aether bit at me with icy teeth as I fished my pendant from around his neck and tugged it off. I could get the clasp fixed later.

A second chain came with it, tangled in mine. My skin crawled at the idea that he'd been wearing my necklace, and I hurried to tuck them both away before anyone could see. I'd figure out what else I'd grabbed later.

"This is mine," I spat, baring my teeth as I slid the full length of my blade between two ribs.

The knife drank all my fear and hatred of him for what he'd done, my disgust at his species supremacy, my guilt at not finding Sybil alive, leaving me strangely empty and igniting his heart. I fell back in shock with the knife still in my grip, dizzied by the rush of power that flowed out of me, pulse fluttering as I wavered on the verge of passing out.

A hand landed on my shoulder and I screamed, whirling with the knife raised.

"It's me. It's just me." Roman, still in wolf form, knelt in front of me.

I wilted in relief as he gathered me to him. We sat, my back to his front, his stubby snout over my shoulder, watching Leith scream while dancing white and green flames extinguished themselves in his blood.

"See you never, asshole," I said when they went out, taking Leith's last hoarse breath with them.

"Your turn, marshmallow," Maria said as she tripped Troy, riding him down to the floor.

Frantic, I pushed away from Roman. "Maria, no!"

Chapter 27

Roman tightened his arms around me. I struggled and said, "Roman, let go! Maria, stop! Stop!"

The vampire lifted her head to regard me, her cap lost, straggly emerald locks pulled loose from their bun to frame her face. Crimson shaded her teeth, and her eyes had gone black, the white of sclera swallowed in her bloodlust. She was as terrifying as she was beautiful.

At my words, her head cocked so fast that it was upright one moment and tilted the next, with no transitory movement in between. "Why?"

"Please," I said, pulling free of Roman. "I need him."

"He wants your death," she hissed, before licking the blood from her lips. "I can taste his thoughts in every beat of his heart and oh, is he delicious. A high blood, like the other. So much power." Her tongue dragged along the slashed fabric over the elf's flank, catching like a cat's would before she looked at me again. "You don't need him. Give him to me. I'll see that Torsten rewards you. Keeps you safe. Our honored guest."

Troy's sandstone-moss eyes flicked toward me before refocusing on Maria. His inattention to me said that he didn't honestly think I'd save him.

Did I want to? No. He deserved to be drained.

Did I need him? Unfortunately, the answer was yes, if I wanted one less elven house hunting me, and not to trade an elven prison for a vampiric one. I might enjoy death at Maria's hands more than I would at Troy's, but either option would have the same ending. No. I wanted my independence.

"Maria."

She looked up, and snarled, staring at me with the intensity of a leopard interrupted at its meal. Her night-dark gaze swayed me for a second before I tore myself away, out of the influence of her glamour. Fighting the pain of burning synapses, I swatted at her with Air.

That got her attention. Roman pulled away from me, crouched to intercept as she chuckled and crawled toward me with a flowing, boneless grace.

"You never did say what you were," she purred. "But with all this wind and those gorgeous, glowing gold eyes? I think I know now. I've never tasted one like you, not in over five hundred years of existence on this miserable earth. A rare treat, indeed. Come to me, little duck."

"Right family, wrong idea," I snarled. I was a kestrel, like the tattoo on my back, not a duck. Nobody's meat, and not some prey for the table. With one last push that started a trickle of blood from my nose, I threw an implacable wall of Air to hurl her against the wall. She hit hard enough to be knocked out.

And then I collapsed myself, overwhelmed by the pain of pushing well past my limits.

* * *

"I don't fucking know!"

The panic in Roman's voice cut through me. Poor Roman. Protecting me was probably turning out to be more dangerous than he'd thought, but he was still here. I wanted to comfort him, but I was swimming in a molten pool of suffering that stole my breath.

"She's the one thing that binds us all together," Maria's wine-dark tones snapped. "I don't trust weres, and I certainly don't trust elves. The djinn would betray their own mothers to better themselves, and Callista has served her own interests since before that fool Colombo stumbled across the New World and called it India."

Breathing hurt. Thinking hurt. The simplicity of being alive hurt.

As soon as I recognized that yes, I was still alive, a strangled groan tore itself from my throat and my back arched. My fingers scrabbled against hardwood, clutching at nothing until a rough, calloused hand grasped one of mine.

"Easy, babe, easy," Roman said in a distracted tone.

I tried to draw a breath, and it came as a sob. Body heat and auras throbbed at both sides and my head. I was surrounded.

"Watch it, she's lashing out!" Troy's usually emotionless tones were colored with the faintest hint of panic. That made me grin. He should be afraid, because I was done fearing elves.

The grip on my hand became crushing, forcing my bones to grind together. It hurt, and it drove me to push harder. I would be free, even if it killed me. A wet trickle brought the taste of iron to my lips.

"Hold her!" Roman said.

"No. Let her go, and back away," said a new voice, one I recognized.

The metallic whisper of a blade being drawn preceded Troy saying, "Shadow-damned meddling djinni!"

The sound of a scuffle erupted as I struggled to force my eyes open. The blur of a dark-skinned form dematerializing and flashing back into existence behind Troy caught my attention. "Duke?" I rasped. What the hell was he doing here? Was I hallucinating?

Everyone halted, holding themselves still as statues. Duke pressed a jagged blade to Troy's throat from behind as the elf held his punch blade where the djinni's kidney would be as long as Duke stayed solid. Maria's taut form hovered on the edge of deadly chaos as her eyes darted from one to the other, edging back to blackness. Roman hunched over me, but saliva dripped from wolf-like jaws, and brutally sharp claws had gouged furrows in the floor. Four pairs of eyes turned to me.

"The fuck is going on?" I tried pushing myself upright, falling back, but managing to stay propped on my elbows.

Nope. My elbows gave out, and I toppled back to the floor. That was fine. It was solid and cool, the most inoffensive thing in the ransacked room. Closing my eyes made everything spin in darkness, so I forced them open again.

"What. The fuck. Is going on?" I repeated, staring at the ceiling, and willing it to stop moving like that. Ceilings had no right to undulate like the sea.

"You have an elf prince, a vampire assassin, an exiled wolfling, and an unbound djinni waiting for you to make a decision," Duke's smooth voice said.

"The fuck are you doing here?" I grumbled. Maybe if I said *fuck* enough times, someone would take me seriously and answer.

"You were gone for a time, and then reappeared. Darkness and cold no longer surrounded you. I came to see what had changed, and found you encircled by new threats," he said. Leather creaked, and snarls erupted at his words.

"Yeah? Well, you can fuck right off," I said. The ceiling wouldn't stop wavering and it, combined with Duke's presence, was pissing me off. "I got here all on my own and I'll get out the same way."

"I think not, darling girl," he said. "Power gathers here this night, the makings of a new era with you at its center, not

Callista. For the first time in millennia, the balance of Otherside is shifting, and not in the hands of gods and goddesses."

I blinked at him. Gods and goddesses—Callista? *Callista is a goddess? Or is she working for one?*

"Don't try to figure her out," Duke said, his voice beguiling in its smoothness. "That way lies madness."

"We're all mad here," I said, the Cheshire Cat's words slurring together in my fight for consciousness.

"Just so," Duke said as he eased his dagger from Troy's throat in an unusual display of trust. The elf spun away, on guard and ready to fight anyone else in the room. Maria still thirsted, if the desire on her face was any indication. Roman, as the weakest person present, was strung out to the ends of his endurance judging by his hyperattention to every movement.

"Stop," I said, tired of it all. Fighting each other was stupid, and there was more than one way to gain the strength I needed to break away from my guardians…but only if they had a reason to back me. "Callista is about to force Otherside out into the open, and y'all are busy fighting each other."

Everyone went dead still at that. "What did you say?" Maria snapped.

"There's a mundane start-up in RTP on the verge of developing a test that will out all of us as not human. They don't know what they have yet, but Callista wants to beat them to it and take control of the situation."

"How do you know that?" Roman rumbled.

"I planted the bugs that gave her the intel," I said. "Or had y'all forgotten that I'm a private investigator *and* a Watcher in addition to being an elemental?"

The grave's silence fell over the room before it exploded in a confused babble that made my head hurt all over again. All my secrets were in the open now, held in the hands of the bizarre little group clustered around me. I had nothing left to bargain with, nothing to protect myself, and I curled up in a wretched little ball, no longer caring what happened as long as I could take a nap first.

"Shut it. Shut up!" Roman's bark cut through the noise.

"Watch your tone, dog," Troy snarled.

"We're all missing the big picture."

I blinked my eyes open, wondering which big picture Roman was seeing, and how it played into his desire to restore relations with his family. He glared at Troy, the effect slightly reduced by his being back in fully human form, wearing tattered scraps, and lacking the menace of sharp teeth. "We're going to be discovered soon anyway, one way or another," Roman continued, meeting each of the gazes on him. "We all know it. If it's not this start-up, it'll be the next one."

"Doc Mike is already weirded out," I slurred, drawing everyone's attention.

"Who's Doc Mike?" Maria asked.

"Her pet medical examiner," Duke said. "Why is he concerned, Arden?"

"Because she got sloppy, and he knows it's not copperheads." My hand flopped as I gestured toward Maria, who flushed, full of Leith's blood. That probably should have grossed me out but all I felt was a grim satisfaction. That asshole had gotten what was coming to him. "He thinks it's a new drug for now but…"

"But he won't for long. Shit," Roman swore. "And that means someone might start taking a closer look at other…irregularities."

Troy rolled his eyes. "Stop worrying. We have it locked down. My kin killed the report, and cast a maze on everyone who had read it."

So, it was *the elves.* "You can't bury all of them, and you can't cover the entire country," I said, flopping onto my back before trying again to push myself up. Everything still hurt, especially when Roman supported me with a hand on my shoulder, but I hadn't done all this just to roll over and disappear again. If I wanted my independence, I would have to take it.

A wave of dizziness crashed over me, and I put my head between my knees to focus on breathing through the nausea. The power hangover was hitting me early and would pack a hell of a wallop this time. Doing my best to shake it off, or at least ignore it, I said, "We need a plan, or one will be made for us."

"We? You must be joking." Troy's derision helped nothing, and I lifted my head enough to scowl at him.

"*We*," I reiterated. "Or those who cooperate can just choose another of the elven houses. Luna, maybe; I don't think they've pissed anyone off. They might be interested to hear about…Javier, was it?"

Roman practically vibrated at my back, quivering with an eagerness I could feel in the flex of his hand on my back. Maria smiled craftily, and Duke just looked thoughtful.

"You wouldn't dare," Troy hissed.

"Wouldn't I?" I asked, hoping I sounded dangerous, and not dangerously on the edge of passing out. I tilted my head toward Leith's smoking corpse. "Why not, when I've dared so much already?"

Nobody moved. I watched them think through the angles, the costs and benefits to themselves and their people. Callista had ruled the Triangle for as long as there had been European settlers here. She meted out punishment whenever and to whomever she chose, overruling elven queens, were clan leaders, vampire masters, and anyone else who crossed her. Nobody knew the source of her magic, or the limits of her powers; sometimes it seemed like she had none. She made secret deals on a whim, and used Watchers like me to extend her power. I didn't like being used, but nobody else liked being under the heel of a capricious mob boss who held a hell of a grudge.

Whatever she'd planned to use me for upon my embracing my powers, I wasn't having it. If I could convince them to work together in defying her, I'd have an even better shot of making it on my own. Duke was right. We were on the knife-edge of history, the first shift in the Détente since it was agreed, and Troy Monteague wanted to play hardball. Fine. I could play too.

"If you think humanity is going to simply accept that we have been living among them for millennia, you're wrong. And when you're all pushed into the open—because it will be all of you; I'm excluded from Callista's plan—you will learn what I have dealt with my entire life."

With a scoff, Troy said, "Please. We're all hiding what we are from the humans."

"But you all have recourse. You can turn them or make them forget. It's not an automatic death sentence for you to be discovered by anyone." I let a nasty smile twist my lips. "Yet."

"What are you proposing, Arden?" Maria asked from where she sat cross-legged, her swords balanced across her knees.

What am I proposing? This hadn't been my original plan. All I'd wanted was to be left alone, and I couldn't quite figure out how I'd become the nucleus of this little group. "A pact," I said, after thinking about the best way to secure my freedom. "We support each other. We don't fracture or sit back to watch one group be destroyed by the humans. And we don't let Callista call the shots."

"You can't be serious!" Troy snapped. "My people will handle this. We already have representatives in every electable position from local to national level. It will go away. We will make it go away. Like we always do."

"You're an idiot, Monteague," Maria snapped. "The humans outnumber us, and their technology improves by the day. How long do you think you'll hold your precious elected positions when there's a blood test that works? How long do you think it will take after that for them to put anyone different into camps? To carry out tests and experiments? You see what they're doing to their own kind at the Southern border. It'll be worse for us."

Nobody answered her. I felt sick as she continued. "Humans enjoy that kind of thing. I saw it in the Inquisition, and the only thing that has evolved between then and the Holocaust, and the Holocaust and now, is the technology. No. I won't be the one responsible for putting my coterie, my people, through that."

"We'll need a representative. A go-between," Duke said, dravite eyes laughing and sly. "Someone completely unaffiliated with any one group."

I pulled my head up from my knees as the weight of their combined stares landed on me. "What, me? No. Nope. I just want to be left alone. Y'all sort out a parliament or something."

"Arie, it has to be you."

I turned and glared at Roman. "I don't see why."

"Because there's only one of you," Maria said.

"There's only one of whatever Callista is," I threw back.

"But she rules as a dictator. You built a coalition. And from what I saw tonight, you can back it up." Maria tilted her head and smiled modestly. "Perhaps with some help, at first."

I rolled my eyes. "Help that you would offer?"

Her grin widened. "Of course. And it looks like your wolf would help as well."

"I don't have much standing left with the Volkov pack, but I can bring them the offer and make the case," Roman said behind me.

"Roman…"

"I know, babe. You didn't sign up for this. But what if it's the best way to keep you safe?"

I opened my mouth. Shut it. Wasn't that what I'd wanted? *It was…I just didn't want to be in charge.* I tried a different tack. "I'm not Callista. Nobody is going to listen to me."

"I sure as hell would," Maria said. "I can't make promises, but I will take this to Torsten. You're the only one who has gotten us what we've wanted since we moved to this wretched backwater." She glanced at Leith's corpse, her expression becoming that of the cat who got the cream.

A thud drew everyone's attention. Troy had pounded on the wall. "There are laws. Conventions. Procedures and processes that need to be followed—"

"Oh, hang your procedures and processes," Duke said. "I can only make an agreement for myself, but I'll take it to our council. If Arden agrees to be our peacekeeper, that is."

I stared at them all, my mouth making stupid movements as I tried to find words. "Are you all insane?"

"No, we're desperate," Roman said, rubbing my shoulders. I shook him off. A massage was not going to cut it. "Arden, come on."

I was being pushed and managed again, and I didn't like it. "What do I get out of it? Huh? What are any of you going to offer me?"

"If messing with you creates an excuse to hunt more powerful blood…mmm." Maria licked her lips. "I can think of several vampires who would sign up for enforcement duty on that point alone, with my name at the top of the list. No promises, yet, but will it suffice?"

"What? Someone fucks with me and the rest of you back me up?" Maria's slow nod made my heart skip a beat, considering the possibilities. More freedom. Being accepted, or at least tolerated, in Otherside. I could practice openly and be my whole self, the way I'd dreamed. And I'd have something of my own. Maybe even a community of my own. I shuddered with both longing and apprehension. "I think we all need to go back to our decision makers, first," I said, not willing to allow myself to pin hopes—or my life—on a breeze.

"And before that, you need to fulfill the rest of your deal with me." Troy reached down to grasp my arm, and dragged me to my feet, ignoring both Roman's protests and my weak attempts to push him away. "Move," he growled at Maria.

With a smirk, she stepped aside in a slow, smooth motion.

Troy let me go to grab Leith's corpse by the shoulders and haul it upright. "You're coming with me, sylph. I won't risk you disappearing before you testify."

"Wouldn't dream of it," I muttered, grimacing and following him out.

Chapter 28

"What interesting company you're keeping these days, my dear."

Callista's voice made me miss a step, and I nearly fell down the stairs. Troy shrugged Leith's corpse off his shoulder and to the ground, where it landed in an unceremonious heap as he drew his blade. "Back off, witch," he growled.

Her laughter was the chiming of bells and the roar of the ocean, a power I'd never heard before echoing in each note. "A witch? You should be so lucky." When the elf didn't put his knife away, Callista snapped her fingers once. Troy's guard came up when Grimm materialized, twirling a lock of blood-red hair around her finger. She took stock of the situation and grinned wickedly.

"Oh, my. He smells powerful. Can I have him, Callista?"

"Only if he doesn't let us have Arden."

Troy and I both stiffened. "No djinni is having me," he snarled. "And the elemental is mine."

Grimm only licked her lips, flickering as she readied herself to go misty if he struck first. For all the mutual antagonism between the two species, I'd never seen a djinni fight an elf in earnest, and the possibility of the two halves of Aether colliding made my heart trip in my chest. I knew Grimm's strength and had an idea of Troy's. The Chaos the collision would create would probably warp reality for at least a mile.

Footsteps on the landing behind us made me jump as a vampire and a werewolf joined the party we had going on. The familiar lemony tang of djinni Aether blended with the metallic scent of vampires and the musky cedar of wolf to drown out the elven meringue.

Duke materialized between the two groups. "Callista—"

"Nebuchadnezzar." That she invoked his full name in front of those who could use it was a warning, and his dark skin greyed at her cold tone. None of us had expected the alliance to be called into question so soon, certainly not by Callista herself. *How did she even know where to find us?*

"I know more than you could ever dream," she said, fixing me with a sharp look. "Even Artemis never saw so much, not until it was shoved in her face."

My mouth went dry as I remembered Duke's implication that Callista was a goddess. Whether she was or not, she was referencing beings from so long ago that she herself might as well be one if she was still alive to disparage them.

Callista smirked. "Come with me, darling. There are those who need answers."

I darted back from her reaching hand, the movement reflexive and violent, nearly spilling me to the earth. She reached again, and I dodged again, stumbling over my own feet and going down.

"Grimm," she said, her lips thinning. I barely had time to look at Grimm before the djinni dematerialized and reappeared behind me. The last thing I saw before reality shifted was Roman's horror and Troy's outrage.

When the planes snapped back together I heaved, throwing up when Grimm released me to fall to my hands and knees. Leith's corpse thudded to lay beside me.

"Welcome to the true Otherside, stupid girl. You should have listened when I told you to stop pursuing the Sequoyah case," Grimm purred in mocking tones.

My fingers clenched in white nothingness so bright it burned, like sand but imperceptible as being physical.

Seeing the movement, she laughed. "You'll get used to it. Or not. Either way, your damned elven father robbed you of having this without help."

Whatever *this* was, my mind spun, trying to latch onto anything I could, but there were no points of reference. I'd be intrigued if I wasn't overcome by the sensation that I'd fallen off the Earth, my stomach whirling as though I was on the swings at the state fair. We were in an in-between, an empty canvas of what could be, not my world of reality and yet not the unreality the djinn lived in. A blank slate. Purgatory? My breath came in short pants as my mind fractured.

"Frame a Crossroads, before we lose her," Callista said as she stepped into the plane like walking through a door.

The djinni clapped twice before spreading her hands wide, and the whiteness rippled outward from her fingertips, delivering me to a forest that could have been a twin for Eno except that it smelled of nothing but dust and static. There was even a shallow river rippling over huge granite boulders. It was like the opposite of whatever Troy did with shadows, structuring an illusion with light rather than darkness.

When I waved my hand out to the side a rough, fallen log appeared. I pulled myself onto it without question, and held my head in my hands, keeping it low in an effort to settle the dizziness. Between the disorientation and the burgeoning power hangover, I had nothing left to fight this, whatever it was. I'd have to ride it out.

Faint pops sounded as more beings appeared. Keeping my head down, I watched them emerge from nothing and morph into shapes that suited them here. My heart hammered. Who the hell were they?

First was a tall, bald black man with a necklace of green and black beads interspersed with cowrie shells, who glanced around and examined the edge of his heavy machete upon seeing the clearing mostly empty. A pair of child-sized ravens flapped to perch on two boulders, and preened feathers that soaked the light around them in endless shadow. A lean, brown-skinned man striped in blood-red streaks, with spooled earrings made of deer hooves and a fanged mask, appeared in a ripple of star-spangled darkness, and checked his arrow points. A short, muscular woman in an ancient Egyptian-style wig and beaded collar strode into the clearing from another plane whirling a staff, a bow and arrows racked on her back.

Power rolled off of them all, like Callista's but greater, the oppressive weight of ages and magic beyond my comprehension. My mind blanked, too overawed for anything else.

"Are the others coming?" Callista asked when no one else appeared.

"Not yet. Not for this," the Egyptian woman said. "I cannot speak for the rest, but I am only here because it has been so long since I have seen one of these." She jerked her chin at me, still spinning her long, slim staff. The movement of her lips didn't match the words, and I wondered whose magic was in play, or if it was special to this in-between place.

Callista nodded, frowning. "Very well. Then you will be the first to hear of any developments that come of this. In the meantime, accept this offering of blood and bone for your indulgence." She gestured to Leith's body and they all nodded, though none of them were paying any particular attention. Things I couldn't see or hear had them glancing around, hands on weapons, or tensed to strike.

Whatever Callista had in mind, I wanted to get it over with so I could finish the night and go home. These people were giving me the creeps; my skin felt like it was trying to tear free and slither away. They could keep Leith's body, even if it would piss off Troy, and leave me the only loose end should the elves decide to quietly clean house.

"Why am I here, and who are all of you?" I rasped, not liking this place, or the waves of power coming off of these beings to beat against me and push my throbbing head to a new level of pain.

The ravens laughed in scraping croaks, and the masked man tilted his head, regarding me with eyes that held the swirl of the Milky Way in their depths. After the barest glance, I looked away before I could fall into them. They were worse than vampire glamour, in the way that a saber-toothed tiger was worse than a rusty-spotted cat.

"You've drawn our attention, sylph," the black man said. His strings of beads clattered softly as he approached me, and tilted my head up, almost fatherly in his gentleness despite the huge blade in his other hand. Goosebumps rippled over me as even that light touch made me waver. "Show us what you can do."

"What do you mean?" I said, scarcely able to breathe around the power coursing through me. Duke had tried to warn me about the gods, and I hadn't listened.

"You know what I mean."

I wanted off of this plane, and I was getting fed up with the backwash of power ebbing and flowing from all of these beings. I didn't survive an elven death threat only to become another offering of blood and bone.

Using my power again, so soon after burning out, hurt. I screamed as I threw everything I had into a buffeting wind. I tasted blood.

The ravens spread their wings for balance and the men and women—or gods and goddesses?—swayed but remained where they were.

"So greatly weakened after such a short battle. She is unlikely," the big man said, turning to Callista, "and would need to be paired with one of equal power, bonded together. What makes you think it is time for our great Hunt, or that she is a worthy Mistress?"

"I don't know that she is, or that the time is now. Only that there are rumors, and she is uniting sundered alliances." Callista stood beside him, glancing at the blood dripping from my upper lip. "I could be wrong. She's only just testing her power. Perhaps this is her limit. We won't know for some time yet."

"Then she could be too late even if worthy." He released my chin, looking disappointed. "And if so, you have disturbed our rest for nothing. We wish to Hunt, to remake the world, not to speculate and dissemble."

Anger snapped in his words, and I flinched involuntarily, an instinctive fear clashing with resentment at being measured against a scale I didn't know for a task of which I had no comprehension. I didn't even know what I should have been prepared for, or how it fit into my personal quest for freedom, independence, and self-actualization. What did they think I could do? What was this about remaking the world?

"We shall see what we shall see," Callista said.

"Will you punish her for undermining you?" the man with the deer hoof spools in his ears said. As with the Egyptian woman, words and lips didn't match up. The threatening rumble of thunder rolled in his voice.

A cruel smile crossed Callista's face. I'd taken aim at her role as keeper of the peace, and she would find a way to punish me for it, allies or not. "Why don't you send her back the hard way, now that you've seen her? Set her a test of survival?"

Survival? Fuck this. Anger surged and forced out everything else. I didn't care who they were, I deserved better, and I was tired of forcing everyone to see things my way.

I scrambled to my feet, or tried to. Hands pressed on my shoulders from behind, and I looked up to see Grimm glaring down at me, bare of the face she showed the world, with ruby eyes set in a shifting swirl of fog.

The creak of a bow drew my attention, and I looked forward just in time to see the striped man release an arrow. It struck me under my right collarbone, burning with the fire of a lightning bolt, and throwing me out of the dimension.

I landed in reality so hard my howl of pain cut off as the breath was knocked out of me.

"Arden!" Roman knelt beside me, and electricity shocked through us when he touched the arrow projecting from my chest. He was thrown backward; I could only writhe in pain.

"Don't do that, please don't do that," I sobbed when the spasms passed, and I could breathe again.

"What the hell is this?" he said, sounding frantic.

"A message." I flinched at the rich hunger in Maria's voice. There were too many frightened people, and she'd been interested in my blood already, before it was pumping on the outside.

"From who?" Roman said, sounding frantic. The idea of an overwrought werewolf and a ravening vampire fighting over me sent my anxiety levels up a notch, but Roman wasn't done. "Who the fuck shoots arrows made out of—*that?*"

"The Old Ones," Maria said. "They who sleep, lost to time until wakened, clinging to a shattered remnant of who they were, and seeking a way back. Who was there?" When I didn't answer, too busy panting in pain and delayed fear at the memory of the strange, powerful beings, her tone sharpened. "Arden, who was there? How many are awake?"

"I don't know," I groaned, not wanting to remember. This arrow had to come out, and I didn't know what would happen when it did. "The man who shot the arrow had the whole galaxy in his eyes. There was a woman with a staff. Another man with cowrie shells and a machete. Birds."

"Birds? What kind of birds?" she pressed, kneeling opposite to Roman and apparently unfazed by how loony everything I'd said sounded.

"Back off, vampire," Troy growled. "I need her alive."

"Oh, the irony," Maria deadpanned. Even so, she shifted to the side to give him room.

Nothing happened other than the tickle of Aether skating along my skin, probing into the wound. I arched upward and hissed when it pressed against the power in the arrow and was repulsed, knocking Troy onto his ass. Roman straddled my hips and leaned into my left shoulder.

"What the hell…" Troy murmured, sounding preoccupied as he leaned in again. Aether pressed harder, sparking something in the arrow. He jerked back as though shocked while I choked on another scream. I was tired of making that noise.

After more gentler probing, Troy sat back on his heels and said, "This isn't Aether. It feels like elemental magic but…bigger. Older. Much older." He grimaced, glancing at a smug Maria.

They were taking too long. I wanted this fucking arrow out. I wanted to be free of all of them, and all of the Old Ones in the other plane. After all of this, I wanted to go home to my own space where I could hide, or cry, or scream, or plot, or stare blankly, whatever came first.

You wanted something done at all, let alone done right, you did it yourself. That was my path forward from here. I might as well start now. Grunting in pain, I reached up with my off hand to grasp the arrow.

Roman gasped. "Arden, stop! What—"

Movement above me. Frustration surged as I reached for determination, and let Troy and Roman catfight amongst themselves. I focused on ignoring the spikes of electricity and getting the fucking arrow out. With Troy's comment that the magic in it was elemental, I was able to find a trace of Air threading through the lightning. *A thunderstorm is air and fire and water.* I could work with Air. It was mine.

The Water scared me, and I shied away, but the Fire made me think of Val. Her Fire warmed rather than burned, and I sought that aspect of the element, letting it curl through me like a cat rather than trying to fight it.

The arrow jiggled, the only pain coming from the obsidian head scraping against my collar bone rather than a jolt of electricity. A gasp turned into a giggle as it slipped out. I'd manage this on my own, beaten and battered, but not broken. None of them would have me, not in this plane or any other.

"We're fucking losing her, you elf bastard!" Roman's voice was tumbling back into the lower registers of a growl. "I won't lose her, and I won't lose my chance to get back to my family. Let me—"

Something twisted in my heart at the mention of his family. It shouldn't have hurt. I should have been big enough not to begrudge him that dream. But some ugly, selfish part of me had hoped that someone was here purely to help me; that for once, I mattered that much.

One last tug, and the arrow was free. Everyone looked skyward as lightning crackled and thunder rumbled in the frozen air, unusual but not unheard of in a North Carolina winter. My arm flopped to the side. Someone tried to tug the arrow from my hand.

That fueled my temper further. "Fuck," I gasped, tightening my grip despite the numbing jolt of electricity it sent down my arm. "All of you." The arrow was *mine*. My pain, my prize.

"Arie!"

"No, Roman. You, and Maria, and Monteague, and the djinn and Callista, wherever the fuck they ended up, can all go to hell." The breath to say all that burned in my lungs as I forced it out. "It sounds like you're all here for yourselves, so you know what? Create your own alliance, I don't care. I just want to be left. The fuck. Alone."

Silence descended. Hands tried to help as I rolled onto my right side and tried to press upward; my arrow-torn chest muscles collapsed with a painful ripping twinge and dumped me facedown in the dirt. Didn't matter. I shook everyone off with a snarl, and pushed myself up with my core muscles, my left hand pressed against the wound trickling blood from my collarbone. I'd been alone all this time, and didn't need allies now.

I made it to my knees and curled over, waiting for the dizziness to pass. When I sat up all the way, Roman was looking at me with worry and heartache, Maria with open hunger, and Troy with, of all things, a wary, disbelieving respect. "Fuck off," I repeated despite the waver in my kneeling stance.

Unsurprisingly, Troy ignored me, and pulled me the rest of the way up. "Get over yourself," he growled, tugging me in the direction of the road with a firm hold on my right wrist. Roman snarled when I groaned in pain, stumbling after Troy if only to stop the pull on torn muscles. A cold sweat broke out, and I choked down vomit as my collarbone twisted painfully. Troy must have heard the aborted heave because he stopped, clasping my temples and forcing a wave of Aether into me.

"No!" I gasped, trying to break free and pull away.

"Will you stop," he snapped. "You did the same thing when I tried to—never mind. There."

My knees nearly buckled from the sudden disappearance of pain. Troy held me upright, glaring over my shoulder as Roman barked, "What are you doing to her?"

"Whatever it takes to fulfill my mission and my oath," the elf snapped. "Don't worry, wolf. She'll live. For now."

The smooth black side of an Acura SUV appeared only when I stumbled into it. My hands plunged through shadow, and I caught myself on cool metal. The arrow still in my grasp sparked, scratching and burning the paint.

Troy must have done something to hide the car. He yanked the door open and handed me up into the passenger seat with rough motions. I barely moved my knee aside before he slammed the door.

"Where's Sequoyah's body?" he asked as he climbed into the driver's seat.

I slumped against the cold leather and propped the arrow between my feet. "I don't know. I think they ate him."

Chapter 29

I picked a fluff of lint from the chest of my black t-shirt, feeling terribly underdressed in the foyer of the Monteague family mansion. Troy had bandaged my shoulder and given back my phone before we got out of the car—not that it mattered, now that I had ordered a spare with a new, unlisted number. I fiddled with the arrow I'd refused to relinquish, trying my best to ignore the ache it sent up my arm, my throbbing headache, the burn of the wound in my chest, and the bright light of the crystal chandelier overhead.

"Troy!"

We both looked up at the excited squeal of his name from an upper landing. A teenage girl in a lilac-colored silk blouse and jeans pounded down the stairs with none of Troy's quiet grace, her hair flying behind her in black ringlets. Once she reached the bottom, she threw herself at him.

He grunted, and spun to absorb the momentum, kissing the top of her head before setting her back on her feet. "Little one," he said, a hint of the first smile I'd ever seen on him cracking his stern visage.

She sucker punched him, and stuck her tongue out. "Big brother. Nice to see that the Darkwatch lets you come home once in a while."

His good humor collapsed, and his lips pressed into a grim line as he glanced at me.

"Oh, sorry. The big open secret," she whispered, grinning at me before refocusing on her brother. "Who's your friend? She's pretty. What's that arrow? Is she bleeding? I smell blood. Ouch. Is she staying for dinner? Grandmother said she has business first, so we're eating late tonight. What happened to your face? What's wrong with your ribs? Were you in a fight? Did you win?"

The rapid-fire questions bombarded the distance I was trying to create around myself, and they were dangerous. I half-turned, hoping for more anonymity.

"You need to watch your tongue, Evie," Troy said, clasping her shoulders and stopping the torrent of chatter. "You have no idea who this is. She could be an enemy of the House."

"Ugh. Please," the younger elf said, fluttering her eyelashes in an exaggerated eye roll. "You wouldn't bring an enemy here." Turning back to me, she stepped back in front of me, and offered her hand. "I'm Evangeline Monteague. I'm the—"

Her introduction was interrupted by Troy sliding between his sister and me, angled to keep her away from me while keeping us both in his sight. I jumped back and winced as my chest pulled, not wanting to touch him as he extended one arm toward her and settled the one closer to me on the hilt of his long knife. "I do as my queen orders and I mean it, Evie. Go study something."

She leaned around him to look at me again, all the laughter washed from her by his cold sternness. "You're Grandmother's business." Her odd violet eyes were serious in her tawny face, and a trickle of Aether crept toward me. Clearing my throat, I tightened my fractured shields, unable to hide my grimace of pain as mental pins and needles pricked me on doing so.

Troy tensed. "Stop, Evangeline."

"I'll be qu—"

"I said, stop. Your future is not your present, and I'm not here as your brother today."

It rankled that his argument was more *I'm the boss* and less *Because we don't cross the boundaries of strangers*, but I doubted that boundaries were a thing Troy thought much of. Especially if they inconvenienced him, as everything to do with me apparently did.

"I see." The younger elf's warmth chilled. "Very well." With a last glance at me, she stalked back up the stairs, nose high.

"Don't look at me," I muttered when he glared at me, as though the whole exchange was my fault.

"If you hadn't brought that damned vampire into this, I would have had Leith alive," he snapped under his breath. "And no need for you." A dark, savage light danced behind his eyes as he caressed the hilt of his knife.

If I hadn't brought that damned vampire into this, we'd both be dead, and your sister would be crying rather than pissed. I had the sense to keep it in my head this time. Being home, if that was where we were, had Troy even shorter of temper than usual, and I worried that killing me might still be on the table if he got his way. After all, I'd just about served my purpose.

I put my hand on the hilt of my own blade. Keeping it and the arrow had been my price for getting out of the car without screaming that I was being kidnapped, and waking the human neighborhood they lived in.

"My—ahem." A pale man dressed in dark slacks and dress shirt approached on silent feet, startling me into taking a defensive stance. He lifted light brown eyebrows, and frowned at my weapons before turning back to Troy. "Sir…she'll see you now."

"Move," Troy said, jerking his chin to indicate I should go in front of him. The butler, or whoever he was, led us deeper into the house, to a large sitting room where several people waited. Everything in it looked too fancy for actual use, and nothing looked comfortable, which might have explained the stern expression on the darkly beautiful older woman in the room's one armchair. Silver-threaded ebony hair was pulled up in an elaborate style. A subtle diadem of twining leaves graced her brow. She had Evangeline's eyes with a streak of green. Any softness they might have had hardened to fluorite as they landed on us.

"This is not Leith Sequoyah." Her voice carried so much command that I stood up straighter without thinking. With a piercing stare at me, she said, "This is not even an elf. What have you brought me, grandson?" She rose, smoothing her viridian silk dress as she approached.

I shifted my feet. *How did she know I wasn't an elf so quickly?*

As he had with Evangeline, Troy slid between me and the woman I assumed was the queen of House Monteague. She cleared her throat, and the scent of ashy marshmallow rose. Troy moved, reluctance making him stiff.

"Something dangerous, then," she said. "How intriguing. What are you, my dear?"

"I'm a Watcher," I said, the words sticking in my throat as I looked for the exits. I didn't know what I'd imagined an elven queen to be, but I had underestimated handily. She wasn't as bad as the gods or Callista, but she was bad enough. Power swirled around her, much like Torsten's had pounded from him.

"And what else?" she said in a harsh whisper. I looked at Troy, not wanting to answer, not wanting him to either.

"She's a sylph," he told her, his eyes on me.

Snaps and creaks of leather preceded a shuffle of movement as the two men and three women who'd been lounging on armchairs rose supernaturally fast. Guns cleared their holsters, pointed at the floor rather than toward their queen, but still out and ready. Aether crackled.

"We had an agreement," I said to Troy, keeping my hands open at my sides in an effort to reduce the threat I represented. "You already tested it once."

"What is it on about?" his grandmother snapped. "You know the law. Why is it breathing? And armed in my presence." Pressure in the room grew as every elf present gathered more Aether.

I was still depleted from the fight, bruised, bloody, and shaking. Attitude would have to carry the day. I lifted my chin and glared right back.

Troy said, "The knife is stained with Sequoyah's blood. She threatened to alert the neighbors if I took it. The arrow is evidence of a new threat, a greater one."

"None of which explains why this animal had to be alive for you to bring me these things."

My breath hissed as I inhaled. I flashed hot with indignation and then cold, too offended to be afraid. I'd thought Troy's casual privilege and Leith's enraged hatred was bad, but this icy, dehumanizing superiority was far worse both for its dispassion and her position of power.

Troy shifted, the first hint of discomfort I'd ever seen from him. "I offered immunity in exchange for testimony. The Redcap is dead, and his outlaws scattered. This one witnessed a confession before Javier was drowned."

"And me. By you," I snarled. No, I was not over it.

That got the queen's attention. "You killed Javier? And saved this creature?"

"I answer to the Darkwatch, Grandmother. That was the best way to complete the mission."

"In this House, you answer to me, boy."

Tension stretched until Troy made the slightest incline of his head. "Even so. I gave my word."

"As though that matters when dealing with animals." She waved her hand dismissively.

I stiffened, outraged all over again, subsiding into a trembling fury when someone behind me cleared his throat as a reminder of all the guns in the room. *This is for your freedom. Your safety from this House will be your revenge.* That reminder gave me the fortitude to run through a breathing exercise, holding my breath until my heart responded, then exhaling slowly through my nose.

Reconnecting with my element refocused me. Violent reaction was what they wanted; it would prove their thought that I was less civilized, less of a person, than they were. It would justify them in their edict that elementals had to be hunted down and killed. I had to be better, even if it was disgusting, unfair, and hateful.

"It matters to me," Troy said softly after a pause. "I did what I had to do to complete the mission the conclave of queens issued the Darkwatch. Leith's was the greater offense. I won't be forsworn."

"You've gotten bold in your absence, boy. Too bold." Troy didn't respond as the queen evaluated me, disgust plain on her face. "Very well. House Monteague will honor its prince's word—this time." She returned her chilly stare to her grandson. "Try this again, and the Darkwatch will be your only house."

Blood drained from Troy's face, although his expression didn't change. "Yes, my queen."

She nodded as though she'd expected no less. "Speak," she said to me, turning her back to return to her chair.

It took me a few moments to find coherent words in my rage at being treated like a dog. "As a sworn Watcher, this is my testimony," I ground out, starting with the formal words. "May the Goddess strike me dead should I lie."

"May She strike you dead either way," someone muttered behind me.

My shoulders hunched higher, and it took me two tries before I could push through the rancor burning through my blood to keep speaking.

By the time I'd finished recounting Sybil's murder and discovery, and all that Leith had said—his desire to overthrow the queens and for war, the exposure of the vampires to human law enforcement by his actions, his charnel house in the lake, and the arrow shot by one of the old gods—her face could have chipped diamond.

"This is outrageous," she growled.

"It's true," I snapped, too riled to be either afraid or decorous.

Troy nodded at my side, reluctant but honest. "And aside from the traitorous acts of their bastard prince, the Sequoyahs had to have known something."

"Even so," the queen said. "The Lunas will want a life for Javier."

And if she wants to punish the Sequoyahs for it, that admission and condemnation will be the pretty bow wrapping up my case to Callista. I kept my face blank even as triumph gave a bittersweet edge to the evening. *Wait…prince?* Leith was a prince?

"I understand." Troy's acknowledgement was heavy as he squared his shoulders. His grandmother gestured to someone behind me without taking her eyes from my face.

We waited in silence until they returned, pushing a young man to the center of the room. From his blond hair and blue-green eyes, he was very obviously another Sequoyah. I hadn't thought it possible, but the bodyguard's faces grew even colder, and overt malice tinged the taste of the Aether in the room. I started to feel sick again.

The boy paled at the look on the queen's face. "Why—how have I displeased you, Queen Keithia?"

"Escort the Watcher out," Troy said as he drew his knife. The Sequoyah started to beg, and I backed toward the door, not wanting to be a part of what was going to happen.

"No. It will stay and witness elven justice." The queen's face remained expressionless as a man held me where I was with a firm grip on my bicep, and another man and a woman grabbed the Sequoyah by each arm.

"Watcher?" the boy said, stiffening as his fear of me outweighed that of the queen before him. Big mistake.

"How long has your family known about Leith, Clay?" Keithia asked, drawing his attention back.

"I don't—"

I gagged as enough Aether was drawn to make me taste marshmallow in the back of my throat. With concentration, I opened my third eye to see an arrow of magic dart through Clay's aura, then a second tinge of Aether settle over him. He stilled.

"How long has your family known that Leith was murdering his own people?" Keithia asked again.

"Some years now," Clay's voice slurred distantly.

"I see. And his treason?"

"Treason?"

Keithia scowled, and changed direction. "Why did Sybil send you here?"

"To be your ward."

"Yes, but why *you*?"

An ugly sound came from Clay as he tried not to answer. Keithia rose, and the pressure of Aether tightened. It seemed that Troy's skill with shieldbreaking and auratic enchantment came from this side of the family. "Tell me, child."

"I was to win Princess Evangeline," he choked out. "What Leith did or didn't do wouldn't matter if our Houses entered alliance."

"Oh, Sybil," Keithia murmured. "Out-plotted and outdone by your own bastard grandchild. I told her not to force that divorce, low-blood or not. Well." She returned to her chair, and flicked a hand.

Before I could blink, Troy moved forward, and stabbed Clay through the heart.

Keithia didn't watch the Sequoyah boy die, or react to the spreading pool of blood on her green antique rug. She watched me struggle to find my breath as I wondered if I'd be the next one dead on her expensive furnishings.

"A life for a life," she said when I dragged my eyes away from the body and to her. "You leave with yours today by my grace alone. Remember this, and pray you don't come to our attention again. Watcher or not, agreements or not, we have our laws and they will be enforced. And speaking of Watchers…we can't have you sharing this with Callista, now can we?"

Her dart of Aether stung through my tattered shields even faster than Troy's had. The shock dropped me to my knees as she wove a maze. "How much does she need to recall?" Keithia's voice reached me, muffled, as I fought to find the edge of the spell.

"There were witnesses at the house. Torsten's third, a Volkov, a djinni. They helped with Leith. She needs to remember coming here. They saw me put her in the car." Troy's voice held a note of something I couldn't interpret. Frustration, maybe?

"Fine. Sylph."

I looked up into her fluorite gaze, not fighting it. She couldn't know that I could break free of this yet, or she'd tie off her loose end in a more final way before I had a chance to consolidate my own power.

"You came to House Monteague to testify on the circumstances of Leith Sequoyah's death. We thanked you for your services, and you left. You remember nothing of a conspiracy or elven justice. You will go straight home, and speak of this to no one."

"Yes, ma'am," I slurred, even as I resisted, holding the knowledge in a secret corner of myself. She wouldn't have this. This was mine, and she could die mad about it when I used it.

Troy's rough hand dragged me to my feet, spinning me around and out the now-open door. The movement startled me into gasping. Keithia's touch was both heavier and finer than Troy's had been, leaving me free to move while scrambling my thoughts. I didn't protest as he shoved me ahead of him.

"Troy, have you seen Clay?" Evangeline called as we approached the front door. He didn't answer, shoving me again as he opened the door, channeling whatever he was feeling into his antagonism with me.

He said nothing at all during the drive, speeding as though he was fleeing something, his expression blank. His silence held even when he pulled up outside a garage in a storage facility and handed me my key ring. I didn't have much of anything to say, either, even at the welcome sight of my car sitting inside.

Turning up on Roman's doorstep was becoming too much of a habit, plus I was still mad at him for wanting to use me, so I shrugged off the memory of the comfort to be had in his arms and headed home.

The yard was littered with fallen leaves and a few broken branches, not unusual with the winds we'd had when the temperature shifted from below freezing to balmy. The wood chips were strange, though, and I frowned. Had a tree management service made a wrong turn up my drive?

As I pulled up to my house, I crunched over a smaller branch, crushing it with a sharp snap. Clearing all this up would be top of the list for tomorrow. For tonight, I wanted a cup of tea and solitude. Peace and quiet, and a chance to process all the shit I'd just been through, to break free of the maze still clouding my mind and dampening my rage. I got out of the car, keys in one hand, knife in the other. I wasn't taking chances with Keithia's so-called grace.

A small shout startled me. "Hey! Get off my property!"

I snatched at the breeze teasing the leaves in the driveway, and cracked it like a whip in the general direction of the voice despite the pain of handling Air just now.

A tiny *eep!* and a scuffle of small feet gave me the crazy idea that raccoons had learned to speak, but then I spotted the kobold. At least, I thought it was a kobold; I'd never actually seen one. Spirited brown eyes glared at me from under a mane of wavy red-brown hair, her lightly tanned face peering out from under my porch.

"This is my house," I said cautiously, trying to remember what I could of the sprites. Slighting them was a good way to get your house burnt down or become the target of a string of bad luck and malevolent pranks.

Not the peace and quiet-filled solitude I'd been hoping for.

"Mine now. Nobody here. No warding to claim it," the kobold said.

I crouched at the top of the driveway, racking my brain for a fast way out of this. A deal, maybe? House fae came and went of their own free will; trying to drive her away with Air would only get piss in my porridge—and that was the best outcome.

Maybe this is a good thing. Kobolds were supposed to be fiercely protective of their claims. With elves, vampires, and weres all aware of who and what I was now, and House Monteague only promising not to kill me for now rather than forever, I'd been considering a dog for early warning. Having a kobold around meant I wouldn't need a dog. Nobody clever pissed off a kobold.

"Perhaps we could make a trade?" I said. "You must be hungry. The woods are bare at this time of year."

Her dark eyes became crafty. "Maybe. Maybe not."

"Why don't you come inside, and see what you might like to eat?" I offered. "Or I have wine?"

"Beer?" she countered, looking so hopeful that I winced. I didn't drink the stuff.

"No, but I could get some, if you like."

"I take wine now. You pay rent in beer. Each seven-day."

Blinking at the idea of paying weekly rent in beer to a kobold to live in my own house, I rose, and made my way up the porch and to the front door. Maybe I'd just think of it as protection money; Goddess knew I was going to need it with my secret out. Spotting the block of Air right before I tripped over it, I made a bigger step and unlocked the door.

Everything was as I'd left it, and my shoulders dropped, losing the tension I hadn't realized I was carrying. The heat kicked on as I stood there with the door open, taking in the sight and smell of home and safety. A tiny throat clearing reminded me of the kobold's demand, and I went to the kitchen to fetch a thick highball glass, filling it from a fresh bottle before bringing it back out.

"Acceptable?" I asked, unsure how much booze it took to buy off a kobold.

"Acceptable," she agreed, wandering back to the crawl space under the porch. I was just glad kobolds preferred the dark, earthy spaces *under* houses rather than the comfort within them.

With the kobold satisfied, I went to my bedroom and hid the arrow in my closet, walling it away behind Air. I had no idea what the hell to do with it, and I had a feeling it would be dangerous to display it openly.

That done, I poured a glass of Merlot for myself, and collapsed into my cushy armchair. I only managed a sip before the shakes and tears started.

No. I grabbed hold of myself, and wiped the tears away with a shaking hand. Yes, what I'd been through was overwhelming.

But I'd won a major victory. Three, really. I had information that House Sequoyah and the Darkwatch were corrupt and failing, a threat to Otherside that I doubted Callista would abide. I'd protected that knowledge within myself despite Keithia's attempts to steal it from me. And Leith Sequoyah was dead by my hand.

I remembered the second necklace he'd worn, and dug in my pocket for them both, holding them side-by-side in my palm. Mine looked just as it always had, an onyx disc the size of a nickel, its edges wrapped in gold. His looked so similar my heart missed a beat. It was a yellow stone, topaz maybe, and wrapped in what I guessed was white gold, but otherwise identical.

What the hell does this mean? Was it just a thing all elves had, or did it signify something? I finished my wine pondering it, then wrapped it in a tissue and put it next to the arrow of lightning in my closet. Keeping trophies was stupid, but both items were more than that. They were evidence, clues I'd keep to help me assemble the shards of my past.

Epilogue

Life had to go on, no matter who might have been trying to kill you.

After giving myself a few days off to recover and see who might crawl out of the woods to find me, I paid Callista a visit. Her icy contempt barely hid a suppressed desire to hurt me, bad, and I almost tried to walk back out.

Freedom isn't free. I squared my shoulders and lifted my chin. My pounding heart and a cold sweat weren't going to stop me, not after everything I'd survived. "I have information."

"Then let's hear it, my dear." Callista's voice was colder than the lake I'd nearly drowned in.

"I want to make a deal."

"You don't get to make deals. You're mine."

"I *was* yours. Shall we take this to your office?"

Her glare told me she wanted to decline out of spite, but information was how she maintained her small empire. For me to push back like this told her it had to be good.

"If this isn't earth-shattering, I'm binding you in bronze and leaving you in the basement as an elemental pretzel," she said in dangerously neutral tones when I was seated. "I will *not* be defied."

I swallowed, hard. I had one good play here, and I prayed that it would work. "The Old Ones might have something to say about that." I sweated under my winter coat, but was proud of myself for keeping my voice steady.

Callista leaned back in her chair, and steepled her fingers. "You threaten me with the gods? Do you know what I am, girl?"

"No. But I know that if you're making offerings of blood and bone, they're more powerful than you."

Outrage flashed, turning her green eyes luminescent. "Tread carefully."

"I do." I swallowed again, and forced the next words out before I could lose my courage. "But I'm also fixing to tread my own path."

"Are you now?" I didn't answer that, forcing myself to hold her gaze until the hint of a bitter smile quirked the corners of her mouth. "I suppose I did tell you to grow a spine."

"You did."

Abruptly, her mien shifted from threatening to conspiratorial, humoring me. "Speak, then."

I rolled my shoulders to ease some of the terrible tension that was already making my head pound. "I've learned something that could threaten the balance of power…or help tip it, if someone had the right pieces on the board."

"It's your duty as a Watcher to report it."

"I'm done working for free. I found this in my investigation, doing my job." She opened her mouth, and leaned forward, but I hurried on. "I don't owe you this. And I'm done being used. Keep your secrets about my past; I'll figure them out for myself. I'll still keep an eye on things, but from now on, you'll pay me for them." My gamble was that by not demanding a complete break, she could keep enough face to compromise.

The dangerous look came back into her eyes anyway. "Is that so?"

"It is."

"Your new friends have made you awfully bold, girl."

I waited without replying. The silence stretched, and I forced myself to bite my tongue and sit steady in my chair.

"Fine," she said. The word cracked like a whip. "What's your price for this information?"

Hope fluttered. I squashed it, and said, "My independence. You *ask* if you need help. You pay the price I set. I can turn you down. No more freebies. No more orders. No more threats."

"You ask a great deal. I want to hear the information first."

I hesitated, suspecting that oaths wouldn't bind her, not like the djinn. "No. I'm sure Torsten or the Volkovs would love to hear what I have to say, or the djinn council. They'd have a hell of a hand to play."

When she seemed set to start another stretch of silence, I rose.

"You have a deal. Talk."

I sat, hoping my shakes were hidden, and told her about Leith's Redcaps and their plan to overthrow the queens. That his House knew he'd been murdering elves for years in pursuit of a species supremacist agenda that violated the Détente. That he'd been a former Darkwatch agent, and Troy hadn't dared bring in more after his team had been killed, for fear the rot had spread beyond Leith. That we hadn't gotten all of the Redcaps, only Leith, and the conspiracy might well have gone underground. That Keithia now had to know at least some of it, and had tried to mindmaze me to stop me from telling Callista.

Callista's eyes glittered with fury when I wrapped up with that last. "You swear this is all true?"

"I swear."

"Very well. The terms stand. Go."

I fled, keeping my pace to a vigorous power walk. I didn't know who was in charge of House Sequoyah with Sybil dead, but I had a feeling they were going to get an unpleasant visit from some terribly unpleasant people.

"Ashes to ashes, dust to dust," I muttered as I hit the street, and got into my car. I sat there for a moment, letting the shakes run their course as a giggle of disbelieving triumph bubbled free, then morphed into borderline hysterics. Joyous tears streamed down my face. I'd done it. I wasn't all the way free of Callista, but I wasn't her bitch anymore either.

I couldn't keep the smile from my face on the drive home. I'd survived making demands of Callista. I had an agreement with House Monteague, and House Sequoyah would be too busy to hunt elementals anytime soon. That left House Luna, but it was the smallest of the high elven houses and an ally of Monteague.

Freedom. Safety. Space to be myself, my whole self. I wasn't naive enough to think I was out of danger, but I felt lighter and more hopeful than I could ever remember. I was a force to be reckoned with, a powerful elemental with agreements and, maybe in time, allies.

A nightly trip to the martial arts studio became a regular thing after the meeting with Callista, or a run in the woods to improve my stamina. Every night, I celebrated my liberation by practicing with Air. I did everything I could to stop feeling like I was an easy mark, including letting Roman be protective when a low-blood elf threatened me on our make-up dinner date.

Nobody was going to take me again without paying for it in pain.

Weeks passed before I stopped jumping at shifting shadows or the scent of meringue wafting from the bakery window I sometimes passed. I stopped wondering when Duke or Grimm would show up to explain themselves, when Callista would break her word and order me to her bar for another assignment, when Torsten or Maria would come calling again, or when an elf would turn up at my office. Nobody did anything and finally, one day, I relaxed.

I got my ass kicked in hapkido that night. All the practice I'd been doing since getting back to what passed for normalcy had gotten me bumped up to the next level. That meant a new level of pain as I learned new moves, and proved myself worthy of stronger competition.

Rolling my neck, I headed out after class sticky with drying sweat, sore, and satisfied. Even the chill bite to the spring air couldn't dampen my good mood or my pride in my new belt.

A tall figure leaned against the streetlamp where I'd parked my car. I slowed, reaching into my gym bag for the gun I was finally permitted to carry.

"You don't need that, Finch," the man said, looking up. "I'm just here to talk."

"Monteague." Regardless of what he'd said, I kept my hand on the grip of the little Ruger LCP. I wasn't sure where we stood, or whether he knew I'd been behind the recent clean out at House Sequoyah. "Following me around the Triangle?"

His smile was mocking, and I flushed when he said, "As though you'd have any room to complain. But no, I don't need to follow you. I have you tagged, remember? I can find you whenever I want."

The chill air suddenly felt a lot colder. "Take if off me."

"No."

"Dammit, Monteague—"

"My grandmother would love for me to break my word to you and bring her your head."

That he was capable of it, I had no doubt. I remembered the way the Sequoyah boy had died to settle a blood debt, that Troy had done it as smoothly as a wind through pine needles. I tightened my hold on my gun and reached for Air at the threat. The streetlight would hide the faint glow of my eyes from mundanes, and he already knew what I was. Burnt marshmallow tickled in my nostrils as he drew Aether to him. We stared at each other, at an impasse until he relaxed. The scent faded.

"Don't worry. You may be an elemental, but you helped the elves when we needed it. When I needed it." The last sentence was almost under his breath, and he looked like he'd swallowed glass as he made the admission. "I'm not here for your head this time, but I'll be watching."

Part of me wanted to laugh—an elf watching a Watcher? But another part of me had grown smarter. I kept my mouth shut and curled my lip. Had I made a tentative ally, or a delayed enemy? "Watch all you want, as long as you leave me alone. You said you wanted to talk. So talk."

"Queen Keithia of House Monteague sends her regards."

I shivered, wondering if the Monteagues knew neither their maze nor Callista still bound me. "And?"

The gold flecks in his eyes seemed to flash with ire. "And she's agreed to come to the table for negotiations to join the alliance, even if *you* are involved. You'll be seeing me around." He walked away, drawing shadows to him as soon as he was out of the streetlight.

"Great," I muttered, disgruntled for the time it took me to shake it off and find the silver lining. I hadn't wanted an alliance, but Roman had been right. Holding off everyone who wanted a potshot at the one outed elemental in town would be easier if I had my own power base. The most influential elven house in the Triangle wasn't a bad start.

Acknowledgments

The idea for this book came to me when I was at a low point in my life. Getting from there to here was a hell of a journey, supported by many people.

First and foremost, my parents and sister, who helped me get back on my feet when I was struggling to rebuild something from all I'd left behind. Publishing a book requires a certain amount of privilege and luck in terms of time, finances, and relationship support, and they gave me that, trusting that I'd find my way again. My sister was also the one who introduced me to North Carolina, showing me her favorite spots and taking me hiking on her favorite trails. It was on those explorations that I finally discovered a setting for *Elemental.* The world wouldn't exist without her guidance, and a number of the places she showed me made their way into the novel.

Jeni Chappelle and Michelle Rascon, both editors for the #RevPit Twitter contest, provided feedback that strengthened the story considerably. Special thanks go to Jeni, who reached out and encouraged me to join in the contest when I lacked confidence that the book was ready. She went on to do the developmental edit, and Arden kicks a hell of a lot more ass (or in editor parlance, has more agency) because of Jeni's work. Thanks also to Dani Moran at Tessera Editorial for her helpful comments during the copy edit.

The lovely folks of Jeni's Writers' Craft Room provided the supportive writing group I'd been looking for. Writers are your community, not your competition, and so many people in the group provided support in various ways.

My friends get a huge kudos as well. I fell off the radar for long periods of time while writing, editing, pitching, and eventually publishing this book. They were still there when I came up for air, providing encouragement and listening to more than a few rants and rambles. Special shout-out to RSL, who offered so much support.

About the Author

 Whitney Hill writes adult sci-fi and fantasy from her adopted home of Durham, North Carolina. Her worlds feature the diversity she has lived as a biracial woman of color and former migrant to Europe's political and financial capitals. She draws on these life experiences to write characters trying their best to find a place for themselves.

Outside of writing, she enjoys hiking in North Carolina's many beautiful state parks and learning about world mythology.

Learn more or get in touch: whitneyhillwrites.com
Sign up to receive email updates: whwrites.com/newsletter

Join her on social media:
- Twitter: twitter.com/write_wherever
- Instagram: instagram.com/write_wherever
- Facebook: facebook.com/WhitneyHillWrites

Learn more about the publisher, Benu Media, at benumedia.com, or sign up to receive newsletters with the latest releases at go.benumedia.com/newsletter.

One Last Thing...

If you enjoyed this book, please consider posting a short review or telling a friend who might also enjoy this story.

Thank you for reading, and for your support!

9 781734 422726